e Graham was born in Northern Ireland and een a keen romance reader since her teens. She very happily married, to an understanding husband who has learned to cook since she started to write! Her five children keep her on her toes. She has a very large dog, which knocks everything over, a very small terrier, which barks a lot, and two cats. When time allows, Lynne is a keen gardener.

USA TODAY bestselling, RITA®-nominated, and critically acclaimed author **Caitlin Crews** has written more than 100 books and counting. She has a Master's and a PhD in English Literature, thinks everyone should read more category romance, and is always available to discuss her beloved alpha heroes. Just ask. She lives in the Pacific Northwest with her comic book artist husband, she is always planning her next trip, and she will never, ever, read all the books in her 'to-be-read' pile. Thank goodness.

Also by Lynne Graham

The Ring the Spaniard Gave Her

Heirs for Royal Brothers miniseries

Cinderella's Desert Baby Bombshell
Her Best Kept Royal Secret

Innocent Christmas Brides miniseries

A Baby on the Greek's Doorstep
Christmas Babies for the Italian

Also by Caitlin Crews

Chosen for His Desert Throne
The Sicilian's Forgotten Wife
The Bride He Stole for Christmas

Rich, Ruthless & Greek miniseries

The Secret That Can't Be Hidden
Her Deal with the Greek Devil

Discover more at millsandboon.co.uk.

PROMOTED TO THE GREEK'S WIFE

LYNNE GRAHAM

THE SCANDAL THAT MADE HER HIS QUEEN

CAITLIN CREWS

MILLS & BOON

First Published in Great Britain 2022
by Mills & Boon, an imprint of HarperCollins*Publishers* Ltd,
1 London Bridge Street, London, SE1 9GF

www.harpercollins.co.uk

HarperCollins*Publishers*
1st Floor, Watermarque Building,
Ringsend Road, Dublin 4, Ireland

ISBN: 978-0-263-30065-9

01/22

This book is produced from independently certified FSC™ paper
to ensure responsible forest management.
For more information visit www.harpercollins.co.uk/green.

Printed and Bound in Spain using 100% Renewable Electricity
at CPI Black Print, Barcelona

PROMOTED TO THE GREEK'S WIFE

LYNNE GRAHAM

MILLS & BOON

CHAPTER ONE

'FORGET ABOUT THEM,' the family lawyer had advised. 'Should a problem arise in the future, provision has been made. Your inheritance is ring-fenced. There is no reason why you should concern yourself with this issue.'

Even today at the newly opened London HQ of Stefanos Enterprises, where the proof of his own exhilarating rise to success should have put him in a very different mood, Aristaeus Stefanos couldn't get that unscrupulous little speech out of his head. Only a month had passed since his father's death. A renowned philanthropist and business mogul, Christophe Stefanos had been a much-admired figure. A loving son, Ari had been devastated by his sudden death, and in all the years he had known his father, he had never once doubted his essential decency.

In retrospect, that complete trust now struck him as ludicrously naive for a male of twenty-eight years of age. Death had, after all, cruelly exposed his parent's darkest secret and had shattered Ari's faith in him. Ari had been forced to acknowledge his father's feet of clay and to make a decision that he might some day regret even while accepting that he could not *live* with any other option. Fierce conflicting emotions still bubbled uneasily beneath Ari's controlled surface. Angry shame and disbelief still rose uppermost whenever he reflected on his father's choices.

Life, however, was too short to agonise over what could not be changed, Ari reflected grimly. For that reason, rather than taking advantage of the many social invitations that had come his way since his return from his father's memorial service in Greece, he had decided to do something he had never done before: get to know some of his employees. It wasn't Ari's style to get close to his workers. A billionaire shipping tycoon and resort developer, he hired professionals to monitor his staff and kept his distance. His need for a distraction, however, had won out, and what could be more of a diversion than his participation in a company retreat to be staged in the wilds of Norfolk?

The new HQ of Stefanos Enterprises brought staff together from several different sites, and his HR director had suggested the retreat as a means of bringing down barriers and improving communication. Ari wasn't quite sure he believed in the value of company retreats. He understood the concept and the potential benefits, but he also suspected that many of his executive staff would view the retreat as a nice little holiday on company time.

His handsome mouth quirking, Ari left his office just as an eruption of giggles sounded from the reception area. His hard, dark gaze arrowed in that direction, and exasperation flooded him at the sight of a security guard flirting with the receptionist, who irritated the hell out of him. What was her name again? Cleo, he recalled, and even the name was inappropriate for a female with a mop of blonde curls and blue eyes. Cleo, short for Cleopatra, was, in Ari's highly experienced opinion, the name for a tall, dark beauty, *not* an undersized one with the curves of a pocket Venus and the dress sense of an eighties swagged and ruffled floral curtain.

It was fair to say that Ari had no time at all for Cleo the temp. But then she had blundered badly on her first day by letting Ari's stalker-type ex, Galina Ivanova, walk into his office unchallenged. Of course, she had apologised. *Thee mou*—had she apologised! While Ari never used two words if one would suffice, Cleo was a hopeless chatterbox and capable of utilising fifty words to do the work of two. She had apologised to him for five solid minutes, staring pleadingly at him with those huge blue eyes of hers that made her look more like a cherub than a grown woman. Having been made aware by Human Resources that he could not simply sack her out of hand, he had grudgingly accepted the apology, but her presence in his vicinity offended him.

'Have a nice afternoon, Mr Stefanos!' Cleo called cheerfully, not having the wit to pull a low profile after being caught in the act of distracting the security guard from his job.

Ari struggled not to respond with something derisive and told himself off for letting so minor an incident darken his mood. But Ari liked absolutely everything in his life shipshape and *tidy*. He had placed things in neat little groups since he was a child. Back then he had found security in making and restoring order. The testing times of his childhood were unforgotten, although he chose not to dwell on them. His wardrobe was colour-coded, his bookshelves alphabetically arranged, his desk immaculate. In his world, there was no clutter and everything and everybody had a place. When anything was out of place, it set Ari's teeth on edge, which was exactly why the receptionist irritated him, he reasoned in exasperation.

Cleo didn't 'fit' Stefanos Enterprises. She lacked dress sense and sophistication. She was too visible, too chatty and too friendly. She smiled too much. Spend five minutes in a taxi rank with Cleo and she would divulge her entire life story without the smallest encouragement. That kind of verbal licence gave Ari the chills. Thrusting her from mind, he reminded himself that he had a Norfolk-bound helicopter waiting for him…

Cleo clambered into the minibus with her overnight bag.

A lot of the staff were travelling to the retreat by car, but she hadn't made any close friends at Stefanos Enterprises and she hadn't been offered a lift. People rarely made much effort to get to know temporary employees and she was accustomed to being somewhat invisible at work when others were socialising. Even so, she had been thrilled to be included in the retreat, which was probably because she would be working at Stefanos Enterprises for another eight months.

She suppressed a grimace, thinking of the incident on her first day that she suspected had ruined any hope she had of ever stepping into a permanent position at Stefanos Enterprises. An enviably confident sleek dark beauty, dressed to the nines in designer fashion, had approached Reception to announce that she was lunching with Mr Stefanos and would go straight through to his office. Cleo hadn't even thought of questioning the woman further. She had simply assumed that the woman was a regular visitor, possibly even a family member. She hadn't been shown the banned list of visitors before she began her shift. She hadn't been told that the boss's lovers never had access to him during working hours either by phone or by personal appearance. And nobody had been more shaken than her when she saw the furious woman escorted off the premises by two security guards and one of his personal assistants came running to ask what on earth had she been thinking when she had allowed that 'madwoman' into Mr Stefanos's office. An ex, a stalker-type ex, apparently, who refused to take no for an answer and kept on showing up in the hope that he would change his mind. Cleo felt that she should have been warned the minute she took over the desk that her employer's adventurous, ever-changing love life included such a deceptive personality.

Cleo suppressed her unproductive thoughts. She preferred to concentrate on positive things. A night away from the cramped little studio apartment she shared would be very welcome. Although she had been grateful to find city accommodation that she could share, she often longed for the peace and quiet of her own space, but with the cost of rents in London and her less-than-stellar earning power, that was a luxury she could only dream about. In any case, she reminded herself, she was lucky enough that her landlady, Ella, spent a couple of nights a week at her boyfriend's place, leaving Cleo in sole possession of the mezzanine bedroom space and the tiny living area they had to share. Ella's parents had bought the property for their daughter and it really wasn't large enough for two people. Ella, however, was a student, who was struggling to get by, and she needed Cleo's rent.

The retreat was being held at a boutique country hotel, situated deep in the countryside and surrounded by woods and fields. The bus arrived late, after an accident caused a long, slow tailback of traffic. As they waited for their key cards at Reception, several remarking on the fact that their belated arrival excluded them from joining the team chats, Lily, one of the clerical staff, turned her head to say to Cleo, 'Come on... You're sharing with me.'

Cleo forced a smile, able to see that her companion was no keener on the arrangement than she was. No sooner had they arrived in the comfortable hotel room than Lily was excusing herself to join her friends. 'We'll be in the bar after dinner... You're welcome to join us,' the pretty blonde told her with a pleasant smile. 'The more the merrier.'

And a strange face was easier tolerated in a crowd,

Cleo reflected ruefully. She was pleased about the invitation, just a little worried that she would not truly be welcome and was only being asked out of politeness. 'I'm going downstairs to see what I can sign up for.'

'The yoga classes are supposed to be very good,' Lily informed her on the way out of the door. 'And they've got one on first thing...'

Cleo wasn't fond of yoga. Having once signally flopped at twisting her body into a pretzel shape at a class and having felt an absolute failure, she had decided that she simply wasn't bendy enough.

After freshening up, she went downstairs to explore the other options on offer. Breathing in deep and mustering her courage, she signed up for paintballing and stand-up paddleboarding the following day. Although she was not remotely athletic, she was a firm believer in moving out of her comfort zone when the opportunity was presented, and goodness knew, she thought ruefully, she was unlikely ever to receive another opportunity to try out such activities free of charge. At the very least, it should be fun.

Throwing herself in head first was Cleo's way when she felt intimidated. Growing up with a single mother perpetually fretting and expecting disaster had taught her to be fearless. Lisa Brown had always had a pessimistic outlook, while Cleo preferred to look on the brighter side of things.

Getting changed for dinner, she tugged out a stretchy comfy dress and heels. The bright colours of the jungle-palm print made her smile, whisking her back to her childhood with a mother who habitually wore black, believing that colours were less elegant. A lot of good that dark, colourless wardrobe had done her poor mother, Cleo reflected wryly. The man she loved, Cleo's father, hadn't loved Lisa Brown back and hadn't wanted a child with her either. Lisa's pregnancy had eventually concluded their clandestine relationship.

Cleo went down for dinner, glancing round the dining room and seeing only a handful of vaguely familiar faces. She was keeping an eye out for Ari Stefanos, who was reputedly joining his staff for the retreat. That had surprised her, Ari not being the most approachable of employers, and true to form, Lily had mentioned that he was not staying in the hotel, but in some separate luxury property in the woods, well away from the hoi polloi. No, Cleo was looking out for Ari simply because it was always a treat to feast her eyes on him. Those cheekbones, that unruly blue-black hair, that piercing dark-as-night gaze set below level ebony brows, not to mention the lush pink of his eminently kissable mouth.

The first time Cleo had met her employer had been the same day she had attempted to tender an apology for the woman she had allowed to walk unchallenged into his office. That had been her first glimpse of him, and sheer fascination had mesmerised her because there was just something about the precise arrangement of his perfect features that had made her stare like an enraptured schoolgirl. Her tongue had tripped over words, her mouth had dried up and her brain had closed down in that same moment. Ari Stefanos exuded irresistible appeal with every breath that he drew.

He was Cleo's secret addiction. It was a harmless piece of fun. All the women in the office treated Ari Stefanos to more than one glance: he was shockingly good-looking and smoulderingly sexy. He cast ordinary men in very deep shade. But he was a safe target for appreciation because his distaste for office flings was incorporated in her employment contract. In any case, Cleo knew that she didn't have the looks to attract such a man.

Cleo had never been in love and had no desire to fall in love either. Her mother had loved her father and it had ruined the best years of her life. No, Cleo would only allow herself to fall in love with a man when it was clear that *he* was keen enough on *her* to make a commitment. That was where her mother had gone wrong, trusting promises made in the heat of the moment, making the assumption that deep feelings were involved when they were not. Cleo had no plans to make the same mistake.

And in the short term, admiring Ari Stefanos from a safe distance was an amusing, perfectly prudent and private source of enjoyment.

Unaware that anyone received entertainment simply by looking at him, Ari led a discussion on the company vision for the future before heading for the bar, determined to have one drink and be sociable before he retired to his own quarters.

For some inexplicable reason, his attention immediately landed on Cleo and stayed locked to her. She was seated with a group, engaged in animated discussion, her mop of golden curls glinting in the low lights as she moved her head. She stood up to walk to the bar and he almost winced at the sight of the vivid giant-palm-leaf print she was sporting. A large blue butterfly was stretched across her curvy behind and, like the leaf cupping her full breasts, the loud design somehow accentuated the lush fullness of her glorious curves. In that instant he understood perfectly why she continually attracted his notice. She might be barely over five foot, but she had a superb figure. Pretty good legs too, he noted absently, watching her at the bar, catching her gurgling laugh and the brilliance of her smile as the bartender surged to serve her.

'She's very pretty and very young,' his senior PA, Mel, commented at his elbow as she looked in the same direction.

Ari tore his gaze from Cleo, faint colour edging his high cheekbones as he registered the throb at his groin, and shifted uneasily. 'She talks too much.'

'Yes, but she's very good on Reception,' Mel countered. 'Friendly, helpful, welcoming. In my opinion, she's a big improvement on that frozen fashion doll out on maternity leave.'

Ari gritted his even white teeth. 'She dresses badly.'

Mel frowned and gave him a surprised look. 'So, let someone give her the advice to tone down the colours a little and look more…er…professional.'

Tiring of the conversation, Ari tipped back the whisky brought to him without savouring the vintage. 'I'm going to turn in now. It's been a long day.'

Cleo didn't spend the whole evening with Lily and her pals, just an hour to be friendly. She went to bed smothering a yawn, wondering where Ari Stefanos had disappeared to, because she hadn't seen him. She woke and went down to breakfast alone because Lily had gone to the yoga class. Clad in a long-sleeved top and cargo pants, she ate and then followed the signs to the wooded, fenced area that held the paintball operation. She was a little embarrassed to see that only one other woman had chosen the activity and she was an athletic former soldier, whom Cleo had met the night before in the bar, and she was jogging on the spot with eagerness. Cleo put on her mask, helmet and protective vest and grasped the gun after it had been demonstrated for her benefit, and then she tried to strike a fit pose as if she too were fizzing with pent-up energy.

Ari Stefanos strode into view with a small group of other men. His black hair was tousled and in need of a cut. Cleo curved back into the shadow of the wall the better to watch him before he disappeared into the equipment shed. She wondered what it was about those features of his that continually locked her attention to him. The dark deep-set eyes, the rawly masculine hard jawline and faint shadow of stubble? The thin aristocratic nose? That beautiful mouth, which she had never seen smile? With the recent death of his father, she supposed he didn't feel he had much to smile about. He was very tall, spectacularly well built, all lean muscle from his wide, strong shoulders, flat stomach and narrow waist to his long, powerful legs.

The group was split into two teams and the game began. Cleo was ambushed behind a tree when she was least expecting it. Three of her own team, young and boisterous types, cornered her and literally sprayed her with paintballs, laughing uproariously as they did it. As the balls struck and spattered over her, she was startled by the force of each hit and by how much it hurt. She cried, 'Stop it!' as she felt the stings of pain and the pressure that would surely bruise her, but they were still laughing hysterically as they ran off again.

When they were gone, Cleo was left in a rage. Her own team members had attacked her, presumably because she was a temp, a safer target for a prank than a permanent staff member and an easy mark! And she was hurt, aching all over from the assault as she began clumsily picking herself up again, furious tears blinding her.

'You're out… Take yourself off to the dead zone,' a curt voice instructed.

'I'm not out! My own team ambushed me!'

'Got witnesses? If not, you're out,' the voice told her without sympathy.

'I'm going to get my own back,' Cleo countered furiously, recalling how turning her back on unkind behaviour aimed at her at school hadn't won her any favours. When anyone deliberately set out to injure Cleo, she had learned to always fight her corner in self-defence. It didn't pay to let people walk over her. If she allowed such treatment, it would be more likely to reoccur.

'That's against the rules. Neither is that attitude in the spirit of proper gamesmanship,' her unwanted companion informed her in a lofty tone of superiority.

'Oh, shut up!' Cleo said sharply. 'If they can ignore the rules and attack me, I can do it back!'

Below Ari's disbelieving gaze, Cleo shimmied up the tree behind her like a miniature ninja warrior. 'They won't even see me up here. I'm going to get them!' she hissed.

'Did you listen to anything I said?' Ari enquired drily. 'Did you even read the rules? You're not supposed to climb the trees or attack from above. Once you're hit, you're out and you should leave the field immediately.'

'A lot of good it did me reading the rules when nobody else is following them!' Cleo shot back, unimpressed. 'Go away and leave me alone. You'll draw attention to me and that'll wreck my plan.'

'Get down and I will see you get off the field safely,' Ari breathed impatiently.

'Like I need your help!' Cleo snapped. 'Anyone ever told you to mind your own business?' Reaching up to a higher, sturdier branch, she clutched the gun awkwardly below one arm. 'I'm about to teach those guys a lesson!'

Ari had never had an employee simply ignore his commands before. Undoubtedly, the helmet and the mask were a better disguise than he had appreciated. Ari was a stickler for rules, and while he understood her burning desire for retribution, he could not condone it. Stretching up, he closed his hands around her small waist, and from that angle, he really could not avoid noticing that in the close-fitting pants her derrière jutted out like a particularly ripe and luscious peach. Disconcerted by the instant swell of arousal against his zip, he tugged her down from the tree and brought her carefully down to ground level again. Of course, he knew who she was. Cleo was unique amongst the top-floor staff. She was too tiny to be mistaken for anyone else.

'What are you *doing*?' She gasped in disbelief.

As she staggered, he bent down to steady her and the faint scent of strawberries emanated from the golden hair curling out from beneath her helmet: he was too *close*. Ari took a sharp and deeply conservative step back from her as he spun her round to face him. The cornflower depth of blue that distinguished her eyes was distinctive. He tensed while he censured himself for his overt physical reaction.

'I'm taking you out of here,' Ari told her curtly. '*Before* I lose my temper with you.'

'Just because you have a different take on how to play games—'

'Breaking the rules could lead to the game being stopped for everyone,' Ari warned her curtly. 'There are safety concerns here. Please…'

And it was his accent, roughening the edges of his vowel sounds with a growl that made her steal a longer frowning glance at him. In one fell swoop she rose above her rage sufficiently to recognise the clothes that he wore and the dark golden eyes flaring like a shower of sparks behind the mask. *Oh. My. Word.* She was fighting with the boss, the great rule upholder!

'I'm so sorry, Mr Stefanos,' she murmured flatly. 'I didn't realise it was you.'

'Maybe I should have worn a warning label,' Ari riposted as he retained a controlling hand on her shoulder and steered her towards the boundary fence and the area marked out for the paint-spattered losers.

As the first arrival in the losers' corner, Cleo gritted her teeth on a snarky reply and compressed her lips, saying stiffly, 'Thank you. I'll head back to the hotel to change.'

Ari leant down to her level from his great height. 'I promise you… I'll cover those bullies in paint!' he murmured fiercely.

'Don't exert yourself on my account, Mr Stefanos,' Cleo remarked thinly as she walked away. 'After all, it's only a game…'

Ari snatched in a sudden sustaining breath, incredulous at her insouciant gall, and he stood there for several taut seconds watching her disappear from view, defiance in every line of her shapely, sexy body. The natural sway of her hips stole his masculine attention. He gritted his teeth and swung away, furious at the fact that she evoked a visceral sexual response from him. She was an employee. Such a reaction was unacceptable.

Still furious, Cleo stomped back to the hotel and straight into the shower, unhappy until she had rinsed the last speck of paint from her body. Faint pink circles of bruising marked her arms, her neck, her legs and stomach. It was her own fault for not wearing thicker clothing and for not taking advantage of the extra protective gear on offer in the equipment shed out of a fear of looking naff. Now she was suffering from an attitude adjustment and a growing retrospective horror about her unfortunate encounter with Ari Stefanos.

Talk about a clash of opinions! She shouldn't have been arguing with anyone in the game, considering that she was the most junior member of staff on the retreat. She couldn't afford to foolishly offend anyone higher up the ladder than she was…and what had she done? Only attracted the wrong kind of attention to herself *again* with the boss! She winced as she donned her swimsuit and got dressed again. Ironically, she was no longer in the right mood to try out a paddleboard following her unfortunate experience with the paintballing. But Ari Stefanos was truly the most infuriating guy! So bossy, so confident and bold in his conviction that only his way was the right way and, while Cleo had never considered herself a rule-breaker, his strictures had made her madder than a hornet.

In the end she decided the encounter didn't much matter in the scheme of things because she had probably already given him the very worst possible impression of herself and her talents on her very first day at work. No point crying over spilt milk, she told herself firmly, reminding herself that at least nobody else had witnessed their exchange of words.

Consoled by that reflection, she went downstairs to an obligatory first-aid class and accompanied Lily's group into lunch. Everyone talked about what a beautiful day it was to go out on the lake. Cleo's spirits lifted when one of the women insisted that you didn't need to be especially fit to succeed at paddleboarding. Words like 'slow' and 'peaceful' increased her optimism as she clambered awkwardly into a wetsuit in the changing rooms. They all helped each other do up the back zips and there was much laughter as they added the life jackets and compared their bulky images.

Ari almost smiled when he saw Cleo walking down to the edge of the lake with her friends. There was nothing sexy about Cleo in her current apparel. Indeed, Ari felt wondrously safe looking at her, and he told himself that he had imagined his former response to her. The instructor stood on the wooden pier to see everyone safely disposed onto their boards. Cleo stepped onto the board like someone stepping onto hot coals, an oddly frozen expression on her face as though she was forcing herself to do something she didn't want to do.

As she used the oar to push away from the pier, it caught on something, jerked and fell from her hand, and she immediately lurched off balance. For a split second, Ari glimpsed the sheer terror on her face, and then he was instinctively moving forward because the instructor had already moved away while he adjusted someone's life jacket for them. Cleo plunged face first into the water with a tremendous splash and scrabbled frantically for the board. Ari recognised the pure panic in her reaction and the ineptness of her flailing hands. The board was right beside her, but she seemed to be too alarmed actually to see it. Someone was laughing, but Ari had already seen more than enough. He dropped down into the water beside her and grabbed her, lifting her above the water with easy strength.

'Relax, the water is barely a couple of metres deep at this point—'

'I'm not a couple of metres tall!' Cleo gasped, spitting out lake water in disgust. 'I'll drown at that depth—'

'No swimmer could drown in water this shallow,' Ari informed her forcefully, capturing her flailing hands. 'And calm down… You're not in any danger—'

'I *can't* swim!' Cleo hissed in a desperate undertone. 'I know I've got the jacket on and I'm sorry, but I'm very nervous—'

Ari dealt her an arrested appraisal. He lifted her up onto the side of the pier and hauled himself bodily up beside her. 'You can't swim? You actually went out on the water without being able to swim?' he demanded in a rising crescendo of incredulity.

'I've got a life jacket on,' Cleo protested.

'Have you a death wish? The minute you hit the water you panicked! Have you any idea how many people drown because they panic?' he raked down at her wrathfully.

'I wasn't likely to drown unless someone deliberately held me down under the water!' Cleo slung back at him in furious denial. 'And while you may not be my biggest fan, I doubt if you were about to do that—'

'You're an absolute bloody idiot and you should stay away from water!' Ari flamed back at her, dark eyes brilliant with anger, kissable mouth hard as granite. 'What you did was stupidly dangerous!'

Alerted by his wrathful volume, every eye in their vicinity had now turned to them, and Cleo cringed.

She was shivering with cold and the aftermath of fright. Ari Stefanos was standing over her in a rage and it was too much to be borne in the mood she was in. Cleo swallowed the lump in her throat, but her stricken eyes still flooded with tears of hurt and mortification.

A woman broke the horrible silence in which everyone on shore had fallen quiet and hurried forward to wrap a large towel round Cleo. 'Let me take you back to the hotel,' she urged. 'You've had a shock.'

'Thank you, Mel,' Ari breathed in a compressed undertone. 'But I'll take care of Cleo.'

CHAPTER TWO

Cleo scrambled awkwardly upright and, because she felt shaky, she removed the life jacket very slowly while breathing in deep.

'Let me help you... You're swaying,' Ari murmured, scooping her up into his arms and striding away from the pier before she could object to his high-handed behaviour.

'I'll be fine when I get back to my room,' Cleo insisted tightly, shivering within the damp towel and closing her eyes to envision a blissfully warm shower and privacy. 'But I hate you...'

Ari released his breath on an audible hiss because he was well aware that he had screwed up. 'I kind of hate me too at this moment.'

Eyes wide with surprise, Cleo turned her head to really look at him as he settled her down into the front seat of an open-topped buggy. 'You disrespected me... You humiliated me,' she condemned thinly.

'It was an overreaction and I apologise. I saw my twin sister drown when I was a child. It...er...upsets me when people take risks in the water, but I shouldn't have taken that out on you,' he breathed, taking a split-second decision to drive on past the hotel sooner than face the challenge of escorting a wet, distressed and tear-stained woman through a busy reception area.

Cleo was stunned by that very private admission. Curiosity had made her look him up on the internet and that information about his sister had not appeared in his history. Of course, what she had read had related to his education, his business prowess and his sex life, which had been encyclopaedically covered. All his exes had struck her as being of a particular type: tall glitzy brunettes, socialites and models, spiced with the occasional up-and-coming actress.

Scolding herself for her wandering thoughts, she concentrated instead on what he had just told her. Naturally, he would have been traumatised by the experience of seeing a sibling drown, and even she, who didn't like him, could begin to understand and forgive what he had termed an overreaction. For the first time she recognised that Ari Stefanos, the gorgeous, wildly successful billionaire, was not omnipotent and, indeed, was as human and prone to errors of judgement as she could be.

Ari shot the buggy to a halt outside an opulent two-storeyed and balconied wooden cabin surrounded by trees and got out. 'Come on. You'll feel better once you have a shower and warm up—'

'But why did you bring me here instead of back to the hotel?' Cleo demanded, climbing out of the buggy at a much slower pace, an uncertain look on her heart-shaped face.

'It's more private.' Ari raked lean brown fingers through his wind-tousled black hair in a gesture of frustration and gave her a rueful look. 'You were crying. The hotel is very public.'

'I'm not crying any more. It was just a momentary thing…caused by shock,' Cleo pointed out defensively. She squelched up the steps to the front door and, in embarrassment, kicked her sodden footwear off to leave it outside before she stepped indoors barefoot.

'There's a shower through here,' he told her, pushing open a door.

'You didn't think this through, did you?' Cleo said uncomfortably. 'I have no clothes to change into and I'll need a hand to get out of the wetsuit.'

'Trivial,' Ari pronounced, tugging her forward and turning her round to attack the back zip of the wetsuit. 'I'll have our clothes brought here.'

He unzipped the suit, blunt fingertips grazing the smooth, soft skin of her back, and she shivered, shockingly aware of him. She tugged loose her locker key and spun round to hand it to him.

The confines of the bathroom suddenly seemed very small and tight, and breathing felt like a challenge when she glanced up uneasily to meet the lustrous dark gold of his black-lashed gaze. Those ridiculously lush long black lashes of his had gold tips, she thought crazily, locked there in stillness.

'I suppose I should ask you to perform the same service for me,' Ari murmured.

'I suppose…unless you're a natural contortionist,' Cleo mumbled thickly through her dry mouth, ducking her head to move behind him and stand on tiptoe to reach the zip on the back of his suit. Every brain cell in her head felt as though it had died as a long slice of golden satin-smooth brown back showed through the parted edges.

Cleo backed off to the side and tugged at the sleeve of her suit to start removing it, reminding herself that she was wearing a perfectly respectable swimsuit underneath. Yet she was feeling as awkward as a woman forced to perform a strip in public.

Catching a glimpse of Cleo's full rounded breasts cupped in smooth, stretchy material, her movements accentuating the luscious depth of her cleavage as she struggled with the sleeve, was not to be recommended, Ari decided when he went as hard as a rock, every libidinous instinct sparking instantaneously. In an effort to distract himself, he reached for the edge of her sleeve and gave it a sharp yank, enabling her to get one arm free.

'Thanks,' she said, warm colour blossoming in her cheeks as she began peeling her other arm free of the flexible fabric.

His wetsuit hung down round his waist, exposing a flawless bronzed masculine torso and the lean muscular perfection of sculpted abs and pecs. In her haste to draw back and put some space between them, she almost collided with him.

'Not enough room in here for the two of us,' Ari pointed out jerkily, backing away in turn to step back into the hallway. 'I'll sort out the clothes and leave them outside the door for you.'

'Th-thanks,' she heard herself stammer while still staring at him as if he had dropped down in front of her from the moon.

Her palms were sweating, her skin had come out in goosebumps and she was running out of oxygen. He was beautiful, like a glossy picture in a book and just as unreal and untouchable. An odd clenching sensation thrummed between her thighs and she knew what it was—oh, yes, she knew what it was, and it was absolutely *not* anything she should be feeling around her employer. Her face burned hotter than ever.

'Can you get out of that suit alone?' Ari pressed in a roughened undertone.

'Yes, of course,' Cleo declared, hurriedly shutting the door, turning the lock, flinching in even deeper embarrassment when it made a noisy click.

But that instant when she had recognised just how powerfully she was attracted to Ari Stefanos had thrown her back in time to her first love, Dominic, and that could only send chills through her. She didn't want to feel like that again about anyone! Dominic hadn't been her boss or a colleague, though, just a salesman who came into the office occasionally. She had fallen for him like a ton of bricks, although with hindsight she reckoned it had only been an infatuation. He had been young, good-looking and full of easy banter. There had been nothing suspicious about him and, as far as was possible for her, she had checked him out before deciding to commit to their relationship and sleep with him. He would have become her first lover had his girlfriend not turned up on her doorstep clutching their toddler.

To be fair, Imogen hadn't been nasty. She had just said, 'Dominic does this… He gets bored with us and strays… But he always comes back again. It's not your fault. He tells lies and he's very convincing, but he will get bored with you too.'

And Cleo had realised to her horror that she had almost fallen into the same trap as her mother. Her mother had only been a convenient outlet for her father, who had also had another woman in his life. Cleo had been badly burned by the experience she had had with Dominic. The fear that she might place her trust unwisely in a man haunted her whenever she dated and made her very wary.

Irritated by thoughts of her less-than-successful dating past, Cleo managed to remove the wetsuit and her swimsuit and rummage for towels on the open shelves before she stepped into the shower.

The warm water combatted the shivers running through her. She shampooed her hair, thinking that she shouldn't be feeling guilty when nothing had happened between her and Ari. Attraction was normal, but people didn't always act on it, and in any case, she doubted very much that he was equally attracted to her. She had seen the sleek, expensively dressed and giraffe-legged females he dated on the internet, women with the kind of beauty that she had never had. On a good day in her very best clothes and all done up, she could shoot at being pretty, but she wasn't distinctive or particularly sexy, and she didn't have classic features.

He had classic features and yet that description severely understated the ability of his features to linger inside her head. She always wanted to stare at him, to linger with pleasure on the full curve of his lower lip, the clean-cut perfection of his angular jaw, the blue-black luxuriance of his hair and his spectacularly noticeable eyes.

Such reflections were ridiculously immature and foolish, she conceded as a knock sounded on the door and Ari informed her that her clothes had arrived. She wondered how he had achieved that miracle at such speed and she reckoned that it was probably something to do with the fact that he was very, very rich and people seemed to fall over themselves in their eagerness to please the very, very rich.

Wrapped in a towel, she opened the door and ducked back inside with her bag, quickly pulling on her jeans and long-sleeved top, regretting that she had worn her supposedly waterproof shoes down to the lake because now she had nothing else for her feet. Without her miracle styling spray that suppressed frizz, she would also have to leave her hair to dry naturally.

Cleo emerged into the silent hall and went straight for the front door to leave, but it was locked and the key had been removed. Rolling her eyes in frustration, she walked quietly down the hall into the large sitting room and sat down on a comfortable sofa to await the reappearance of her careless host. A wave of tiredness engulfed her because she hadn't slept well the night before with Lily just across the room from her engaged in constant texting with her boyfriend.

Ari strode downstairs, his black hair still damp from the shower, and stared in surprise at Cleo, who was curled up in a ball on the sofa fast asleep. He studied her, struggling to identify what it was about her that roused his libido to such an extent. She wasn't his style, and yet when she had turned those big blue eyes on him, lust had roared through him in a surge of heat that had left him thunderstruck. He breathed in slow and deep, steadying himself. Of course, that urge was not something he would ever succumb to, he reasoned confidently.

Ari was as organised and restrained in his sex life as he was in everything else. He had a select band of willing lovers in his life with whom he spent occasional casual nights and he had never had an exclusive relationship. Sex was a release from tension, a sporadic pastime, something enjoyable rather than exciting. Perhaps that was the secret of Cleo's appeal, he mused. She excited him and he could not recall when a woman had last had that effect on him. Possibly actual excitement in that field had evaded him since he'd left the adolescent years behind.

Wry amusement tilted his mobile lips. He was well aware that he was spoiled in the female department, never being asked for anything more than he was willing to give because women wanted him to continue to call. He received endless invitations and selected only the most tempting from women he viewed as 'suitable'. Cleo wasn't and never would be suitable, he conceded calmly.

He was hungry. He swept up the phone and glanced at Cleo's tumbled mop of guinea-gold curls over the back of the sofa. He would order dinner for her as well, make up for his outburst down by the lake by being sociable with an employee for a change. He was very much a loner, he acknowledged. But then he had been an only child born to two only children, so there never had been much of a family circle to enjoy, which was naturally why the family lawyer's revelations had been so very intriguing.

Ari viewed his slumbering guest with amusement. There was something impossibly sweet about that innocent lack of intent. Women never fell asleep in Ari's radius because they were invariably keen to utilise every possible moment to impress him. Certainly, he could not imagine any other woman he had ever met cheerfully telling him that she hated him, as Cleo had done without hesitation. She was outspoken, again not a quality he was accustomed to because people were not honest around him, not if there was the smallest risk that that honesty could offend or indicate anything that could prove to be personally prejudicial. Cleo didn't guard her tongue or pay lip service to his position even as her employer.

As she shifted and stretched like a little cat in wakefulness, Ari leant over the sofa to say quietly, 'I'm ordering dinner—'

'Ah!' Cleo squealed and shot off the sofa and upright, huge blue eyes locking to him in consternation. 'You gave me a fright!'

'My apologies… What would you like for dinner? Or should I ask what would you *not* like?'

'Dinner?' Cleo gasped, backing away in apparent dismay, wide blue eyes pinned to him as though he were a ghost.

Ari was hugely entertained. 'I'll just order for you,' he decided, lifting the phone to contact Reception and order steak with all the trimmings for two.

'Why would you offer me dinner?' Cleo framed as he replaced the phone again.

Ari gave her a slanting smile that unleashed butterflies in her already tense tummy. 'I don't know. Do you think it could be an attempt to make amends for being rude to you?'

'That's not necessary, Mr Stefanos,' Cleo declared woodenly, her discomfiture unconcealed as she contemplated her bare toes digging into the plush luxury rug beneath her feet.

'I think it is,' Ari asserted. 'So, sit back down and relax…'

He had to be joking on that front, Cleo thought, incredulous at the idea of sharing a meal with a billionaire, who was also her boss. Even so, if he was trying to be nice when he was so obviously *not* a nice person on her terms, it would be mean of her to deny him the opportunity. Grudgingly, she sat down very stiffly in an armchair.

'You've had a pretty rotten day of it,' Ari pointed out quietly, determined not to smile at his recollections. 'You got ambushed at the paintballing and you fell in the lake when you tried to go paddleboarding.'

Stony-faced at those unwelcome reminders of her lack of athletic talent and physical grace, Cleo nodded. 'I'm not an outdoorsy person, but I like to give things a go—'

'That's an admirable trait,' Ari remarked, thinking that she was about as 'outdoorsy' as an exotic plant plunged into the frost, but he was impressed that she had been willing to try.

'Except when it comes to activities in the water,' she dared to remind him of his opinion.

'I may be in a minority, but I did think that your participation in those circumstances was dangerous and, worst of all, the experience gave you one hell of a fright,' Ari told her drily, letting her know that he hadn't changed his opinion of her daring in the slightest. 'Would you like a glass of wine?'

'Thank you.' Cleo nodded again and tucked her restless hands between her thighs because she had never been more conscious of a man's scrutiny. Those dark golden eyes that lit up his lean, darkly handsome features held her fast as glue.

Cleo watched him uncork a bottle of red wine and fill glasses, his every move smooth and dexterous, his polished assurance as much of a draw as his devastating good looks. Cleo had never met a male that confident and there was something oddly reassuring about that quality. 'I suppose I should have panicked when I found the front door locked,' she confided abruptly.

Ari glanced back at her with a raised brow of enquiry.

'Locked in a house with a strange man…' Cleo clarified in a belated attack of mortification because she could see that that aspect had not once crossed his mind. And why would it have? she asked herself ruefully. Women rarely wanted to escape from young, rich and very handsome men.

'I'm sorry. It didn't occur to me that you would wish to leave immediately,' Ari countered, walking away from her and back to the door to replace the key that he had removed in an act of personal security that came to him as naturally as breathing. 'There, it is possible for you to leave now whenever you like…'

In receipt of that demonstrative response, Cleo had turned as red as a ripe tomato while secretly cursing his decision to take her word so literally. She took a strong glug of her wine.

'Is the wine okay?'

'I don't drink much, so I don't have an opinion to offer,' Cleo admitted tautly.

'I thought everyone in your age group indulged,' Ari remarked.

'I don't like the feeling of being out of control. I remember my mother…' Just as she voiced those words, her lips compressed. 'Sorry, you don't want to hear about that—'

Ari elevated a brow, deciding that yanking Cleo out of her shell could take more effort than he was capable of awarding her. For all her bubbly friendliness on Reception and her surprising backbone and defiance in adversity, she was amazingly shy. Clearly, only fear of losing her employment had turned her into a chittering chatterbox in his office the day they had first met.

'I do. I'm trying to get to know you. Did your mother have a problem with alcohol?' Ari prompted with deliberate boldness.

Cleo paled, shrugged. 'Only for a while, when I was younger and I didn't really understand what had happened. She had broken up with my father and obviously she was upset for a time because she knew she wouldn't see him again.'

Ari angled suddenly intent eyes on her troubled face. 'You grew up without your father?'

'Yes. He had a relationship with my mother, but not with me.' Cleo winced.

'And how did that work?' Ari Stefanos asked her with apparent interest, his entire focus on her, which was a rather unnerving experience.

Indeed, the sudden intensity of those black-lashed burnished bronze eyes of his was mesmerising and her skin broke out in goosebumps of awareness. She shifted uneasily in her seat, mortified by her reaction to him.

'I can't see how you would be interested in that,' Cleo commented edgily, not knowing a polite way of telling him that the subject was too personal since he seemed to be clueless in the empathy stakes.

'I have very good reasons for asking such questions,' Ari declared. 'There is a situation in my life at present which appears to bear some resemblance to *your* childhood experiences.'

'Oh...' Cleo drained her wine and set the empty

glass down on the coffee table with a snap, demurring when he offered her a refill. Her brain was concentrated on striving to work out what situation in his life could possibly lead to such questions.

In the dragging silence the doorbell rang.

'That will be the food.' Ari strode off to answer it.

I'm dining with a billionaire, Cleo reminded herself, pinching a slender denim-clad thigh to reassure herself that she was not dreaming while the buzz of voices, the sound of a trolley and the chink of china and glass sounded in the background.

'Cleo!' Ari called, and he sounded just like a boss and she grinned then, her discomfiture vanquished by *that* tone.

She crossed the hall into the dining room and sank down at the table, her chair pulled out by a hovering waiter.

'If you answer my questions, I would be very grateful,' Ari informed her once the front door thudded closed again on the waiter.

Cleo had to swallow hard on her mouth-watering steak because she was unable to imagine any situation in which her input could possibly be helpful to Ari Stefanos. 'What relevance could my very ordinary life have to do with anything in yours?' she asked quietly.

Ari studied her. 'Is it possible for me to trust you not to run to the nearest tabloid newspaper to sell a story?'

Cleo stared back at him in wonderment. 'You've had someone do that to you?'

Ari gave her a brusque nod of confirmation.

'I wouldn't sink that low!' she declared with convincing sincerity. 'I *swear* I wouldn't!'

Ari reached a decision and set down his cutlery. 'Okay. Recently I learned to my astonishment that, through my father, I have half-siblings...'

'My goodness...' Cleo almost whispered. 'So have I, although I've known about them since I was a teenager...'

Ari dealt her an amused look. 'Which in your case is not exactly a hundred years ago. Tell me about what it was like growing up without a father, which I assume is what happened?'

'Yes. Mum worked with my father and had a long affair with him. It ended when I was about three. I'm afraid I have very few memories of him. He wasn't married but he did live with another woman with whom he had already had two children. When I was fifteen she admitted that in her late thirties she decided to get pregnant before she missed out altogether on having a family of her own.'

'Then you weren't an accident...'

'No, but she *may* have told my father I was,' she confided with a wrinkled nose. 'I didn't like to ask too many painful questions because she was a brilliant mum, apart from that period after she and my father broke up and I think she was depressed and that's why she was drinking then.'

'Probably. Did your father take any interest in you?'

'He paid maintenance but there was no visitation. He wasn't interested obviously in having a relationship with me and I can accept that—'

'But do you *really* accept it? And how does it make you feel that you were rejected?'

Cleo winced at that rather cruel question. 'Try for a little tact, boss.'

'Don't call me that when we've strayed so far from workplace boundaries.' Ari pushed away his empty plate. 'There's desserts somewhere…possibly in the kitchen—'

'Not for me. That steak filled me up.' Cleo stood up. 'I'll have coffee, though.'

Cleo set out the coffee cups on the top tray of the trolley and proceeded to pour for both of them before walking back into the sitting room. 'You asked me how I felt about my father? Rejected about sums it up. It hurt a lot when I was growing up when I saw other kids with their dads. And then years later I saw my father again with a woman and two children in the park. They seemed happy. It was only then that I truly understood my background. That woman and those kids were his *real* family, while I was only the by-product of his affair—'

Ari frowned. 'That's harsh.'

'It's reality,' Cleo contradicted quietly. 'It was healthier for me just to accept that that's how it was. I gather your half-siblings come from a similar set-up?'

Ari expelled his breath in a sharp hiss. 'A long-running secret affair, yes. I was shattered when I found out—'

'Shattered?' Cleo queried in surprise.

'I believed that my parents had had a very happy marriage—'

'Yes, but you were on the outside,' Cleo pointed out gently, reflecting that, in the realm of personal relationships, Ari seemed rather naive. 'I assume that this affair was your father's and that you only found out about it because he had…er…passed away?'

Ari released a heavy sigh as he paced. 'Yes… Do you mind me asking if you've ever contacted your half-siblings?'

Cleo twisted to look at him and frowned. 'No. Why would I do that?'

It was Ari's turn to look surprised. 'They're your flesh and blood.'

'Yes, but I've always assumed that they don't know about me and probably have no idea that their father cheated on their mother with another woman. Why would I want to upset them with that knowledge?' Cleo asked ruefully. 'Yes, I'm curious about them, but approaching them would probably hurt them by revealing stuff they don't need to know. I doubt that I would get a very positive response.'

His level ebony brows pleated. 'All the same—'

'No, Ari,' she cut in, using his name for the first time because she was so caught up in the discussion. 'Look at how *you* are feeling now. You said you were shattered when you discovered that you had siblings and that it's trashed your belief in your parents' happy marriage…'

As Cleo made those deductions, Ari angled admiring dark golden eyes over her and sank down on the hide sofa beside her. 'You really understand all this stuff… You see, I don't. The whole thing just came at me out of nowhere and I'm not sure how to handle it—'

'But you're on the *other* side of the fence from me. You are the *accepted* child. What about your half-siblings? What do you know about them?'

'I've got a private investigation team trying to trace them, but nothing that I have so far discovered is reassuring. I don't know when the affair ended or even how it ended, but my father appears to have left the woman and the children without money, which very much shocked me,' Ari imparted in a driven undertone. 'The very *least* he should have done was ensure their financial security.'

'I suppose I respect you for caring and not just thinking about yourself,' Cleo told him truthfully.

'I feel bloody guilty. I had an idyllic childhood. I have never lacked anything I wanted in life.' Ari breathed rawly, his disquiet unhidden. 'I have had every educational opportunity and advantage handed to me on a plate…while my father's other three children have had next to nothing in comparison—'

'There are *three* of them?'

'A boy and girl set of twins and a younger girl,' he proffered curtly.

Compassion filtered through Cleo. She was staggered by the amount of emotion he was revealing, because she had always assumed he was as self-contained and cool and calm as he appeared to be on the surface. The revelation that he was not at all that way humanised him and erased her awareness of their differing status while touching her heart. His spectacular golden eyes were liquid with emotion and she lifted an instinctive hand and rested it in a soothing gesture against his jawline, fingertips lightly grazing his stubbled skin.

'It's all right,' she whispered softly. 'It's not your fault. Nor is it your duty to carry the responsibility either. It was your father's choices that made it that way for his other children. I can't believe that they would blame you for his oversights.'

That this tiny young woman was actually striving to comfort him knocked Ari sideways. No female had ever approached him in that light since his mother had died several years earlier and it drew him like a fire on a winter's day, his dark eyes flaming pure glittering gold as he tipped up her chin with a flick of his fingers and brought his mouth down on hers.

It was like sticking her finger in a light socket, being hit by lightning, taking a ride on a shooting star, Cleo thought crazily as her whole body pulsed and lit up with a burst of heat and longing that blew her away. Nothing had ever tasted as good as that beautiful mouth of his, about which she had fantasised so often. Hard and yet soft, his lips caressed hers with lazy sensuality, and then, as her own parted to let him inside, the stab of his delving tongue kick-started an infinitely more primitive response. A needy ache stirred between her thighs and her nipples tightened, pushing at the lace of her bra while her heart thundered inside her chest.

'Are you okay with this?' Ari husked in her ear as

her hands clung to his shoulders as if he were the only stable thing in a collapsing world.

And in a way, he was, because she knew exactly what he meant, only there was no time to think about the many, many things she knew she would normally be thinking about. She knew that any perceptible hesitation would end the opportunity. She also knew she definitely didn't want that. She didn't want to be a virgin any longer either, she conceded grudgingly. For goodness' sake, she was twenty-two years old and had held on to her innocence, her *ignorance*, whatever people might choose to describe it, for longer than most in her age group. For once, too, she didn't want to play it safe; she wanted to tear up the rule book and take a risk. After all, with every man she had ever spent time with, she had always been waiting for the magic moment when passion sparked and swept away every other concern, giving her that shot of adrenaline-driven desire that other women had described. So what if her magnetic irresistible lure was Ari Stefanos? Surely she was as capable of having a one-night stand and walking away afterwards as any other woman? After all, there was nothing surer than that *he* would be walking away…

A guy who lived in a world utterly removed from her own. *Are you okay with this?* He took it for granted that every woman was prepared to consider travelling from a mere kiss to full sex when he asked! Hiding her reluctant amusement, Cleo pressed her face into his shoulder, drinking in the divine scent of him and quivering with an awareness absolutely new to her. 'I'm fine with this,' she framed shakily.

Ari was refusing to think. That kiss had powered him up like a rocket. He hadn't ever felt *that* before with a woman and he could not overcome the temptation to explore it even though every brain cell in his head was telling him 'no'.

'Let's go upstairs,' he heard himself say in defiance of his shrewd brain.

'You had better not get me pregnant,' she warned him in a near whisper, because that was her biggest fear relating to sex. She didn't want to be a single parent as her mother had been with no other adult to rely on. 'I'm not on the pill.'

'I don't make mistakes like that,' Ari assured her while trying not to laugh at the gaucheness of that warning.

Cleo was wondering whether to mention that she was a virgin, but she decided he didn't need to know that and would hopefully not notice. She was also afraid that if she admitted that truth it might make him think better of what they were doing. He closed a bold hand over hers and headed for the stairs, and she got all breathless and incredulous about what she was doing. But this was the guy who had haunted her dreams from the first moment she laid eyes on him, and there was no way she was willing to deny herself the chance to be with him just once. She *could* handle the 'just once', she told herself squarely.

The bedroom had a wooden cathedral ceiling and a massive divan bed. Ari tugged her gently back to him and lifted her top off her so smoothly she only fully registered what he was doing as he freed her from the sleeves. Cheeks colouring as he eased round her to appreciate the fullness of her breasts in a bright scarlet bra with deep cleavage, she only forgot to be self-conscious when he kissed her again, and—*my goodness*—he could kiss. He made her head swim and her body hum like a purring engine. She didn't notice the bra dropping to the floor or the loosening of her waistband, only reconnecting with reality when her loose jeans dropped round her ankles and he lifted her out of them and brought her down on the bed instead.

'You have gorgeous breasts,' he husked.

In the act of trying to cover them like some shy maiden, her hands dropped again and she lifted her chin, striving for a confidence that she did not have in her body. She had always thought that her boobs and her hips were too big for the rest of her, and that if by some miracle it were possible to stretch her to a much greater height, she might have had a terrific figure. As it was, she had always felt dumpy in stature and top-heavy.

He sank down on the bed beside her and curved his hands to the full firm globes, his heavily lashed dark golden eyes colliding with hers. It was as if a shower of sparks went flying through her and suddenly she was leaning forward and finding his gorgeous mouth again for herself. It had not even occurred to her that she could ever feel anything as powerful as the instincts driving her now with him. He tasted so good and the scent of him was even better, ensuring that one kiss led to another and that his hands were all over her just as hers were equally all over him. She had never felt that fierce urge to touch and explore before. But the smooth flex of muscles below his shirt, the tented evidence of his arousal beneath his trousers, held an extraordinary pull of attraction for her. He groaned beneath her touch, hunger blazing in his dark golden eyes as he gazed down at her.

'You are so incredibly sexy,' Ari husked feverishly, rearranging her to close his lips round a pouting pink nipple and tug on it until she gasped out loud.

A river of molten fire snaked through Cleo's veins as he simultaneously stroked the delicate folds between her legs. A fingertip dipped, a thumb skilfully brushed her clit and her body raced from zero to sixty in seconds as a flood of reaction gripped her. A croak of sound was torn from her lips, her back arching, a spasm of such raw response travelling through her that she was mindless in that moment, a being controlled by wild want and need.

'Never wanted anyone as much as I want you right now,' Ari growled, peeling away what remained of his clothing. He was entranced by her passion. She couldn't seem to keep her hands off him any more than he could keep his hands or his lips off her: she was more than the object of his desire; she was a partner, and for him it was an exhilarating experience.

Yet on another level of his shrewd brain Ari could not quite credit what he was doing. He did not mix business and pleasure, yet he was in bed with an employee—an absolute no-go in his rule book. But

Cleo's innate allure for him, he conceded, overpowered every misgiving and smashed his control.

Cleo was way beyond the ability to speak, pulling him closer, finding his sensual mouth again for herself, hands roaming down over his long, smooth back and spreading there while she remained feverishly attuned to her awareness of the erection pressed against her thigh. For an instant there was a pause as he drew back to don protection. Her breath was feathering in her throat, her heart pounding as he came back to her and suddenly he was *there*, where she most wanted him to be, nudging against the most sensitive spot, pushing in, stretching her in the most remarkable way, somehow answering the overpowering need coursing at the very core of her.

A sting of pain made Cleo jerk and grit her teeth. For an instant she tensed and then the discomfort was gone, washed away in the tide of amazing sensation that followed. He shifted his lean hips and a wave of elation gripped her as the pleasure began to build with every driving motion of his powerful body on and in hers. A sense of wonder rose within her as her heart hammered and the piercing need that had controlled her only minutes earlier returned with a vengeance, forcing the level of excitement to a pitch she could hardly bear. Ultimately, she reached the heights, and white-hot electrifying pleasure shot through her every limb as her body seemed to splinter in a shower of physical and mental fireworks that left her falling back against the pillow in shaken wonder.

A wicked grin slashing his sensual lips, Ari sat up

and feasted golden bronze eyes on her dazed face. 'We need to talk,' he declared unnervingly.

'We've got nothing to talk about!' Cleo told him in a defensive rush, clawing the duvet to her and sitting up. Had he guessed that he was her first? How would he have guessed that? There was no way on earth he could have guessed, she told herself urgently.

'Think about it,' Ari urged softly, springing out of bed and disappearing into the bathroom.

There was blood on him, and he knew, he simply *knew*, that she had been a virgin, but he could see that she was ready to deny it. And how did he fight that? Admit that her lack of sensual sophistication had been an equal betrayal? Yes, a seeming critique of her performance would really raise him in her estimation! Frustrated, because he was a male who always preferred honesty in place of other less presentable approaches, Ari switched on the shower. All he could realistically think about at that moment was how soon he could have her again…and he knew that was out of the question so soon, only that didn't stop him recollecting how absolutely amazing the encounter had been. He had never felt passion like that; he had never had sex that good…

The scent of her skin, the feel of her, her ability to stay natural and her lack of desire to impress him, all combined with her effortless sexiness, were a temptation he could not resist. As a rule, women didn't tempt Ari. He felt like sex and he had sex and it was usually that basic in that no one particular woman had special appeal for him. Yet Cleo attracted him like a magnet, and in surrendering to that attraction, he had not been sated, as was the norm for him. In fact, he was already wondering how soon he could be with her again…

Distract him, Cleo was thinking in consternation. The last thing she wanted was any kind of intimate discussion, not following on from the biggest mistake she had ever made in her life! She had to get out of the cabin and back to the hotel just as soon as she possibly could, write her ghastly error off to temptation and inexperience and never ever think about it again. In a frantic race she located her dropped clothing and hastily got dressed again.

Ari emerged from the bathroom, a towel knotted round his lean waist because he suspected that too much nudity would freak her out. He was utterly taken aback and unprepared to find her fully clothed again. Women didn't usually rush away from him. *He* did the leaving, not the other way round. Shock stilled him in his tracks.

'So,' Cleo stated rather abruptly. 'You never did get around to telling me what you were planning to do about these siblings you've discovered you have.'

Ari shot her an arrested appraisal, that having been the very last thing he had expected her to mention at that moment. He shook his tousled dark head slightly and regrouped. 'I'm trying to track them down with a view to getting to know them…if that's what they want.'

Cleo gave him a bright smile of approval that struck

him as incredibly fake while she sidled closer to the door with the air of someone not wishing to be noticed. 'That's a lovely idea—'

Ari stepped between Cleo and the door. 'Going somewhere?'

'Yes, I want to get back to the hotel before my roommate wonders where I am,' she pointed out stiltedly.

'Staging a cover-up is unnecessary,' Ari intoned with conviction. 'This is a private matter.'

Cleo tilted her head back, because she was barefoot and he was so tall that she couldn't look him in the eye any other way. 'Well, that's one way of putting it. I'd call it a huge mistake, but fortunately, we can forget it ever happened,' she told him even more brightly, seeking and expecting his approval. 'As far as I'm already concerned…it *didn't* happen—'

His well-shaped black brows pleated. 'It *did* happen, and why should you want to run away from it? I have no regrets whatsoever—'

'It was wrong. We both got carried away—'

'I'm not a teenager and neither are you. I'm way past the age where I get carried away. We started out being inappropriate and then somehow it began feeling right and *being* right,' Ari imparted with level emphasis, revealing far more than he usually did with a woman because everything felt different and new and fresh with Cleo.

'How can something so absolutely wrong be right?' Cleo demanded fiercely, reaching past him for the door handle.

Ari rested a lean brown hand down on hers to forestall her. 'I can make it right. I can make it possible. I will find you employment somewhere else—'

It was the perfect solution, Ari reflected with satisfaction. They would no longer be working in the same place, which meant that he could cherish his rules of office conduct again. A voice in his brain queried that, even though he had already thoroughly *broken* his own rules by getting intimate with an employee. But what was done was done, he ruminated, and he already knew that he didn't want it to be only a casual hook-up. For the first time ever with a woman, he was willing to sign up for a repeat experience, and in the light of that, it would be infinitely wiser to move Cleo into another job.

'No…you don't get to do that and interfere!' Cleo gasped, stricken. 'I'm not like my mother… I won't change my life or base my decisions on what some man wants!'

'I'm not asking you to do that,' Ari incised tautly as she ignored his attempt to reason with her and yanked the bedroom door open. 'I'm only offering to remove any obstacles which you may feel prevent us from being together like this—'

Cleo stalked out onto the landing. 'You're crazy but you're also my boss. I want to forget this happened and never have it mentioned again.'

'That seems rather like overkill,' Ari commented drily. 'We're young and single. We haven't harmed anyone.'

'Thanks for dinner,' Cleo pronounced awkwardly.

'Cleo…' Ari breathed in fierce frustration as her

bare feet slapped down the wooden staircase, her golden curls a messy mop that glimmered in the fading daylight, her slender spine rigid in its rejection. The solid thud of the front door closing on her heels was the only answer he received.

Cleo didn't trust herself to say another word, particularly when Ari had forcefully disagreed with every word she had said. But every inch of her rebelled against the secret sordid fling she believed he was offering her. *My goodness.* Had the sex been *that* good on his terms?

CHAPTER THREE

ARI WAS STILL recalling that exasperating conclusion with Cleo when his limousine dropped him off at his London Headquarters. He had been out of the country for five days, negotiating the purchase of an exclusive Portuguese beach resort that had unexpectedly come on the market. He hadn't been able to contact Cleo because he didn't have her phone number, and using his status to acquire that number had struck him as beneath his dignity. In any case, he was keen to believe that a few days to cool off would have put Cleo into a more reasonable frame of mind.

For that reason, Ari was taken aback to see a strange face presiding over the reception desk when he arrived on the top floor. 'What happened to Cleo?' he demanded of his PA, Mel, when his personal staff joined him in his office.

Everybody's surprise that he should even ask that question about a junior staff member made him bite back further comment.

Mel shrugged. 'She quit and the agency replaced her the next day with profuse apologies.'

Ari knew that he had much more important matters to handle than Cleo's disappearance, but he also knew that workplace ethics would not, in this instance, stop him from discovering her address. He had an appointment with the family lawyer at lunchtime. Apparently, the private detective agency he had engaged had lodged a timely and pretty comprehensive report, although enquiries were still ongoing. Receiving information about his siblings was definitely something to look forward to, he reflected confidently.

By mid-afternoon, Ari's sense of anticipation had died in receipt of a truckload of bad news. Indeed, he had learned things about his siblings' lives that would most likely give him sleepless nights. One fact in particular had hit him very hard and he left the office mid-afternoon to seek out Cleo. He could not imagine discussing such personal stuff with any of his friends but, somehow, Cleo was in a different category in his mind. She had impressed him as practical rather than overly emotional and he liked that trait. Somewhere in the back of his brain, he was querying that immediate wish to discuss the situation with a woman he barely knew, but Ari was not accustomed to questioning his own decisions or to stifling urges that might impress some as unwise. Nor was he the sort of male who dwelt overlong on the mysteries of life and his connections to other people.

Cleo was tired. With her free hand she massaged the ache in her back, acknowledging that she had forgotten how exhausting bartending could be when it was busy. Mercifully, the rush was over, and she was thinking longingly of the end to her shift because her feet were killing her in the high heels she so rarely wore. But then she had had no choice because without the heels she wasn't tall enough to reach for certain items.

The office temp agency had been furious with her for breaking her contract, but Cleo had no doubt that she had done what she *had* to do when she resigned from Stefanos Enterprises. She was mortified by her own behaviour and it had been easier to leave than risk an even more complicated and embarrassing situation developing. And yet on another level, which she did not wish to examine, she was also grieving the reality that she would never see Ari Stefanos again, and feeling like that against all common sense just made her hate herself all the more!

After all, she had barely been a blip on Ari's radar even to begin with. He had scarcely registered that she was female or indeed shown any sort of interest in her until events thrust them together and somehow—she didn't honestly know *how*—they had ended up in bed. She should have said no. She was well aware that she *could* have said no, because he had given her that opportunity, but she hadn't and there was no denying that. She had made the wrong choice, put *herself* out of a good job and a reference, and she could not find an excuse to hide behind.

When she glanced up and saw Ari Stefanos in front of the bar counter, she could not initially believe the evidence of her own eyes. 'How did you find me?' she croaked in horror.

'Your flatmate—'

Her eyebrows airlifted. 'You found out where I live?' she condemned resentfully, because walking away from him had been a challenge and she was proud she had managed to do it. Ari seeking her out and showing up again was way more temptation than she needed and it felt very unfair. 'That's not…er… very professional, is it?'

Pleased with that sally, Cleo turned away to draw a beer for a customer and ignored him. But then Cleo didn't need to look more than a second at Ari Stefanos to see him inside her head in all his perfection. Dark grey designer suit cut to outline every muscular angle and line of his tall, powerful body, a white-and-grey pinstripe shirt teamed with a royal-blue tie. Ari didn't believe in dressing down for work and there were no casual-wear days in his offices. He was a formal guy, who laid down pretty demanding conservative rules to be followed in the workplace. Rules, however, that he had chosen to ignore in her case.

Sam, her current employer, stretched above her to retrieve a glass and murmured, 'With your friend here, you can take your break now if you like.'

Cleo turned brick red at the concept of Ari Stefanos being any kind of a friend. He was more like a nuclear submarine who had sneaked up on her, blown her sky-high and destroyed her nice quiet life. But she supposed she had to speak to him, to act normally instead of angry and resentful, before he worked out that she had had a lowering sort of immature crush on him before they had become intimate. How humiliating would that be? He wasn't stupid. He would soon guess too if she kept on behaving as though he were some serious threat instead of simply a man she had once slept with. 'Thanks, Sam.'

'Ari…' she muttered, glancing up only to be ensnared by rich tawny eyes semi-veiled by black curling lashes, and her heart literally clenched in her chest. 'Why are you here?'

'When do you finish?' he pressed, his keen gaze scanning the colourful geometric top she sported, the fitted skirt exposing her shapely legs, the strappy shoes accentuating her slender ankles. Hunger punched through him with raw vigour, disconcerting him because he had believed, *genuinely* believed, that some weird combination of reactions had coalesced in him at the retreat and made him act out of character. Only now he was looking again at Cleo in the flesh, the guinea-gold curls surrounding her heart-shaped face, the big blue eyes striving to avoid his, the delicate flush of her pale skin, and his response was almost instantaneous, setting up a throb of almost painful arousal.

His lean, darkly handsome face gripped her gaze. 'I need to talk to you—'

Cleo struggled to drag her hungry eyes from him. But it was as if he were a magnet and she were made of metal. Compulsion made her gaze cling to his sinfully gorgeous face. 'We've got nothing to talk about—'

'I've had some news about my siblings, but not anything I want to share in a public place,' Ari intoned drily. 'When will you be free?'

She knew her own vulnerability as her heartbeat quickened and a shimmer of prickling awareness sifted wickedly through her taut body. He was still making her feel things she had never felt before, but even worse, he was making her feel them when she was striving not to be affected. He broke down her every defensive barrier and she didn't know how he did it.

'Six. But—'

'I'll have you picked up,' Ari incised, and turned on his heel.

Cleo wanted to smack him for his arrogance even while curiosity was tugging crazily at her because she was almost as inquisitive about the unknown relatives he had discovered as he was. She bristled at having been taken by surprise. Would she have acted any differently had she been prepared for his appearance? She suppressed a sigh and tried to be honest with herself. Truth was that, on the spot and in the flesh, she found Ari Stefanos downright irresistible.

Only a few minutes after she walked out of the bar, a luxury car purred into the kerb. A male she recognised from the office as belonging to Ari's security team emerged from the vehicle, tugged open the rear passenger door and called, 'Miss Brown?'

Cleo settled into the car as it pulled back into the traffic and didn't really draw breath again until the vehicle purred through a select city square of Georgian town houses and finally drew to a halt outside one of them. She had expected some penthouse apartment, not an actual house, she reflected in surprise as she climbed out and mounted the steps to the front door. The car departed again just as the door opened and an older woman murmured, 'Mr Stefanos is waiting for you, Miss Brown.'

Her slender spine stiff with self-consciousness, Cleo walked through an echoing tiled front hall, becoming belatedly aware that the house was a rare double-fronted town house of enormous size and grandeur. Her surroundings were like a shock wake-up call to her. This was Ari's true milieu, the rich and opulent environment of a male born with an entire silver service in his mouth, never mind a single silver spoon! What did he know about scrimping to survive in a city as expensive as London? What did he know about shopping with coupons and buying clothes in charity shops? How on earth had she ended up in bed with a male with whom she had so very little in common?

She was shown into an unexpectedly airy sunroom where tall exotic plants offered filtered shade from the sunshine. Comfortable seating overlooked a secluded rear garden that was a glorious oasis of greenery. The sound of a sliding door sent her flipping round. Ari strode in from outdoors, more casually clad than she had ever seen him in faded jeans and a forest-green sweater. Although his lean, dark features were clenched with a brooding tension she had not seen there before, he still looked younger and even sexier than normal in that get-up. The instant that bold thought raced through her head, she squashed it flat and reddened.

'Cleo…sit down,' he urged. 'Coffee?'

'No, thanks. I'm on a caffeine high by the time I leave the bar,' she confided.

'It's time we exchanged phone numbers,' Ari decreed.

Cleo breathed in deep, on the brink of refusing, and then, belatedly, she acknowledged that she wanted that link, and she dug out her phone.

The woman who had ushered her indoors reappeared with a laden tray, which she set down on the low table before withdrawing again. Cleo was relieved to see a pot of tea on offer.

'Help yourself,' Ari urged, passing her a plate. 'I thought you might be hungry…'

'Only a little,' Cleo confided, tempted by the delicious snack foods into selecting a couple and then setting down her plate to pour the tea. 'I get a pretty good lunch at midday.'

'It's none of my business, but why would you leave a decent position in an office to do bar work?' Ari shot at her with a frown.

'If you take tips into account, I actually earn more at a busy city bar,' Cleo explained apologetically, glad to employ an excuse that glossed over her real reasons for leaving Stefanos Enterprises. 'My stepfather runs a pub. Thanks to him, I'm experienced behind the bar.'

'I think we both know that the salary is not why you chose to jack the job in,' Ari murmured softly.

Cleo stiffened. 'Let's not get into the personal stuff. What did you want to talk to me about?'

'You're the only person apart from my lawyer who

knows about my father's second family. It seems wiser to keep it that way,' Ari explained heavily. 'Tragically, I received bad news on that score today.'

'Oh…' Cleo framed in dismay on his behalf. 'What did you discover?'

'That their mother died over ten years ago and that the three children went into foster care because there were no other relatives. So far, the investigation agency has only been able to trace one of them… Lucas, the elder twin and the kid brother, whom I was *so* eager to meet,' Ari breathed through clenched teeth, a muscle tightening at the corner of his unsmiling mouth, his amber gaze dark with suppressed bitterness and regret. '*Dead* at the age of twenty-two from a heroin overdose, both him and his girlfriend—'

'What hideous news to receive,' Cleo responded in a shaken whisper, leaning closer, wanting to offer comfort but not sure how to do it without crossing the imaginary line that imposed the boundaries she felt that she needed around him.

'Their bodies were found together in a squat. I feel sick with shame that something like that could have happened to my own flesh and blood!' Ari admitted in a savage undertone. 'How could my father neglect the needs of the children he had brought into the world to that extent?'

Cleo frowned at that searing condemnation. 'You take such a negative view of things,' she scolded softly. 'You don't know all the facts, do you? And unfortunately, with both your father and the woman he had the affair with dead, you may *never* know the facts.

A hundred and one different things could have happened. Maybe the woman broke up with your father and refused his support… Nobody knows their own future. Maybe they lost contact and she was too proud to ask for help. It was a secret relationship as well, so there was probably nobody else able to inform your father that the children had lost their mother. Until you know for sure what happened, you must *try* not to make harsh judgements.'

'When you receive news of that nature, it is difficult *not* to judge! My siblings went into the care of the authorities. My little brother dropped out of school at fifteen and ran away from his foster home to live on the streets. He had a string of convictions for drug-dealing before becoming an addict. He was identified by his criminal records—'

Cleo reached for his hand, where his fingers were biting angrily into the arm of his seat. 'Ari…it's *not* your fault. None of this is. You didn't even know Lucas existed. But it's very sad that you never had the chance to meet him and that he seems to have lived what sounds like a pretty unhappy life—'

'I haven't even told you the *whole* story yet,' Ari admitted heavily. 'There was a baby found with my brother and his girlfriend, a baby girl on the brink of starving, whose birth hadn't even been registered. She may be their child… She may not be. DNA tests are being done to identify her and to establish whether or not she is of my blood. She's still in hospital and then destined for foster care—'

'A baby?' Cleo repeated, with frowning eyes of

concern. 'It breaks my heart to think of a poor little baby suffering like that...but, all the same, it's *good* news—'

'Good?' Ari repeated rawly as a warm smile chased the shadows from her face. 'How can it be good news?'

'If she's your brother's child, she's your niece and you should have a say in what happens to her, unless there are other, closer relatives involved—'

'I have given a DNA sample and requested a meeting with the child,' Ari admitted. 'But what do I know about babies? What would I do with her even if she does prove to be my brother's kid?'

'That's for you to decide in the future. One step at a time. Don't waste energy even thinking about what hasn't happened yet,' Cleo murmured calmly.

Ari locked stunning dark eyes highlighted with flecks of gold on her and studied her from below his curling black lashes.

Cleo flushed. 'What?' she pressed uncomfortably.

'You're a remarkably soothing woman in a crisis,' Ari murmured with frank appreciation.

'My mum used to flip at the smallest thing going wrong. I learned to be quieter, more practical,' she muttered defensively. 'It's just how I react when there's trouble.'

'It helps,' Ari breathed, his rich drawl dark and deep in tone as he closed a hand round the small fingers still engaged in stroking the back of his hand. She was very touchy-feely and he wasn't used to that, because in his family they had all been of a stand-offish bent, rarely touching and certainly not embracing.

There was no denying that her natural warmth and sympathy attracted him in some bizarre way.

Cleo gazed down uncertainly at the hand gripping hers. Ari tugged on it and she glanced up warily to be engulfed in smouldering dark golden eyes. 'Come here…' he murmured, soft and low and intense.

Something dangerously hot curling low in her pelvis, Cleo half stood up and hovered nearby rather than immediately accepting his invitation. 'Not a good idea,' she muttered shakily, inwardly fighting herself to keep her distance from him.

'Stay with me tonight,' Ari urged.

And that fast, she thought, where was the harm? That ship had already sailed and she no longer worked for him. It was the most freeing thought she had had in days, and the weight of her guilt, regret and insecurity fell away even faster, leaving a wonderful lightness in its place.

'Yes,' she murmured with a sudden shy smile of agreement.

With a flashing smile, Ari tumbled her down on top of him and claimed her readily parted lips with raw, breath-stealing hunger. Her fingers speared into his thick black hair and held him fast. A rush of heat surged at the heart of her and she swallowed back a moan as he groaned into her hair. 'Upstairs before I shock my housekeeper…'

'I assumed that you would be living in a modern apartment,' Cleo confided, feeling the heat rise in her face as he led her up the imposing main staircase, and she hoped like hell that nobody would see them.

For goodness' sake, she wasn't a misbehaving teenager breaking rules, she told herself, irritated by that sneaking-around sensation and her adolescent lack of confidence.

'I was and then my father died. I didn't want this place lying empty and I didn't want to sell it, so I put the apartment on the market instead.' Ari thrust open a door and drew her into a very large bedroom, splendidly decorated with gleaming inlaid furniture. 'Tomorrow evening, we'll go out to dinner—'

Cleo swivelled startled eyes in his direction, taken aback by that announcement. 'No,' she told him without hesitation.

'No…to dinner?' Ari prompted in wonderment, suddenly falling still.

'No to dinner… Yes to everything else,' Cleo qualified with hot cheeks.

'Why no?' Ari pressed for further clarification even as he scooped her off her feet and settled her on the side of the bed before crouching down to loosen the ankle straps on her shoes.

'I don't want to be seen out with you!' Cleo told him in a rush. 'This…*us*…it's a crazy fling. Let's keep it under the radar.'

His flaring black brows elevated. 'I don't think I've ever met a woman who was ashamed of me before—'

'For goodness' sake, it's not like that!' Cleo protested. 'I just don't think this is a relationship meant for public consumption. You know that you and me won't last for five minutes, so why bother? I don't want the media attention either. When I go for another office job, it wouldn't do me any favours if I've been labelled as one of your cast-offs on the internet.'

'Why am I the one feeling like a cast-off right now?' Ari enquired drily.

'Because you're so used to being marched out and shown off like a trophy by women that you now think you're being slighted,' Cleo told him squarely. 'But no insult was intended.'

Ari laughed, helplessly amused by her blunt and irreverent outlook. Cleo was new and fresh in a way that consistently grabbed his interest. And his desire for her and hers for him were off-the-charts hot. Her careless designation of their intimacy as being a fling had sharply disconcerted him, but, in truth, he was probably in agreement with that sentiment. Presumably, what they had would burn out and die as quickly as it had started, and in the short term, why should they need to complicate that? He lifted her small curvy body up to him and ravished her parted lips with his, his tongue delving deep.

Cleo shuddered in his grasp, her nipples tightening, damp infiltrating the heat building between her thighs. He came down on the bed with her, reaching behind himself to haul off the sweater he wore in a very masculine movement. Muscles flexing, he cast it aside and studied her, tawny eyes ablaze with hunger, and her tummy flipped as if she were on a big dipper.

'I wanted to eat you alive again the instant I saw you standing behind that bar, *koukla mou*,' he growled. 'I don't know what it is about you—'

'Or I you,' Cleo cut in, slender fingers stroking

down over his bronzed torso and the cut lines of his muscles with a tactile delight that she could not help savouring.

Ari lifted her top over her head and embarked on her skirt. She wriggled out of it, her heart racing with wicked anticipation. As her bra fell away, he cupped her full breasts and groaned, pressing her back on the bed to explore her lush curves, lingering on the stiff little buds of her straining nipples and then lowering his mouth there. As he captured a straining peak between his lips and gently tugged, she gasped out loud and her back arched. He lingered there, grazing her with the edges of his teeth, licking the hard buds with hungry energy before he shifted down the bed to pay attention to an even more sensitive area.

Cleo's head whipped back and forth on the pillow as her breath sobbed in her throat. Waves of increasing delight were gripping her pelvis. Her fingers were locked into his black hair, shock at what she was allowing silenced by the amount of pleasure flooding her. And then it came, the ultimate wash of sensation that lit her up like a firework display, and she cried out, her body convulsing and writhing in ecstasy. Liquid heat and relaxation surged in the moments afterwards.

'No, you're not going to sleep on me now,' Ari warned her, lifting her with strong hands and turning her over, urging her up onto her knees before reaching for the top of the nightstand to grab a foil wrapper and tear it open with his teeth.

He tugged her hips back to him and plunged boldly into her tingling damp channel in almost the same movement, and a charge of indescribable excitement roared through her as her body stretched to accommodate him. She felt possessed, dominated, and it was a huge turn-on that added to an already intense experience. His hands firm on her hips, he quickened his pace. Claiming her with fierce thrusts, he made her body hum and pulse with raw hunger and impatience for the satisfaction that only he could deliver. As the sensual tide of sensation swelled and overwhelmed her on every level, another orgasm engulfed her and she cried out his name, helpless in the hold of that thundering charge of elation.

As she slumped flat on the bed beneath him, Ari snatched in a shuddering breath and flung himself back on the bed beside her. He snaked out an arm and gathered her to him. 'That was amazing,' he muttered thickly.

'I should go home,' Cleo announced with conviction, spooked by a sudden clingy craving to turn into the shelter offered by that arm of his and embrace that closeness.

His hold tightened. 'Stay—'

'I have a shift in the morning. I need a change of clothes—'

'I'll take you home early to change,' Ari spelt out insistently.

But Cleo had already made up her mind. They were having a fling. They were not in a relationship. The way she saw it, that meant she shouldn't stay overnight. Observing those limits would keep everything tidier and ensure that she never forgot where she stood with him. She couldn't afford to get too comfortable with Ari Stefanos. She didn't want to get attached to him and then get hurt. Sleeping over was a step too far in the wrong direction. Her warning was that dangerous desire to cuddle him! Best to keep everything casual, she reasoned ruefully, troubled by her craving to stay with him longer.

'No, I've got to go,' Cleo spelt out briskly in defiance of an instinct that she interpreted as weak. She slid out of bed, still half concealed by the sheet, and reached for her discarded clothes.

'You're not even staying for a shower?' Ari shot at her.

'I can freshen up at home,' she told him firmly.

Seated on a corner of the bed, she dressed, only as she stood registering that the silence that had spread was leaping and bouncing with hostile undertones. She turned her head and encountered brooding dark golden eyes that glittered like the heart of a fire.

'If you walk out of here now, you don't come back...*ever*,' Ari framed in a deceptively quiet voice.

Cleo froze in shock at that warning. 'I don't respond well to threats—'

'Then be reasonable, rather than offensive,' Ari advised, pulling himself up against the pillows.

He looked so beautiful lounging there against the white bedding that he stole the very breath from her lungs. Black hair wildly tousled by her clutching hands, she recalled in mortification, dark deep-set eyes fiercely intent on her below his slashing ebony brows, his bronzed muscular perfection never on more magnificent display.

A knot formed in her throat, threatening to choke her, and tension held her fast. 'You don't mean that—'

'Walk away and find out,' Ari invited in a raw undertone of challenge she had never heard from him before.

'Why are you behaving like this?' Cleo demanded in consternation. 'I haven't done anything offensive!'

'You won't be seen out in my company. You won't spend the night either? That's offensive,' Ari contradicted without hesitation.

'Are you telling me that you a-always spend the night with the women you—?' she began, stumbling over the words that she did not wish to say out loud, and even that sensitivity inflamed her. Ari Stefanos didn't belong to her. She had no right to feel remotely possessive about him.

'We're not talking about me right now. We're talking about you and your hang-ups,' Ari cut in smoothly.

Cleo bridled. 'I don't have hang-ups—'

'Maybe I should have called them *trust issues*,' Ari countered drily. 'But yes, it doesn't take a rocket scientist to see that you definitely have those.'

Outraged at her insecurities being read that accurately, Cleo thrust her feet into her shoes.

'The car will be waiting outside for you,' Ari completed quietly.

For a split second, she sat there, her every instinct at war and plunging her into conflict. She didn't want to leave him, which only persuaded her that she *should* overcome that weakness and leave at speed. In a quick movement, she rose and left the room without a backward glance because she wouldn't allow herself to look back at him. She hurried downstairs to collect her jacket from the sunroom. She was furious with him for cornering her and furious with herself for surrendering to her anxieties.

CHAPTER FOUR

ARI EMERGED FROM an erotic daydream in which Cleo was splayed across his bed like a sensual enchantress and he gritted his even white teeth at that unlikely image.

Two long weeks waiting for Cleo to apologise had sharpened his temper because intelligence was warning him that Cleo would sit him out. Even that he should guess that about a woman's reactions unnerved him because generally he didn't really get to know his lovers on a deeper basis. With women, Ari had always been more of an easy come, easy go guy. He was heading down a very unfamiliar path, he acknowledged grimly, and yet he could not overcome the visceral desire to see Cleo again. Cleo was stubborn and proud. He was equally stubborn and proud.

But wasn't it fortunate that one of them was feeling generous enough to offer a face-saving escape from their current deadlock?

Ari sent a text.

A very discreet dinner? No witnesses?

Cleo's heart jumped inside her chest as she read the text and quickly plunged her phone back into her bag. She breathed in slow and deep. Then out came the phone again.

At your house?

She wished she could inject a sarky note. Surely his own home was the only place he could hope to offer her that kind of privacy?

And the phone started actually ringing in her hand and she stood there paralysed, staring down at it, her heart rate pounding crazily before she surrendered and answered it.

'Not at my house. A restaurant, a surprise,' Ari specified, smooth as glass.

'What happened about the baby?' she almost whispered, revealing her intense curiosity with some embarrassment.

'It's complicated. I'll tell you over dinner,' Ari murmured, smiling as he recalled the way she had lit up with interest when he told her about the baby two weeks earlier. Cleo *liked* babies. He had picked up that much just from her expression at the time.

'When?' Cleo pressed, mouth running dry while she told herself that she wasn't going to agree even while she somehow knew that she had already made that decision from the moment that dark, deep drawl of his had sounded in her ear. He had made the first move, she reasoned feverishly, so she could afford to be magnanimous. Or was she just making pathetic excuses for herself? Cleo winced.

'Tomorrow evening. I'll pick you up at seven.' It would take that long to organise a venue, Ari acknowledged wryly, wondering if he had ever gone to so much effort to see a woman again and why he was doing it for her. Why was she a challenge that he could not ignore or forget? Why wasn't he simply walking away as he had done a hundred times before?

A huge smile tugging at her tense face, Cleo dug her phone back into her bag. She knew she had been guilty of an overreaction at their last encounter. Refusing to consider either a date or an overnight stay had been excessive. Panicking over an entanglement that seemed to have sneaked up on her and caught her unawares with her defences down, Cleo had wanted to run away. Unhappily, her attitude had allowed Ari to see just how hard she found it to trust a man and that was humiliating. He had also been offended and she could hardly blame him for that, considering that he had, from the start, been honest with her. He hadn't told her any lies, hadn't given her any unrealistic expectations or any excuses. He hadn't argued either when she had declared that they were having a fling that wouldn't last longer than five minutes. Clearly, his opinion was similar, she reflected tautly.

Her bar shift flew past while she mentally thumbed through her wardrobe for a suitable outfit and decided that she owned nothing smart enough. She was off the following day and she went shopping, trawling through charity shops until she found her best option, a short fringed blue dress that had a dash of style and was a little less colourful than her usual choices. Turning in front of the wardrobe mirror that evening, she watched the fringes glide silkily across her thighs with every movement, revealing glimpses of her legs, and realised that for the first time in her life she felt sexy. Ari had done that for her ego, she acknowledged ruefully. She had never felt sexy in her life until he had come along and enabled her to accept that side of her nature.

Ari wasn't in the car that picked her up and that disconcerted her. When the vehicle entered a tight network of narrow streets and she was finally ushered out into what appeared to be an alley, she surmised that Ari's surprise could be more of a splash than she had expected. As soon as she was guided through a narrow corridor past a busy kitchen area, where hatted catering staff peered out at her with intense curiosity, she appreciated that she was being brought into the restaurant through a rear entrance as though she were a celebrity desperate to escape the paparazzi. A discomfited veil of colour had swept across her face by the time she was led into the low-lit restaurant, which was unnervingly empty of other diners.

'Cleo…' Ari rose to greet her from a corner table, effortlessly elegant in a dark designer suit, cut to mould his wide shoulders and broad chest, his long, powerful legs outlined by narrow black trousers.

'Where is everyone else?' she almost whispered as a waiter whisked away the jacket she was laying down on the back of a chair and hurried to usher her into her seat.

'Tonight, it's just us. I promised discretion and here it is.' Ari moved a lean brown hand to indicate the unoccupied tables surrounding them. 'We're alone, aside of the servers.'

With that staggering admission, Ari settled back down at the table opposite her and reflected that every effort he had made to achieve such privacy had been worthwhile because Cleo looked incredible in a sapphire-blue dress that accentuated her eyes and revealed tantalising glimpses of slender thigh as she walked. He wondered why it was that no matter how often he had her he wanted more of her, as though she had some weirdly addictive flavour. But, in truth, at that moment he didn't care. He was relishing the surge of sensual anticipation gripping him, the newness of it, the very exhilaration of such an unusual feeling with a woman.

'How can we be here alone? I mean, why would the owner exclude other diners?' Cleo queried nervously as Ari ordered wine.

'I made it worthwhile for the owner to reschedule his other bookings,' Ari explained.

And sudden comprehension sent pallor climbing up her throat into her troubled face. 'You bribed him just for my benefit?' she almost whispered in horror.

Ari frowned. '"Bribed" isn't the word I would employ in these circumstances. I offered a business proposition, which the owner accepted. Nothing wrong with that,' he declared with unblemished assurance.

'The world turns every day on questions of profit and loss. I assure you that the proprietor is not making a loss...and *here you are.* Would you be here if I had not promised you this option?'

Mortification seized her. He had offered and she had accepted, and she had not spared a thought as to how he could achieve such a phenomenon for her benefit, had she? Any criticism would be unjustified and, what was more, did she want to criticise? For the first time in her life, a male had gone to considerable lengths simply to see her. Did she really want to diminish that compliment or criticise it? She glanced around the empty restaurant and finally understood that Ari wielded the kind of power with money that she could barely imagine. Ari didn't play games and he didn't offer false promises. He had met her demand for privacy, and if she shrank from the means he had chosen to utilise, that was her problem, *not* his.

'I didn't think through what I was asking properly,' Cleo conceded uneasily. 'Considering who you are, it wasn't a reasonable request. Your social life is always in the gossip columns. People are interested in your life and your companions—'

'Let's order our meal,' Ari cut into her troubled observations quietly as the waiter extended a handwritten menu. 'And let's forget about how we got here.'

Perhaps that was easy for him, but it wasn't easy for Cleo, who was ridiculously conscious of their quiet surroundings and his admirable ability to behave as though eating in an empty public dining room was normal for him. She selected her menu choices, sipped at the rich wine that arrived and tried not to stare at Ari.

Only that was a challenge she could not meet, for he was breathtakingly beautiful no matter what angle she looked at him from. The way his black luxuriant hair fell across his brow, the exotic slash of his high cheekbones, those perfectly moulded lips surrounded by a faint shadow of dark stubble, but most of all she was enthralled by his eyes, a dark and volatile mix of bronze, gold and caramel, accentuated by glorious black lashes longer than her own. She looked at him and it was his spectacular eyes that captured her every time.

'Tell me,' Ari urged quietly as he glanced up after the appetisers had been delivered. 'Why, after we were first together, were you so dismayed by my suggestion that I help you find other office employment?'

Cleo tensed and tried to savour the tiny sliver of wild mushroom on her fork. She pondered for a moment and then murmured, 'My father meddled with my mother's employment choices and it was to her detriment. I grew up with her bitterness. To protect his position in the same company, he persuaded her to resign hers. She agreed to keep him happy and because she believed they had a future together,' she advanced ruefully. 'But, of course, they didn't have a future and, unluckily for her, she never got that high up the career ladder again.'

'A sobering tale,' Ari remarked thoughtfully. 'Only we don't have a similar history and why would I wish to damage your prospects?'

'I have to be sensible and look out for me because nobody else will,' Cleo parried, refusing to get into the topic because it would be embarrassing. Nobody would take her seriously in any new job if she only got the job in the first place on Ari's personal recommendation. She would have to be stupid to think otherwise.

'I don't like feeling responsible for your resignation from my HQ,' Ari admitted bluntly.

Cleo shrugged. 'I was only a temp. It's not that big a deal, but I did the right thing when I left—'

'Only it didn't work,' Ari pointed out silkily. 'After all, here we still are…together.'

'And it's *still* against all common sense,' Cleo said roundly.

Ari lounged back in his chair and grinned, that slashing charismatic smile making her heart clench inside her chest. He looked utterly gorgeous and utterly unrepentant. 'That's a risk I'm prepared to take.'

'Will you tell me what you've found out about the baby?' Cleo pressed inquisitively as the first course arrived.

'She's only recently left hospital and she is still receiving medical attention in foster care. She's suffered a lot in her short life…but yes, she is, according to the DNA tests, my flesh and blood. Her mother was also an orphan. I am presently the only relative waiting in the wings, although her aunts are obviously still out there but it will take time to track them down,' Ari conceded. 'I have expressed an interest in meeting my niece—'

'When?' Cleo prompted with interest.

'Possibly later this week. I was hoping that you would consider accompanying me—'

Cleo was taken aback by the suggestion. *'Me?'*

'I know nothing about babies, and your presence would make me more relaxed—'

'I spent years babysitting as a teenager. That's my only experience of young children,' Cleo confessed in a rush, but she was pleased by his request. 'I would love to meet her, though. How old is she?'

'They think she's ten months old, but apparently she's very small and she has developmental delays, which makes it hard to be more accurate.'

'Does she have a name?' Cleo asked.

'Someone came up with Lucinda by contracting her parents' first names… Lucas and Cindy,' Ari proffered wryly. 'Considering that their addiction almost killed her, I'm not sure how happy an association that is to give their daughter.'

'They were still her parents, and I think that until you know all the facts, it's probably better not to make judgements,' Cleo suggested quietly. 'Particularly when you're hoping to find your other siblings, because it's possible that Lucas's sisters may have a very different outlook on what happened to their brother.'

Ari nodded. 'A fair point,' he commented with a smile. 'Making snap judgements is a habit of mine—'

'You're an only child. You've never had to bite your tongue to keep the peace. I haven't either,' Cleo remarked reflectively. 'But I saw what it was like when my mother married my stepfather, who has three adult children. Watching them interact was an education.

You and I had nobody to argue with us and challenge us as kids.'

'It doesn't even occur to me to think about stuff of that nature,' Ari admitted. 'When did your mother meet and marry your stepfather?'

'When I was seventeen. He's a kind man and she's very happy with him.'

By the time they were leaving by the rear entrance, Cleo was on a high following a relaxing evening. Ari was letting her into his life, trusting her with secrets and taking her opinions on board. Of course, she felt a little giddy and had a sense of accomplishment. When he curved an arm round her in the back of the limousine that collected them, her cheeks blazed as she voiced the awkward words that had been in the back of her mind all evening. 'I can't stay with you tonight...'

'No expectations here, *glykia mou*,' Ari responded.

'It's just...er... It's just that—'

Ari laughed. 'It's fine, Cleo. You're dealing with a fully grown adult male...but, to be frank, you're a welcome guest in any condition.'

Cleo's face was beet red and she dropped her head, knowing that she would never take the risk of having to hug a hot-water bottle to ease cramps in his radius. Long fingers tipped up her chin to meet her troubled blue eyes, and without warning, he kissed her breathless. A piercing surge of sweet heat arrowed through her quivering body, setting her alight wherever it touched. That quickly, she ached shamelessly, wanting what she couldn't have, reliving their last encounter with every sense thrumming and her body throbbing.

'I'll call you,' Ari told her as he saw her right to the door of the building where she lived.

She floated into bed that night feeling as light as a breeze and resolved not to sink into negative 'what if?' thoughts that would make her feel as though she were doing something wrong. It was an insane attraction and it wouldn't last for ever—she knew that… *Of course* she did. Maybe she would never hear from Ari again. There were no guarantees in her future, but she could live with that, couldn't she?

Ari called the following day to tell her that his meeting with his niece was scheduled for the Thursday afternoon. Cleo rearranged her shift to make herself available, agreeing to work that night instead, and Ari picked her up. He looked tense, his lean, dark features taut.

'Why are you stressing about this?' Cleo asked him quietly. 'All you need to do is smile and be gentle and unthreatening.'

Ari settled troubled dark golden eyes on her and his lips took on a wry curve. 'I'm stressing because I really don't know where I'm going with this and I'm not used to that. I like to plan ahead.'

'Stop trying to conquer the mountain before you even start climbing,' Cleo told him. 'You can't pre-plan everything. Maybe you're just curious to see your brother's child. I don't think that's a sin if that's all it is. She's a baby. You're not harming her by visiting her one time.'

'I hope not,' Ari breathed as the limousine filtered to a halt outside a bleak municipal building.

An older woman greeted them in the reception area and discussed her role as the baby's caseworker. Ari introduced Cleo as his girlfriend, which disconcerted her. His girlfriend… Was she really? Or had that merely been a convenient label to excuse her presence? They were shown into a meeting room and invited to sit down. Impervious to that suggestion, Ari paced restlessly in front of the window until another woman arrived with a baby in her arms. Ari strode eagerly forward to get a first look at his niece. Not wishing to muscle in, Cleo remained seated. Ari sat down beside her and the baby was handed to him.

Lucinda was tiny but her eyes were bright and huge in her tiny face. As Cleo finally got a proper look at the baby, she was betrayed into an exclamation. 'Ari… she's got your eyes!'

And it was true. Lucinda had eyes just like Ari, a golden mixture of browns, heavily fringed with black lashes that matched the wayward strands on her little head.

'Yes,' he said heavily. 'I've seen a photo of my brother and we looked alike. The Stefanos genes seem to be strong.'

Keen to angle his thoughts in a more positive direction and away from the premature death of his half-brother, Cleo murmured, 'She's a very pretty baby.'

'And so she should be,' the social worker chimed in.

'I believe her mother was a model and quite a looker before substance abuse destroyed her career.'

'Would you like to hold her?' Ari asked.

Cleo swallowed hard and opened her arms. The baby was a slight, warm weight curled into her arm and gazed up at her with Ari's tawny eyes. 'She's beautiful,' she whispered.

'She doesn't cry much,' the foster parent proffered. 'But she likes her bottles.'

'She probably became used to her cries not getting a response,' the social worker opined. 'She is gaining weight steadily, though, and getting stronger.'

As the little rosebud mouth opened, Cleo gently rocked the child to soothe her again. The long lashes drooped and a thready little sigh sounded. Ari reclaimed his niece with visible awkwardness and sat in silence gazing down at her. A few minutes later, he passed the child back to the foster parent and, after organising a further meeting with the social worker, they returned to the limousine.

'What do you think you will do?' Cleo asked.

'I believe that I will try to adopt her. She deserves a loving home… I only hope that I can provide that,' Ari murmured tautly. 'Do you want to join me for dinner now?'

'No, drop me off at the bar, please. I'm working tonight. I swapped shifts so that I could come with you this afternoon,' Cleo explained.

Ari sighed but, contrary to her expectations, he made no critical comment. 'I'll see you at the weekend,' he told her.

But indeed, Cleo saw him much sooner than that. Someone hammered on the door before nine the next morning. Ella had already left for her classes and Cleo clambered up with a groan, straightened her pyjamas and hurried down to answer it. The last person she was expecting to see was Ari Stefanos, who shook a newspaper in her startled face and strode in past her.

'I trusted you!' he shot at her in furious condemnation.

Cleo leant back against the door to close it and stared at him. Unlike her, he was fully dressed, all designer chic in a silver-grey fitted suit, dark grey tie and shadow striped shirt. He looked drop-dead gorgeous from the gleaming black crown of his head to the toes of his hand-stitched shoes. But his expression was murderous. He was pale below his bronzed complexion, his eyes were dark and as hard as iron, his mouth compressed and his hard jawline heavily shadowed with stubble as if he had not yet shaved.

'What did you say…about trusting me?' Cleo prompted, because she was only just beginning to wake up properly. 'And what are you doing here this early in the day?'

Ari slammed the newspaper down on the breakfast bar of the tiny galley kitchen for emphasis. 'I'm here about *this*!' he stressed with savage distaste.

He could never recall being in such a rage before, and a bitter sense of betrayal ran hot as a lava flow through his veins. His suspicions had zeroed in on Cleo first because it was so rare for him to share confidences with another individual. He had trusted her and she had let him down. Why hadn't he kept his own counsel? Why had he put his faith in a complete stranger? He had never before taken a risk like that. *Thee mou*, what quality did she have that had contrived to come between him and his wits? Had his libido persuaded him that she was a safe harbour for his secrets? The suspicion that he could be that basic, that stupid, outraged his pride.

Cleo padded closer in her bare feet and picked out the headline in the colourful tabloid newspaper that evidently had Ari breathing fire.

Billionaire baby almost dies from neglect!

Beside it they had run a large photo of Ari. Beneath ran a story about Lucinda's mother, Cindy, stating that she had been a model and an ex of Ari's before heroin became her downfall. The item described how the baby had been found starving in a squat beside the body of her mother. Ari was named as the baby's father.

'Well, they've got the story very wrong,' Cleo pointed out. 'What I don't understand is why you should think that this nonsense has anything to do with me…'

'I imagine that if I checked your bank account I'd find the proof that you were paid for that story by a journalist, who decided to put his own, more interesting twist on Lucinda's background! It's much more newsworthy if I'm cast in the role of a neglectful father!'

'I can assure you that you won't be checking my bank account any time soon,' Cleo retorted crisply. 'But I'm not responsible for this article. I haven't told anybody about Lucinda or your father's second family—'

'Perhaps you decided to keep my father's affair and the children born from it a secret as a special favour to me. I don't know,' Ari grated with distaste. 'I only know that you were the *only* person who knew about my niece and her unsavoury beginnings, and now here it is, spread across the newspapers for all to read about, and now *I'm* being accused of having abandoned her vulnerable mother and left my child to starve and suffer.'

Cleo folded her arms. 'Well, the article's nine tenths rubbish, so I don't know why you're so bothered about gossipy conjecture when you know the truth and the authorities do as well. You didn't even know Lucinda's mother, never mind have an affair with her,' she pointed out with quiet common sense. 'But while I understand that you're upset to see this kind of stuff being printed, I don't understand why you're bringing it to my doorstep when I had nothing to do with it—'

'It has to be you who leaked certain facts… There are no other possible profiteers in the picture!' Ari slammed back at her accusingly.

Cleo refused to be intimidated, although her temper was steadily climbing and had she had the physical strength she would literally have thrown him out of the apartment. Even so, she could already feel the sharp piercing sting of hurt and disappointment that he could believe her capable of breaking his trust and profiting from his family's tragic secrets. But she buried that vulnerability as fast as she could and refused to acknowledge it. 'Don't be so naive, Ari. There must be dozens of people who know enough about Lucinda to have sold this story,' she parried curtly.

'What the hell are you trying to say?'

'Well, a lot of people have been involved in Lucinda's life because of her near-death experience. Start with your lawyer and those who work for him—that's one set of people in possession of facts you would prefer to keep confidential. Then there's the private investigation agency you hired to find your siblings, who identified Lucinda as potentially being your brother's child… That's another set. What about the paramedics and the police who found Lucinda and her parents? Or the medical staff, who cared for your niece in hospital? Or even the DNA-testing facility you used to find out whether or not you and her were related? Then there's the social services staff involved in finding a home for her and her foster carers. Why don't you start counting up just how many different people already know enough about Lucinda's background to cause you grief?'

Ari stared back at her in brooding silence. Cleo looked so tiny standing there, even with her slight shoulders thrown back and her body stretched to its maximum, not very impressive height as she squared up to him. She was wearing pyjamas with horrendous zebra stripes on them, her mop of curls an explosion of gold round her face, her bright blue eyes wide and shocked. She didn't look remotely like a young woman who had been caught out in a shameful money-grabbing exercise. 'I—'

'No, don't you accuse me of anything more,' Cleo warned him in a brittle tone as she struggled to hold her composure together. 'I'm not responsible for this stupid story, and I would suggest that you concentrate your energies on finding out who *is*.'

With that advice, she lifted the newspaper, folded it and thrust it back at him before walking back to the door and yanking it open to encourage his departure. She slammed it shut behind him even as he began swinging back to say something else. In all her life she had never felt more exposed or more hurt. With a few simple sentences Ari Stefanos had trashed her every hope and belief, revealing his true opinion of her character.

She was poor, which apparently meant that she was also untrustworthy and a potential gold digger without a conscience. Tears stung her eyes. Ari had encouraged her to develop a false impression of their relationship. He had emptied a fashionable restaurant for her benefit just in an effort to see her again. But what had that been worth? He was an incredibly wealthy man, a man accustomed to doing exactly as he liked, regardless of cost. It hadn't meant that he set a high personal value on her or her character. Nor had his confidences about his father's second family meant anything more concrete. She had simply been in the right place at the right time at the retreat when he had been in the mood to talk to someone.

But she *had* made a big mistake, hadn't she? The mistake of thinking that she was somehow special in Ari's eyes.

Only now that pathetic conviction had fallen down around her ears like a collapsed house of cards, warning her that she had been vain and foolish to overestimate her importance to him. The instant someone had talked to the press about Ari's private life, she had become his prime suspect! Yet if he had thought it through, he would have realised that had she been guilty she would have made much more money from selling the *real* story, which he had shared with her. And not a story that merely twisted a tiny part of the whole to falsely depict him as a mean-spirited, neglectful father who had failed to look after his illegitimate child's well-being.

So, lesson learned the hard way as always, Cleo reflected unhappily. She was nobody and nothing in Ari's eyes, just a girl he had slept with a couple of times. Everything else had been icing on an empty cake and she had been an absolute idiot to believe that it could ever be anything more.

CHAPTER FIVE

'THESE ARE GORGEOUS!' Ella chorused in wonderment over the extravagant arrangement of tiger lilies in the vase that had been delivered with them. 'You can't put these ones in the bin as well.'

'Well, I've nobody left to give flowers to,' Cleo pointed out, having handed out the previous bouquets to neighbours and workmates. 'And I don't want to look at them here and be reminded of him.'

'I wish you'd tell me what he did that is *so* unforgivable,' Ella said and not for the first time. 'He is certainly saying sorry with style.'

'He can say it until he's blue in the face… It won't change anything,' Cleo said, her generous pink mouth suddenly tight and flat as a steel bar. Ari Stefanos had wronged her in the most unforgivable way. He should never have risked sharing his wretched family secrets in the first instance if he was so ready to suddenly flip and blame her for selling them to the press.

'If you're sure you don't want them, I'll give them to my mother when I meet her for lunch. She'll be thrilled,' her flatmate declared. 'Are you certain?'

'Completely certain,' Cleo asserted as she finished her make-up and gave her reflection a cursory glance in the mirror.

'You don't even want the vase?' Ella checked. 'It's crystal.'

'Not even the vase,' Cleo confirmed.

'He's gorgeous, Cleo,' Ella remarked abruptly, having got a look at Ari when he called at the flat to find out where Cleo worked. 'In your shoes, I think I'd cut him some slack.'

'Looks aren't everything,' Cleo parried, grabbing up her bag to leave, wondering exactly how long it was likely to take for that hollow sensation of loss that she had been nursing inside her to dissipate. Ten days had passed and that awful feeling hadn't yet faded even a little bit. 'And he's already had a second chance and he blew that as well, so I'm not about to put myself out there again.'

The bar was quiet when it opened, and she was up on a stool dusting shelves when the doors swung and she flipped her head expecting to see a customer and seeing Ari instead. Ari, devastatingly spectacular in a dark suit that fitted him like a glove, his bronzed and handsome face unusually grave. She froze and then lurched down off the stool clumsily, almost turning her ankle, wincing as she made contact with the ground again.

'How can I help you?' she asked in a frozen voice as he approached the bar.

'Have you blocked me on your phone?'

'Of course I have. Why would I want to hear from

you?' Cleo asked, genuinely surprised by that question as she bent down to rub her aching ankle.

'Did you hurt yourself?' her boss, Sam, asked from the other end of the bar. 'I warned you about getting up on that stool… It's dangerous—'

'I'm fine,' Cleo insisted with hot cheeks as she limped away to put the stool back.

'Take a break,' Sam urged her across the counter. 'Give the leg a rest for a few minutes.'

'I'll have coffee with you,' Ari murmured very quietly, watching her like a hawk and marvelling at the rapidity of the changing expressions on her heart-shaped face. She had given her boss a genuine smile, but the one she had given him had been fake. That infuriated him. Yet she still looked astonishingly pretty, her halo of curls burnished by the low lighting, her eyes blue as violets against her pale porcelain skin, her sexy little mouth tight with constraint.

She had blocked his calls as if he were a nuisance caller, Ari reflected bleakly. That had *never* happened to him before with a woman. Nor had the attempt to apologise with flowers got him anywhere as he'd waited in vain for her to contact him. Of course, he had never got in deep enough with any woman to the extent that he was having arguments with her and trying to apologise, he acknowledged impatiently. He was disturbed by the suspicion that he was behaving clumsily because he had absolutely no experience of ever being in such a position. There was something to be said for sticking to one-night stands, only no one-night stand had ever had the effect on him that Cleo had. And it was Cleo and Cleo alone whom he wanted.

Ari breathed in slow and deep. Hunger slivered through him and bit deep enough to make him wince as his pants tightened across his groin. He couldn't sleep for thinking about her. She had got him obsessed. He didn't know how, he didn't know why, he only knew that she tied him up in knots and her absence took every spark of excitement and anticipation out of his life. And now that he needed a favour from her, he didn't know how the hell he could persuade her into helping him out of a tight corner.

Cleo's head flew up, angry words on her tongue until she realised that Sam was watching and that, as far as he was concerned, Ari was a customer to be served. She gave Ari a bright meaningless smile. 'No problem, sir,' she said and watched his beautiful face tense at her formality.

As she made the coffee she tried to eradicate that image of his beautiful face and wilful, wonderfully sensual mouth from her mind, but it was too big a challenge. She saw Ari and a sharp little arrow of hot, desperate craving shot through her, scrambling her brain and ensuring that she just wanted to rip his clothes off and climb him like a vine. There was nothing mature or controlled about that reaction. It was a primitive urge that she struggled to suppress every time she met his extraordinary eyes.

'I'm trying very hard to apologise,' Ari proffered when she brought the coffee to the table. 'Why won't you listen?'

'You hurt my self-respect. I can't forgive that,' Cleo advanced as she sat down opposite him, eyes very bright and level, her chin at a challenging angle. 'I thought you knew me. I trusted you. Then I find out that just because I'm a nobody without money, I was your one and *only* suspect. That tells me all I need to know about the way you think and about exactly where I stand with you.'

'It wasn't like that… I flew off the handle—'

'You have a short fuse,' Cleo condemned. 'And this isn't the first time we've been at odds. We don't match, Ari. You live in a different world—'

'I made assumptions, assumptions I had no good reason to make. I think I've tracked down where the leak came from—'

Cleo waved a dismissive hand, which set his even white teeth on edge. 'No need to explain…as long as you know it wasn't me. I wouldn't have betrayed your trust in me like that. I do have standards and you trusted me with secrets, and I haven't shared a word of them with anyone!'

'I was uneasy about the confidential matters which I had shared with you because I don't make a habit of confiding in people,' Ari bit out tautly.

'I guessed that, but I still don't understand why you're approaching me again.'

'I'm in a bind,' Ari admitted grimly. 'I may have somehow given social services the impression that you live with me and, now that I've expressed an interest in adopting Lucinda, they want to come out and interview us together in my house.'

Cleo stared back at him with parted lips of dismay. 'How on earth could you have given them the impression that we live together?'

'I think the lady simply assumed, when you came with me to see the baby the first time, that we were a couple—'

'But we're not,' Cleo cut in, sharp as a knife.

'That's not to say that we couldn't be,' Ari sliced back at her with determination. 'I will do literally *anything* to be considered as my niece's adoptive parent. If that means doing whatever I have to do to gain your willing participation, I *will* do it.'

Ari was thinking about the echoing emptiness of the giant house in Athens where he had grown up with his parents. He had been a lonely child, only making friends at school. There had been no family circle of relatives aside of a few remote cousins whom his parents had not encouraged to visit. He had visited Lucinda only the day before, but he had felt constrained without Cleo's soothing presence, although he had been ridiculously thrilled when he had managed to get his niece to smile at him. He had realised then that he was more ready to have a family than he had ever suspected.

Surprise engulfed Cleo because she had not appreciated that he was already prepared to make such a serious commitment to the little girl.

'Giving my niece a home means that much to me,' Ari admitted in a driven undertone. 'Her parents were unable to take care of her and do what was best for her.

Until I can track down my half-sisters, there's nobody else in the world likely to be as interested in that little girl as I am. I can't let her down the way her parents did. I can't turn my back on her just because I'm single and inexperienced with children. I can rise to a challenge as well as any other man. Bringing her up as a Stefanos is the only thing I can do now for the little brother I never had the chance to meet.'

Involuntarily, Cleo was impressed. Ari had thought the situation through in depth and acknowledged the difficulties ahead, but he was still keen to give his niece the advantages that his own father had chosen not to offer the children born of his second family.

'If you move into the house, I promise not to try and take advantage of the situation,' Ari declared. 'And *you know* I want you and that it will be a battle to keep my distance...'

Cleo flushed to the roots of her hair, awareness shimmering through her in a heady swell, but she was shocked by the suggestion that she actually *move* into his house. She understood why he was asking, because if she lived under the same roof nobody in authority was likely to question the veracity of their relationship. Even so, it was a huge ask for him to make. Her nipples prickled and tightened and, as she connected with his spectacular tawny eyes, her heartbeat thundered and a bolt of sensual heat surged between her taut slender thighs. The wanting, she was painfully conscious, was *not* one-sided. Unfortunately for her, being angry with Ari didn't stifle her desire for him. It never had. He made her angry, but he still inflamed her.

'But I will do nothing to make you uncomfortable,' Ari swore, his lean, dark features taut. 'If you decide to agree to this arrangement, you will have your own bedroom, your privacy, whatever else you require. You will have no bills, nothing to worry about. I will take care of everything.'

Cleo gazed back at him in astonishment at the suggestion. Live in that fabulous house without expense or expectations being attached? For anyone in her precarious financial position it was a prize-winning proposition. It would allow her to build up some savings, something that she had always wanted to do but had never achieved, living as she did from job to job, just about managing to keep her head above water on a day-to-day basis. 'How long would I have to live there for?' she asked abruptly.

'At least a few months,' Ari replied. 'Right now, I can't be more accurate than that.'

Cleo frowned. 'That's a long time and I'd lose the accommodation I have now—'

'I'll help you find somewhere else when the time comes for you to move on,' Ari slotted in.

'I don't want to be put in a position where I'm expected to lie to anyone—'

'Let's not worry about what hasn't happened yet,' Ari urged.

'I'm only considering it for Lucy's benefit,' Cleo warned him defensively.

'Lucy?' Ari queried.

'She's too little to be called Lucinda yet,' Cleo opined in a rush, her cheeks colouring. 'At least, I think so.'

'I suppose you'll want to think about this for a while,' Ari breathed, pushing away his untouched coffee and rising to his full height.

Intimidated by his even more commanding height while she was still sitting, Cleo quickly followed suit and stood up. Her brain was a morass of conflicting urges and needs, all trying to jerk her in different directions. She blinked rapidly, thought even faster. She had to protect herself. She knew that. But she still wanted to help out for Lucy's sake. In the set-up he had outlined, she could not lose, could she? She had loved that house of his, too. That shouldn't count in the scheme of things, but she was human and she could be tempted like anyone else at the idea of her own bedroom and possibly even a bathroom and a garden as well. Those were the kind of luxuries she had never had.

'When do you finish?' Ari prompted. 'I'll pick you up and we can discuss this more.'

Holy moly, those eyes of his, Cleo thought wildly, momentarily lost in his smouldering dark golden gaze and an intensity that revved up every nerve cell in her body and left her feeling both dizzy and confused. 'I don't need to discuss this more…but it'll be a struggle for me to keep my distance too,' she heard herself confide inanely and almost cringed for herself.

Ari muttered something in Greek as he stood staring down at her and the fluctuating colour in her triangular face. Hunger lanced through him and settled into a fierce pulse at his groin.

'B-but we're adults. We'll keep our distance because it's the sensible thing to do. I'll move in as soon as it can be arranged… I'll do it for Lucy,' Cleo informed him shakily.

'I'll make the arrangements.' With a sudden flashing smile lifting the tension from his lean, darkly handsome features, Ari strode off.

Mission accomplished, he thought fiercely. Cleo would move in. Unfortunately, he didn't feel remotely sensible in her radius, but he knew what she was trying to tell him. In such a situation he *had* to be cautious. He had a friend who had ended up with a live-in girlfriend he didn't want in the wake of a wild weekend. False expectations had been fostered by careless comments and compliments made in the heat of passion. Misunderstandings had followed. It had taken weeks for the male involved to regain his freedom and the unfortunate woman concerned had been very upset.

Ari was not that clumsy or naive. Nor was he foolish. He wouldn't make those mistakes. He thought Cleo was fantastic in bed and out of it, but nothing would persuade him to express those sentiments out loud. This time around, he would keep his hands off her and respect the boundaries. How hard could that be?

CHAPTER SIX

FIVE DAYS LATER, Cleo scanned her beautifully appointed bedroom and suppressed a sigh of appreciation. She had moved out of Ella's tiny apartment less than forty-eight hours earlier and already she felt as though she were living in a different world. A world in which meals were made for her and where nothing was too much trouble. Gracious living at its best, Cleo reflected, shaking her head in wonderment.

Her suggestion that she provide her own meals had been received with dismay by Ari's housekeeper. Mrs Thomas had insisted that she would be glad to have someone to look after because the house was often empty. Since she had agreed to move in, Cleo had only talked to Ari on the phone because he was in Paris on business.

A limo had arrived to collect her, her suitcases and her single box of mementos. Cleo had learned young not to acquire too much stuff because there had rarely been much storage in the apartments she had shared with her mother and she had had even less space to enjoy since she left home. Her mother had moved frequently when she was young. It wasn't until her mother had married her stepfather and settled in Scotland with him when Cleo was seventeen that Cleo had felt that she too had a permanent base.

Her phone rang and she stiffened at the name that appeared, answering it with reluctance.

'So, how are you doing?' her stepbrother Liam asked in a hearty tone.

He then announced that he was coming down from Scotland to look for work in London and he asked if he could stay with her. Wincing, Cleo told him that she was sorry but she couldn't help.

'But you gave your mother your new address this week and I assumed that you would have more space now that you've moved,' Liam commented accusingly.

'I do, but it's not my house and I couldn't invite you here to stay.' Cleo hesitated awkwardly in the strained silence. 'I'm living with my boyfriend now, Liam—'

'I didn't even know you *had* a boyfriend!' Liam complained angrily. 'And you certainly didn't tell your mother that you were moving in with some guy!'

'Well, I don't tell my mother everything,' Cleo answered quietly. 'And I'd be grateful if you could keep that fact to yourself until I see whether or not the relationship is going to go the distance.'

Her stepbrother was annoyed and made no attempt to hide his feelings. She was tempted to tell him to mind his own business when he began questioning her about Ari and demanding to know how long she had known him. Ducking his invasive questions as best she could, she remained pleasant, reminding herself that Liam was her stepbrother and that falling out with him would cause grief for her mother.

Liam was the reason why Cleo rarely went to Scotland to see her parent. Her stepbrother had announced within hours of first meeting Cleo after he left the army that she was the woman of his dreams. Sadly, he was *not* the man of Cleo's dreams. But he currently lived with his father and her mother and worked in the pub they ran, and avoiding Liam when she visited was impossible. Unluckily for her, nobody seemed to understand why she couldn't date Liam and at least give him a chance. He was an attractive, decent enough guy, who worked hard and had no obvious bad habits, but Cleo didn't find him remotely fanciable and for that reason she had refused to go out with him. Teased and ultimately criticised for her resistance to her stepbrother's charms, Cleo had found it easier by far to avoid visiting her mother's Scottish home. Sometimes, her stepfather and mother came down to London to see her and she always visited them for Christmas and birthdays. In truth, she resented Liam for coming, however unintentionally, between her and the mother she loved.

Now, keen to avoid any further controversy, she made suggestions about where Liam could stay in London and reluctantly agreed to meet him for a meal on the weekend that he arrived. The knowledge that she would have to put up with Liam's flirtation, heavy-duty persuasion and criticisms purely to keep the family peace made her tense and anxious. Getting off to sleep was a challenge and at two in the morning she surrendered and got back out of bed to go downstairs and grab a snack from the well-stocked fridge.

Mrs Thomas lived in an apartment in the converted stables behind the house and was not disturbed by anyone getting up at night. Clad in shorty pyjamas because Ari's house was always kept at a comfortable temperature, Cleo switched on the low lights in the kitchen and dived into the refrigerator, laying out eggs and broccoli and cheese, thinking hungrily of an omelette. Locating a suitable pan, she almost dropped it when she heard a sound from the door behind her and she whirled round, clutching the frying pan like a weapon.

Ari grinned at her and lounged in the doorway. 'You could batter me to death with that,' he remarked.

Her wrist aching from the weight of the pan, she set it down on the hob. 'I didn't know you were back.'

'About an hour ago. My meetings finished early and I decided to move up my flight, even though it was late,' Ari imparted smoothly, faded jeans clinging to his lean hips, the top button undone, his impressive brown torso as bare as his feet. 'Are you cooking?'

'I was about to make an omelette. Are you hungry?'

'I wouldn't say no to something to eat,' Ari replied lightly. 'How are you finding it here?'

'How could I complain? I've never been so comfortable in my life,' she told him truthfully. 'You said that we had that interview with the authorities the day after tomorrow. Is there anything else I need to know?'

'We have another meeting with Lucy tomorrow

morning. I was hoping you would want to come to that as well.'

'I wouldn't miss it,' Cleo said with an easy smile, striving not to be so conscious of his presence or of her own state of undress.

For goodness' sake, they were adults, not feckless teenagers to whom an inch of bare flesh could be an incitement. She was wearing shorts and a loose tee, not a bikini. Why, then, was she alarmingly aware of his gaze on her slender thighs? He wasn't staring. No, Ari was far too polite and controlled to betray himself like that. She chopped ingredients while stealing feverish glances at him where he sat at the island, one long leg braced on the floor, a powerful muscular thigh flexing below the worn denim that emphasised the bulge at his crotch. Her face burning scarlet, she dragged her attention from him and threw together the omelettes without further ado.

'This is good,' Ari remarked as he ate heartily, allowing himself only a brief glance in her direction because he was ridiculously aware of the curvy, highly feminine little body concealed by her pyjamas. The level of his awareness astounded him. He was accustomed to regular exposure to half-naked female bodies in clubs, on yachts, beaches and at parties. Wherever he went he met women who wore less clothing than she did, and he shouldn't be susceptible to even the smallest show of Cleo's body...but he *was*. Cleo only had to move for her full breasts to shift beneath her top, pert nipples poking out beneath the cotton, and he was as mesmerised as a teenage boy.

'It's a quick, easy option. Your housekeeper is treating me like royalty. This is the first time I've cooked since I moved in.'

'I'm glad you're here. I have a party to attend on Saturday evening. It would seal our couple status if you appear with me in public. I'm not sure we can be very convincing without a public appearance or two.'

'No can do. I'm meeting someone for dinner on Saturday night.'

Ari stiffened, a shard of outrage flaming through him, even though he knew that he was not entitled to that reaction. 'You have a...*date*?'

'Wrong word for it, although *he'll* probably treat it like a date,' Cleo replied ruefully, her mouth tightening with resentment. 'My stepbrother is down in London and, much though I'd prefer not to, I have to be friendly to keep the family happy.'

'If he's family, he can attend the party with us,' Ari suggested.

Cleo cringed at the prospect. 'No, that wouldn't do. He might be rude to you. I told him that we were living together and he was furious. It's none of his business but he pulls the big-brother act when it suits him and reserves the right to criticise. I don't want a truckload of misinformation going back to my mother if I can avoid it.'

'If you don't like this guy, you shouldn't have to spend time with him,' Ari asserted.

'I wish it were that simple, but I'll use my living situation to put some more distance between me and

Liam,' Cleo confided. 'If I talk about us like we're a proper couple, it'll put him off...hopefully.'

'Or if he's the average male, it might only make him try harder.'

'I can handle Liam,' Cleo said ruefully. 'I just wish I didn't have to and that the family would accept that I'm not interested in him.'

'Why do your family want you to be together?'

'Because he decided that he wants to be with me and the family approve. To be fair, other women find him fanciable.'

Reluctant amusement glimmered in Ari's gorgeous eyes. 'I may not come from your world, but at least you fan—'

Cleo leant across the gap between them and rested her fingers against his parted lips to silence the words she could see ready to tumble off his tongue. 'Don't you dare say that I fancy you!'

A slanting irreverent grin illuminated his darkly handsome features and he nipped at her lingering fingertip, making her jump. 'Even if it's true?'

'Don't be vain,' she urged, leaning back from him, overpowered by his masculinity that close. The scent of him was tugging at her nostrils, an intoxicating combination of musk, mint and the faintest hint of some exotic cologne. Even the smell of Ari Stefanos made her fill her lungs like an addict and left her dizzy.

'I was being frank,' Ari countered huskily.

'And don't be provocative either,' she added jerkily, stiffening in the midst of a sizzling encounter with his glittering dark golden gaze. With an effort she dropped her head only to find herself looking instead at the impressive pecs and abs delineating his chest and stomach below his sleek bronzed skin. Her mouth ran dry, hunger stirring in an almost painful surge, her breasts swelling and her nipples pinching taut while a hollow ache throbbed at the heart of her. She pressed her bottom down hard on the stool in an effort to ward off that craving.

'I wasn't trying to be provocative.' Ari breathed in slow and deep, his chest swelling. 'But I take just one look at you when I get this close and all I can think about—'

'Me too,' Cleo cut in, instinctively leaning forward to close the gap between them, on such an edge of anticipation that she could barely breathe.

'I promised not to make you feel uncomfortable here,' Ari reminded her in a frustrated undertone.

'I'm only uncomfortable because you're not touching me,' Cleo mumbled, craving his mouth so badly she ached.

'Is that an invitation?' Ari growled as he slid off the stool to stand in front of her.

In answer, Cleo succumbed to temptation and rested her palms against his warm chest, letting her hands slowly trace down over the ridged planes of his abdomen. Her heart was racing, her breath coming in short choppy waves, her body tight with an urgent tension that literally hurt to withstand.

Without further hesitation, Ari knotted long fingers into her sleep-tousled curls and crushed her soft pink lips under his. Her tongue tangled with his as a big hand curved to her hip to urge her into connection with the urgent hardness pushing against his zip. Excitement leapt and flared inside her and a hot melting sensation in her pelvis turned her body boneless.

Desire simmered and boiled through Ari. He remembered the boundaries he had sworn to observe, the caution he had planned to exercise, and he marvelled at the effect Cleo had on him. None of those reservations could stand against the charge of unfamiliar recklessness powering him. Her hands ran lightly down his body to his thighs, scorching him wherever her exploring fingers touched. She dropped to her knees and pure anticipation ran riot through him.

She unzipped his jeans, found him with her stroking fingers, tracing the powerful heat and urgency of him. He wanted more, he wanted more before she even got properly started. And she was definitely a little clumsy at what she was doing, but her sheer enthusiasm could have levelled entire cities. The fleeting graze of her teeth didn't have the slightest impact on the wild flare of excitement flaring through Ari and expanding at an exponential rate. He exulted in the satisfying suspicion that he could be the first male she had dared to appreciate in such a way.

Long brown fingers smoothed through her tumbled hair and he groaned out loud with pleasure. Cleo glowed with a sense of achievement and then he was pulling her up, lifting her up onto the granite counter behind her to peel off her pyjamas.

'Remind me to buy you some proper lingerie,'

Ari husked as he spread her thighs and bent his dark head, shifting with predatory grace to utilise his carnal mouth on the tiny bundle of nerve endings screaming for his attention.

On the brink of telling him that he would not be buying her any clothing and that any he did buy would not be worn, Cleo lost her concentration. She lost it so completely that the heart-pounding, pulsing wave of bliss that seized her utterly consumed her, and for a few timeless moments in the grip of that powerful climax she honestly felt as though she had left her body.

'I need to go upstairs and get protection,' Ari breathed raggedly.

'I'm on the pill now,' Cleo told him. 'After what happened at the retreat, I decided it would be safer to protect myself, but if there's a risk that *you* may—'

'I was tested last month and I haven't been with anyone but you since.'

That information pleased Cleo enormously and she smiled at him.

Mere seconds later, Ari lifted her and sank into her hard and deep, and her spine arched and she moaned, because her swollen flesh was already so exquisitely sensitive. The pleasure was intense, and excitement roared through her afresh as Ari ensured that she did not have time to begin worrying. As another exhilarating surge of pleasure rocked her, she gave herself up to the moment, suddenly rejoicing in the freedom to do exactly as she liked.

With every lithe erotic thrust, sensation piled on sensation and she quivered at the shocking intensity of what she was feeling. Her heart was pounding, her pulses racing, and suddenly she was in a fever of excitement for the finishing line again. And she was there in the heart of the flame, fireworks flaring inside her and the colours of the rainbow in her dazed eyes as the wild fevered hunger rose to an agonising peak and then slowly brought her down to earth again.

Ari felt intoxicated by pleasure as he began to pull back from her. He had never wanted anyone as much as he wanted her, had never dreamt that he could go from day to day reliving intimate moments with one particular woman and counting the hours until he could see her again. In truth, he had flown back late the previous evening purely to ensure that he could have breakfast with Cleo. What had transpired since that modest goal inflamed him all the more.

As Ari stepped back, Cleo slid naked off the counter, shocked by her surroundings, and she stooped to grab up her pyjamas. Long fingers closed over her wrist. 'Where are you going?'

Cleo breathed in deep. 'I thought—'

'No, you're staying,' Ari incised succinctly as he bent down to lift her up into his arms, naked and flushed. 'Tonight, I don't want to feel like a one-night stand whom you can't wait to escape again.'

'I didn't mean it that way. I just thought—'

'You think the wrong things sometimes, especially around me,' Ari told her lethally. 'I want you here in the morning, so that I can have you again...although I could always grab you out of your room at a mutually agreeable hour—'

Cleo grinned. 'Seems a little complicated…but like this…er… It's totally casual, no strings…okay?'

'You're quite happy for me to be with other women?' Ari intoned in apparent surprise. 'I'm sorry, but I'm not happy to offer you the same freedom—'

'I didn't say that.'

'So, not so totally casual, after all,' Ari murmured in soft and sweet conclusion.

'Why does everything have to get so complex? Why does everything have to have a label?' Cleo lamented.

'Does it matter as long as we're both content with the status quo?' Ari dropped her down on a big bed in a low-lit bedroom.

Cleo abandoned her crumpled pyjamas and curled up into a tight ball of anxiety. She didn't want to get content with him or used to him. She didn't want to get hurt again. Ari made demands and then got annoyed when she failed to deliver. If she had more backbone, she would return to her own room.

While she considered that defiant option, Ari ran a hand down over her hip and flipped her round and back into his arms. 'Go to sleep. I can feel you stressing from here.' He sighed. 'What time do you start work? I'll drop you off after we've seen Lucy.'

An hour later, aware that Ari had fallen asleep, Cleo crept out of bed to go back downstairs and tidy up the mess they had left behind in the kitchen. Ari hadn't even switched off the lights. She stacked the plates in the dishwasher, restored the work surfaces to sanitised perfection, doused the lights and crept back upstairs.

Now, at least, nobody would suspect the shenanigans that had taken place there. Her face burned at the X-rated images still locked in her memory banks. There was no need to advertise her total inability to resist Ari Stefanos.

As she slid back into bed, Ari murmured, 'Where were you?'

'Cleaning up the kitchen. You didn't even switch the lights off!' she told him in a scandalised whisper.

Ari laughed out loud and curved an arm round her. 'Why are you worrying about that?' he asked in wonderment.

Cleo marvelled at his masculine incomprehension.

The next morning, Lucy was very quiet when they arrived for the visit. Cleo got down on the floor and propped the baby up with cushions and began to roll the electronic toy she had persuaded Ari to purchase. As the coloured sections lit up and a nursery rhyme sounded, Lucy began to smile and show interest. Ari joined them, kept the flashing lights going and lifted Lucy's little hand to press the button down to change the tune playing. The baby grinned and Cleo felt her heart clench at that smile and could no longer resist those bright brown eyes in that tiny face. She lifted her up for a cuddle and told her what a wonderful little girl she was, and the way the baby reacted, it was as if she knew that she was being praised to the skies.

Ari was fascinated by the warmth of Cleo's cheerful interactions with his niece. She was so natural and confident with the child that a baby who did suffer from being rather timid and wary positively glowed in her presence, attracted by her sure handling and affection. Lucy, he registered, needed a loving mother figure like that to feel properly secure.

'My turn…' Ari gently eased Lucy into his arms and wondered how Lucy would handle being cared for by a nanny and how she would cope with his absences, practicalities he had not previously considered. His single status was not an automatic bar to adoption, but he also knew that it was not an advantage. And there was Cleo right in front of him: great with kids, fabulous in bed, absolutely not a gold digger. Could it get much better than that for him? He wanted to keep Cleo and what better way would there be?

The appointment passed unbelievably fast and another was arranged while Lucy yawned and yawned, exhausted by all the one-to-one attention and ready for another feed and a nap. Ari dropped Cleo off and she warned him that she would be working later to make up for her late start. He frowned but made no comment, and she looked at him and marvelled that Ari Stefanos was, however temporarily, hers. In jeans and a long-sleeved top in line with her suggestion that he dress more casually for his meetings with his niece, he was heading home again to put on a suit before he went into the office.

Hers, she savoured helplessly. The guy with the colour-coded wardrobe that had sent her into whoops of laughter only hours earlier. He was terrifyingly tidy and organised and…she *wasn't*. He hadn't learned yet how to be flexible, how to compromise. She had watched an expression of appalled disbelief freeze his lean, darkly handsome features when she emptied her capacious handbag to find something and he glimpsed the conglomeration of disparate articles she dragged around with her every day, everything from a mini first-aid kit to a bottle opener.

Hers? Of course, he wasn't, not in any meaningful, durable sense, she acknowledged, only hers in a weird and incredible time-out-of-time way. She remembered him strolling out of his en suite first thing stark naked, like some glorious Greek god and infinitely more sexy. She had been tempted to pinch herself to check that she wasn't dreaming, only the ache of her still humming body the evidence that she was not. And he had dragged her out of bed, displaying all the irritating characteristics of an energetic early riser who put punctuality on the same level as godliness. Yes, what they had, she reflected tautly, was very, very real, but it wasn't likely to last and it would hurt when it ended. As long as she didn't forget that she would be fine, she reasoned as he dropped her off at the bar and made yet another comment about finding her a more suitable job, which she totally ignored.

At lunchtime, Liam turned up and got chatting to her boss. Sam had a friend in need of a temporary bar manager at a Soho pub, and before Liam left again, he had secured an interview that afternoon. Cleo wasn't surprised because her stepbrother had considerable experience in the bar trade. When he showed up at finishing time and pressed her to join him for a drink, she agreed because she could see that he was dying to talk about his interview.

Liam, convinced he had the job in the bag, was in an ebullient mood, and he was annoyed when she said she had to leave at seven.

'Ari's picking me up outside,' Cleo protested when he endeavoured to persuade her to stay longer.

As she grabbed her coat to leave, Liam trailed out after her.

'What's this guy got apart from money and a big house?' Liam demanded argumentatively.

'I'm not with Ari because of his bank balance!' Cleo told him angrily.

'I looked him up online. He's nothing but a womaniser, Cleo. He'll use you and dump you again. He's never had a serious relationship in his life!' Liam proclaimed loudly. 'He's a Greek playboy, who doesn't want to grow up like the rest of us—'

'Will you stop raising your voice?' Cleo hissed at her stepbrother, noting passing heads swivelling in their direction and wishing Liam would calm down. 'And lay off Ari. You don't know anything about him!'

'Except that he dresses like some fancy-dancy model,' Liam quipped nastily, his attention on the tall, dark male drawing level with them.

'Keep your opinion to yourself,' Ari told him curtly.

And without the smallest warning, her stepbrother swung a wild punch at Ari.

Ari ducked and was coming back up to return the attempted blow when Cleo caught his arm. 'No, please… He's drunk and jealous—'

His lean bronzed face taut, Ari stepped back. 'The car's parked round the corner,' he murmured evenly while studying her swaying, pugnacious stepbrother grimly. 'As you heard, Cleo's very loyal to me. That's why we're getting engaged. I may have been labelled a playboy in the past, but Cleo has changed me for the better—'

'Engaged?' Liam repeated in thunderous disbelief.

'Engaged?' Cleo queried incredulously, twisting her head round to focus on Ari's granite-hard profile.

'So, you see, I'm not *playing* with Cleo. This is the real thing,' Ari breathed curtly, closing a taut hand over Cleo's and urging her away.

CHAPTER SEVEN

'HAVE YOU GONE CRAZY?' Cleo hissed at Ari as he led her round the corner of the crowded street and into the comfort of the limousine.

'No. Hopefully I've got him off your back now *and* without having to brawl with him in the street,' Ari parried without an ounce of regret. 'You shouldn't see him again on Saturday when he can behave like that. I don't trust him—'

'You shouldn't have told him we're engaged, and you can't tell me who I can and cannot see!' Cleo slung back at him sharply.

'He was drunk. You couldn't handle him,' Ari countered.

'He was drunk because he's landed a job and he was celebrating,' Cleo retorted. 'Believe me, that's not the norm for him. He wouldn't last long in the bar trade if it were.'

'I don't trust him with you,' Ari responded with finality. 'He lacks boundaries. Although you've never been with the guy, he's already making you very uncomfortable. It's none of his business if you choose to be with me. It's time someone *made* him back off.'

'*Not* you!' Cleo lanced back. 'That's just salting the wound. You're rich, you're good-looking, you're successful, everything most men want to be. Have some compassion.'

Ari's beautifully shaped mouth quirked and he studied her with glittering tawny eyes full of naked appreciation. '"Everything most men want to be"? *Really?*' he queried with amusement.

Cleo flushed to the roots of her hair and punched his shoulder in mock retaliation. 'You know what I mean… What the heck possessed you to tell him that we were engaged?'

Ari lifted his chin. 'It struck me as a good idea.'

'Well, it was the worst idea imaginable! Liam will tell my mother and then I'll have to come up with a whole story about how we broke up and everyone will feel sorry for me and assume you did the dumping,' she complained bitterly.

'But what if we don't break up? What if we *make* it real?' Ari murmured silkily just as the limo drew up outside the town house.

Cleo frowned and fell silent as she preceded him into the house. 'What were you trying to say in the car?' she prompted.

Ari pressed open a door into a room obviously used as an office. Lined with pale bookshelves and dominated by a desk, it had a contemporary aspect very different from the rest of the house and she suspected that Ari must already have had it redecorated. Now he leant back against the solid desk, his lean muscular body taut, sunlight behind him gleaming over his blue-black hair and bronzed skin, his spectacular eyes vibrant.

'Close the door,' he instructed.

'Ari…' she began impatiently.

'I'm asking you to marry me. No more pretending, no need for us to fake or lie about anything.'

Cleo was stunned by the concept. Her upper lip lifted as though she was about to speak and then met with her lower again as she thought better of the hasty refusal ready to tumble off her tongue. 'But you're not in love with me… Why would you ask me to marry you?' she asked stiffly, as though she were afraid that he could be pranking her for some nefarious reason of his own.

'I don't do the love thing…*or* the love thing doesn't do me,' Ari murmured calmly. 'I'm almost twenty-nine and I've never been in love. I've met women I like more than others, but I've never wanted to keep one of them. But you're different.'

'How am I different?' Cleo pressed tightly, and she felt as if her world were riding on his response. His opinion shouldn't matter that much to her, but she was discovering that it did—indeed, that his opinion mattered very much.

Ari had grown up expecting to fall in love, but it had never happened to him. He had decided that possibly he was too grounded to focus that amount of emotion on another human being. Or perhaps it was because he had never witnessed that kind of love in his adolescence. His parents had not been demonstrative with each other, although he had read love in the looks they often exchanged. Now he was asking Cleo to marry him, and even as he did it he was shocked that he was doing it. Yet the commitment he was suggesting didn't scare him in the slightest, which he marvelled at because he had always thought that even thinking about marriage would condemn him to sleepless nights worrying that he was making a mistake. But then Cleo *was* different in his eyes from other women.

'You get on great with Lucy and she needs you. I can be a lot of things for her benefit, but I can't be a mother,' Ari intoned wryly. 'She deserves a mother after her poor start in life, and even though she's not your child, I believe you are capable of loving her. Not every woman could offer that to a little girl who is not her own. The minute I decided that I wanted to adopt Lucy, I realised that I would have to be very careful about any woman I brought into her life.'

Cleo focused her attention on a corner of the desk to the far side of him and her eyes prickled with stinging tears. He was giving her the truth, but it was a truth that could only hurt. He was asking her to marry him for his niece's benefit. He needed a wife, whom he could trust to be kind to Lucy. And on one score he was correct. She was very capable of loving that little girl and would be eager to take up the opportunity, if only it didn't entail marrying a man who didn't love *her*.

'I'm quite sure that there are other women who

would be equally caring with Lucy,' Cleo declared, striving to rise above her instincts. Instincts that cruelly told her to immediately accept Ari's proposal because she wasn't likely to get him any other way. And she was realising for the first time that she wanted Ari, like really, really, *really* wanted Ari for much more than a casual affair. When had that happened? When had feelings crept in to weaken her objectivity? Why had she kidded herself that she could stay uninvolved when every scrap of evidence had indicated the opposite?

'No doubt there are other women, but I doubt if any of them would attract me to the extent that you do. We share dynamite chemistry—'

'And you would marry me just for that?' Cleo questioned in disbelief.

'Sexual compatibility is pretty high up my list of non-negotiable necessities,' Ari acknowledged without embarrassment. 'I have no plans to play away outside my marriage like my father did. No child of mine will ever have to deal with the situation I've found myself in.'

Cleo sealed her lips on the urge to tell him that he was too rigid in his viewpoint. Had his father planned to have a second family? Or had that been something that just happened?

'And of course, eventually, I would like children of my own with you,' Ari informed her levelly. 'I'm suggesting a perfectly normal marriage—possibly one built on a more practical foundation than most, but that doesn't mean that it couldn't be a good and successful marriage.'

Silence fell while her thoughts raced like trapped animals running in circles inside her head. She wanted to say that she would think about it for a while, but she knew she would only be saying that for the sake of her pride. She had always assumed that some day she would marry and have a family. She had also assumed that the man she married would love her, but nobody got everything they wanted, she thought ruefully. With Ari, she was boxing above her weight. He was rich and gorgeous and very honest about his expectations. He wanted what she wanted and she very much wanted him *and* Lucy. She had fallen headlong in love with that little girl and needed to be involved in bringing her up. Ari could make them both happy, was already making Cleo happy, if she was honest with herself, only that happiness had felt very, very risky and short-term in nature because she had naturally assumed that what they had together would not last for long. Now Ari was offering her something permanent and secure and she was discovering right there in that moment that she wanted that chance with every breath in her body. She wanted him and she wanted Lucy and it really was that simple.

'Okay,' Cleo said shakily. 'I'll marry you.'

His exotic caramel eyes glittered gold below his lush black lashes and her heart skipped an entire beat. 'Right, let's go and get a ring—'

'Aren't you being a bit hasty? It's after closing time too!' Cleo reminded him.

Ari pulled out his phone, and a moment later, he was talking to a jeweller. Within minutes he was herding her out of the house again, pausing to speak to his housekeeper to tell her that they would return for dinner. 'Or do you want to eat out to celebrate?' he asked Cleo suddenly.

'No, no, I'll be perfectly happy to eat here,' she assured him, feeling more than a little light-headed at the speed with which events were moving.

Two hours later, seated in a private room in the opulent jeweller's in Hatton Garden, she sipped champagne and contemplated the magnificent pear-shaped palest blue diamond on her engagement finger in fascination. Blue diamonds were rare and she loved it, simply because Ari had expressed interest in it and admired it on her finger. As he walked her back out to the limo in the fading light, he murmured, 'We'll get married in Greece and fly your family out to join us. What do you think?'

'I'm thinking about how much there is to organise beforehand,' Cleo muttered weakly, dazed by how quickly he made plans. 'Like a dress and invitations and—'

'Mel will organise all that for us,' Ari incised with satisfaction as he referred to his senior personal assistant. 'She was a wedding planner before she came to work for me and she's amazingly efficient.'

'I'd better phone Mum,' Cleo said, surprised that her head wasn't spinning with the stream of changes that was suddenly threatening to turn her world upside down.

'We'll go and see Lucy before we leave and we won't stay away long,' Ari stipulated, single-minded as always, and Cleo's romantic haze cleared a little at that point because, however unintentionally, Ari was reminding her *why* he was marrying her.

'Ari didn't really notice me until we were at the retreat, and then, after he'd hauled me out of the water, he took me back to the house he was staying at and… er, well, that's when we got to know each other,' Cleo revealed in an embarrassed rush to her mother.

'I can see why Liam didn't make the cut,' remarked Lisa Brown, a small blonde woman with her daughter's blue eyes and generous mouth. 'Ari's very, very good-looking.'

'I had a bit of a crush on him from the day I first saw him,' Cleo admitted with a sigh. 'It went from there…'

'I just want him to make you happy. At the end of the day the fancy frills don't matter,' her mother opined. 'It's only feelings that count. But my word, this place is out of this world.'

Lisa's blissful sigh of appreciation as they sat outside the luxury suite made Cleo grin. The opulent cabins of the Stefanos beach resort enjoyed the most beautiful view and they fronted a world-renowned hotel. Best of all, the twinkling turquoise sea and the smooth sandy beach lay only yards away, and both women were barefoot after a refreshing walk through the surf. With the sun beating down on them below a bright blue sky, Cleo's mother, an inveterate sun lover, was in seventh heaven.

'This is the holiday of a lifetime and I get to see you married as well,' Lisa murmured, squeezing her daughter's hand affectionately. 'And you'll be nearby for most of it, which is even more wonderful—'

'But she'll be on her *honeymoon*,' Cleo's stepfather, Davis, reminded his wife gently as he emerged from the cabin to join the two women, a greying, still trim older man in swim shorts. 'We'll go to the wedding and then work on our suntans. If Cleo gets a spare minute, I'm sure she'll try and drop in to see us before we fly home again.'

'Of course I will,' Cleo said warmly.

Ari's father had built an exclusive beach resort at the far end of the private island of Spinos and it had been Mel's idea for most of the guests to stay there. Ari had flown her family out in his private jet. With her mother and stepfather, her stepbrothers and their partners all attending, Cleo had felt much more grounded and comfortable with the arrangements. She was also relieved that Liam had opted to stay home and look after the pub to allow his father and stepmother to come to the wedding and enjoy their first proper holiday in years.

'Just one thing I wanted to ask you before we join the others,' her mother murmured in an undertone. 'How much does it bother you that your father isn't here for your big day?'

Cleo sent the older woman a look of astonishment. 'But he's never been part of my life,' she pointed out.

Lisa grimaced. 'Yes, but in recent years I've come to believe that I may have given you a false impression of him when you were a child. I was still very bitter, you know, when he ended the affair and returned to being faithful to the woman he had been living with all along,' she confided awkwardly. 'To be honest, he told me then that it would break his heart to walk away from his child and that he was deeply ashamed but that my pregnancy had made him appreciate how much he loved the family he was already with. The only reason he didn't visit you was that he couldn't face telling the woman he loved about his infidelity and he didn't want any more lies between them.'

Cleo studied her mother in shock because what she was hearing was a very different version of what she had previously been told. Her mother had not told her any lies, but Lisa had given her a much more negative image of her absent father.

'I'm sorry that I let my bitterness over his rejection colour my judgement. It's not fair for you to have to judge your father badly for a relationship that I freely entered. I *knew* he was with her. I *knew* he had kids. But I made the mistake of believing that because he hadn't married her, he was not committed to them.' Lisa breathed out audibly. 'There—I've got that confession off my chest and I can relax now and we need never discuss it again.'

Cleo nodded twice, taken aback by the information she had received and knowing that she needed to mull it over in private. She felt sad at what she had learned, but she also better understood her father's choices. He had chosen to be true to the children he had presumably planned to have rather than the unexpected pregnancy that her mother had presented him with. Could she really blame him for that? That he had admitted that he was ashamed to walk away from her gave her a much more positive image of the man.

Two crazy weeks of high-octane wedding preparations during which Mel had consulted her about every possible bridal preference had already left Cleo dizzy and very much aware that her bridegroom enjoyed an extremely privileged lifestyle. Time and time again she had had to swallow her misgivings and embrace the art of compromise. Just as often, she had taken Mel's advice and chosen to go with more upmarket options. Neither she nor her family had been allowed to pay for anything. Of course, they couldn't have afforded to pay for anything that would have passed muster in Ari's elite world. In a battle between her pride and her common sense, practicality had won. But Cleo had, however, picked her own wedding gown and her mother had paid for it.

And tomorrow was her big day, Cleo acknowledged in wonderment. The one downbeat note in her life was that she missed Ari. She missed him much more than she had expected to miss him. When Lisa had asked her to spend some time with her family, she had wanted that precious time with her mother but, unfortunately for her, she wanted Ari too. And with him having been in Brussels on business and their separate travelling arrangements, she had only seen him when they visited Lucy together shortly before her departure. They were hoping that on their return to the UK they would be allowed to foster Lucy until such time as it was possible to adopt her.

After an evening spent over a long dinner, Cleo's phone buzzed as she climbed into bed at midnight, and she answered it, surprised that it was Ari. *Oh, my goodness.* He wasn't getting cold feet, was he? She came out in a cold sweat of horror at the suspicion.

'I thought you were with your friends tonight,' she said tightly.

'I am, but I don't want a hangover tomorrow, so no wild partying for me. I know it's late, but I want to see you—'

'It's bad luck for us to see each other before the wedding,' she told him gently.

'You can't be that superstitious,' Ari censured.

Cleo winced. 'I am...and I want a good night's sleep.'

'Okay,' Ari conceded, although she knew him well enough to know that it wasn't okay with him, but then Ari was not accustomed to refusal.

'I want you back in my bed where you belong,' Ari admitted in a roughened undertone.

Cleo flushed and felt heat surge in her pelvis. 'Tomorrow night... My mum is enjoying having me here with her.'

She lay back on the bed, perspiration on her upper lip and a wrenched feeling tugging at her loyalties. She knew exactly what would have transpired had she met up with Ari. As her face burned, the ache between her thighs intensified. He had transformed her into a wanton hussy. And there was nothing wrong with that, she reminded herself, as long as she didn't get carried away and start advertising what a pushover she was for him. In her opinion, Ari didn't value anything that came to him too easily and she still needed to offer him an occasional hint of challenge.

Flying in that afternoon, Cleo had noticed the imposing Greek Orthodox church built on the hill above the village. It was a much larger and more elaborate building than one would have expected to find on a small Greek island. Apparently, Ari's grandfather had built the church to commemorate his wife's passing.

The following morning, as the car that had collected her mother and her from the resort drew up outside the church, Cleo breathed in deep and stepped out into the sunlight. She shook free her dress. The iridescent beaded and intricately embroidered bodice shaped her full breasts. It rejoiced in a vee neckline, bell sleeves and a layered and tiered tulle skirt, which flowed softly round her feet. Worn with a short veil, the gown had a romantic bohemian vibe, which she had fallen in love with. On her head she wore the superb sapphire-and-diamond tiara that Ari had had delivered to her the night before.

'You look like a princess today,' her mother had sighed in contentment.

A loud buzz of voices carried from inside the church. By the sound of it, the interior was packed. Ari had said most of the guests were business acquaintances and friends, with only a handful of his distant cousins sprinkled through the mix. Cleo, on the other hand, only had her stepfamily and a couple of old schoolfriends who had elected to come but who hadn't arrived until late the night before.

Now as she walked down the aisle with her mother she was insanely conscious of the number of heads turning to look at her, and her first impression was that there was an inordinate number of very beautiful women in the pews, all staring at her so intently that a veil of colour turned her pale cheeks a soft pink. And there was Ari waiting for her at the altar. He looked amazing in a formal morning suit, very tall and dark and extravagantly handsome, his spectacular eyes locked to her with unhidden appreciation.

And that was that for Cleo. Evidently, Ari liked how she looked, and a cast of thousands in the pews couldn't have daunted her from that point on. He didn't need to speak. His brilliant and attentive gaze told her everything she needed to know.

'You look like a fairy queen,' he murmured softly, his breath fanning her cheek, and a ripple of powerful awareness shimmied through her taut body. 'Or like you belong in a field of wildflowers.'

A narrow platinum band studded with diamonds eased onto her finger some minutes later and the short and sweet ceremony was done. She was Ari's wife now, for better or for worse, she reflected headily.

The reception was being staged at the hotel at the centre of the resort. Gathering her skirts, Cleo settled into the SUV that would take them there along the island's single road, which wound along the sandy shore. 'It's gorgeous here. How long has the island been in the family?'

'My great-grandfather bought it for peanuts in the days when such acquisitions were not considered desirable. Ironically, he did it to prevent tourist development. He didn't have an eye for the future or the people who live here and need employment.'

'But your father built the resort,' Cleo recalled.

'Yes. The family home used to stand where the hotel now is in the bay. After my sister died, my father demolished the house, had the resort built and built a new house at the far end of the island, but my parents only ever made fleeting visits here after that. Losing Alexia here on the island devastated them and they never got over that. My mother was heartbroken because she had always wanted a daughter. I know that they tried to have another child because my mother went into hospital with a miscarriage a couple of years later. I think she had a breakdown after that.'

'That was really tragic after they had lost your sister.' Cleo sighed with sympathy. 'The last thing your parents needed was another hard blow.'

'I know.' Ari compressed his sensual mouth.

'You've never told me how your sister drowned.' Cleo almost whispered the reminder.

Ari tensed. 'We were very close. Alexia was a tomboy, the perfect playmate for me. On the day that it happened, she dived into the pool and struck her head on the side. I tried to get her out of the water, but I'm afraid she was too heavy for me to lift.' Tiny muscles pulled his strong profile taut with the regret he couldn't hide. 'Sadly, I hadn't had lessons in life-saving either. By the time help came, it was too late… Alexia had gone—'

'So, the two of you were playing without supervision in the pool?' Cleo gathered in some surprise at the idea.

'Yes, we both swam like fish and it was assumed to be safe. But we were only six years old. My parents' guilt over that decision probably made it worse for them afterwards.'

'The trauma of that loss may also be why your father got involved with another woman in the first place,' Cleo suggested with a wince. 'Grief doesn't always pull people together. Just as often, it pushes them apart.'

Ari was frowning at that comment. 'The dates would tally with that possibility,' he conceded reluctantly. 'I haven't looked at the situation in that light before.'

'It makes sense. I doubt that your father deliberately went out to have an affair, unless that sort of behaviour was the norm for him.'

'As far as I know, it wasn't. He was a conservative man. Why are we even talking about this on our wedding day?' Ari demanded with a frown as he grasped her slender hand and squeezed it in emphasis.

'I was being nosy.'

Ari laughed, his tension vanishing, his dark golden eyes gleaming. 'You look incredible in that dress,' he told her. 'I like the fact that it's more casual. It suits you.'

In a very grand function room, they greeted their guests. Cleo saw very few recognisable faces around her, but her impression that there was a great number of beautiful women increased, particularly once she had identified four, not from personal acquaintance but by the fact they were celebrities who were often in the newspapers. Two were models, one was a soap actress and another a very rich socialite. And from the amount of snooping she had done into Ari's private life on the internet, she was also aware that at some stage he had been linked to all four women.

'You invited ex-girlfriends,' she remarked in a mild tone that could not be interpreted as censorious for she was reluctant to register an objection to that decision.

'Most remain friends and discreet about our past connection,' Ari parried without batting a magnificent curling black eyelash at her comment.

'There seem to be quite a few of them,' Cleo pointed out, very much aware of the extra degree of critical curiosity such ladies subjected her to and of their often overly familiar manner of greeting Ari. An avalanche of sultry looks, kisses and lingering touches had come his way, every woman vying with the next to claim that revealing physical bond. Their enthusiasm for touching him was a dead giveaway. Body language did reveal a great deal, Cleo conceded unhappily, far from content that Ari had chosen to invite so many of his former lovers to attend their wedding. Shouldn't *her* feelings have been taken into account? What had happened to the bride's right to enjoy a tranquil day of happiness?

'How come they're all still friends with you?' she enquired, unable to swallow back that obvious question.

'Why wouldn't they be? I never promised them anything that I didn't deliver.' Ari parried that further question with perceptible impatience at her continuing interest in the subject. 'Nothing was ever exclusive. It was casual. We'd go out, have a good time, enjoy a few intimate hours together. It was meaningless.'

Just as *she* might have been had Ari not developed a greater hunger for her after their single encounter, Cleo found herself thinking wretchedly. Troubled by his entitled attitude, she visited the cloakroom to freshen up before they took their seats. She was in a cubicle when she heard several female voices belittling the bride and she stayed put, reluctant to embrace the embarrassment of meeting the rude guests but guessing that she was undoubtedly listening to Ari's former lovers dissecting her. It was jealousy, envy, she told herself soothingly, but she could not forget that Ari was only marrying her to improve his credentials as a prospective parent for his niece, Lucy. That was a sobering slap in the face lest there was a risk of her getting too big for her boots.

'I think she's pregnant. She barely sipped the champagne and that hippy dress of hers is cut loose at the front,' a woman chimed in confidently. 'It's the oldest trick in the book, but it *would* explain why he's marrying her.'

A door opened and then another, and the voices

faded away. Cheeks flushed with temper and mortification, Cleo emerged from her hiding place, annoyed that she had remained concealed but all too conscious that Ari would not have thanked her for confronting friends of his about their nasty outlook and cruel comments.

It didn't help her mood to return to the reception and find a lithe brunette in a daringly styled cerise-pink dress flirting like crazy with Ari. The bright smile already fixed to her generous mouth stiffened a little more at the sight.

As the brunette grudgingly gave way to her for them to take their seats at the top table, Cleo murmured, 'Before you met me, you lived like a sultan with a harem, didn't you?'

Straight ebony brows lowering over his spectacular tawny eyes, Ari shot her an incredulous glance. 'What are you trying to say?'

'All those women vying for your attention, nobody daring to complain lest you lose interest, nobody demanding fidelity or anything else that might curtail your freedom,' Cleo clarified with acid sweetness. 'Marriage promises to be a big boring shock for you. How on earth are you planning to manage without your harem?'

Ari gazed back at her in disbelief. It had never once crossed his mind to see his sex life in such a light. He reckoned he could see some point in her censure. He had virtually picked women out of a wide selection of willing contenders, but what was that to do with Cleo now? At the point when he had been admiring Cleo's wondrous lack of vanity, competitiveness and drama in comparison to other women he had known, she chose to blindside him with an attack he hadn't foreseen, and he was very much taken aback.

CHAPTER EIGHT

'So what if it *was* like that?' Ari countered with a lethal cutting edge to his dark, deep drawl and a careless shrug of dismissal, as though his bride's opinion of his past mattered not in the smallest way. 'How I conducted my sex life prior to our marriage is, thankfully, not your problem.'

Cleo went white at his derisive tone, but she tilted her chin up in challenge. 'You made it my problem when you chose to invite every darned one of them to the wedding,' she retorted in a terse undertone.

Silence fell then and Cleo busied herself chatting to the elderly cousin who had been chosen, as Ari's most senior surviving relative, to sit by her side. Ari's best man made a very amusing speech, but that was the only speech, as her mother had had no desire to speak up amongst strangers and Cleo hadn't had any bridesmaids. As the bridal couple stepped onto the dance floor to open the dancing, the silence between them thundered, but she could see that as long as they both spoke to other people and smiled readily, nobody was the slightest bit suspicious that the bride and groom might already have fallen out.

Beneath the show, however, she could feel Ari's tension in the tautness of his lean, powerful body against hers and in the tightness at the corners of his sculpted lips. He held her lightly and did not pull her close, and as soon as the dance was over, he went off to socialise and Cleo joined her family. It was a ridiculously *civilised* row, she conceded ruefully.

The sunshine was fading softly into dusk when Ari suggested they leave. A full-scale party was taking place by then. Her family had gone down to the beach, where a barbecue was burning, a bar was operating and Caribbean music was playing.

'I should get changed,' Cleo said awkwardly.

'I'm afraid you can't yet. All your luggage has already been transferred to the house,' Ari informed her, long fingers brushing her spine as he urged her in the direction of the exit.

Cleo had taken her leave of her mother when the whole group chose the informality of the beach party. Another SUV awaited them outside the hotel with the rear passenger door wide for their entry. Ari strode round the bonnet and climbed into the front passenger seat.

Clearly, she wasn't exactly flavour of the month, Cleo acknowledged, but, rather than her feeling rebuked and put in her place, Cleo's annoyance was growing. How dared he behave as though what she had said was unreasonable? Prior to meeting her, Ari had behaved exactly like a sultan with a harem, cherry-picking whichever willing beauty he chose from a wide pool of choice as and when he wanted without any need to offer anything more than a fun few hours. He had no experience with ordinary relationships. He was unable to see why she should feel angry and hurt by the presence of his previous lovers at what should have been *her* special day. So, she would have to show him in terms that he could understand.

After a drive along the sea road, the SUV cut down a lane surrounded first by dense oak woods and then by orchards. She saw orange and lemon trees and other fruit trees she couldn't identify before the car moved back into the fading sunlight to approach a very large and long stone-and wood-built house overlooking a secluded bay. It was a beach house, she reckoned, going by the many open patio doors and the wide surrounding terraces, but it was a Stefanos property and therefore it was a beach house on steroids.

They walked into the house, where Ari shared a brisk exchange in Greek with the older woman awaiting them. He introduced her as Delphine, who then took her leave.

'There's a cold meal and snacks prepared for us, but she's happy to come back and cook us a hot meal if we want,' Ari told her smoothly.

'Cold will be fine,' Cleo responded, strolling into an airy reception room with a glorious view of the sea and the surrounding hills. 'I wasn't expecting something so contemporary.'

'I had it renovated a couple of years ago,' Ari retorted. 'My father rarely came here, and he signed the island over to me on my twenty-fifth birthday.'

'We need to talk about our difference of opinion,' Cleo told him quietly.

'No, we don't. Let it go,' Ari countered curtly.

'That's not how I operate,' Cleo said apologetically. 'I want you just to picture another scenario. Imagine if I had invited all *my* past lovers to attend our wedding—'

Ari actually rolled his eyes. 'Let's be real. You haven't *had* any other lovers,' he pointed out very drily.

Cleo's blue eyes blazed like sapphire bolts. 'That's not relevant,' she sliced back at him with hot cheeks. 'You can still use your imagination to picture how you would have felt had I paraded my past lovers in front of *you*.'

'I did not parade—'

'You did,' Cleo cut in. 'You invited a lot of women, who were not well-wishers and who spent our entire wedding loudly speculating about why on earth you had married someone as ordinary as me. I found it offensive. You didn't think about my feelings and you should've done.'

'I—'

'No, don't you say that it wouldn't have bothered you if I'd trailed a load of exes in front of you,' Cleo protested. 'You didn't like me spending time with Liam, even though you knew I'd no interest in him.'

'I'm possessive...about you,' Ari added jerkily, because it wasn't the norm for him and he didn't like admitting it. He didn't get attached to women, although he had to confess to having somehow become somewhat attached to Cleo, he allowed grudgingly. When it came to emotions, having grown up in a family where emotion was not freely expressed or shown, Ari had learned to conceal his feelings. That had become his default setting in every situation, he recognised belatedly.

Cleo curved a small hand over his arm. 'I'm possessive too…'

Ari breathed in deep and looked out to sea as the sun sank in a blaze of glorious colour. Peach, gold and scarlet rays radiated out into the darkening sky. Slowly the fierce knot of tension inside him eased. He got her point. He remembered how flirtatious some of those women had been, the inviting glances and touches, the hints that they would still be available were he to get bored, and he was suddenly amazed at how thoughtless he had been. Cleo, he recognised then, operated on an entirely different mental wavelength from him.

'I assumed it wouldn't matter to you because you were my wife, which gives you an unassailable role in my life that no other woman has ever come close to achieving,' he admitted. 'But perhaps that was arrogant…and I was careless and unkind.'

'Or perhaps I lack sufficient confidence to see myself in that lofty light,' Cleo allowed thoughtfully. 'But you do need to consider your attitudes before Lucy grows up.'

'Lecture over yet?' His mouth quirking, Ari gazed down at her, his extraordinary tawny eyes gleaming pure mesmeric gold in the light of the sunset over the bay. 'You're already trying to change me.'

'Polish up the rough edges a bit,' Cleo contradicted softly. '*Not* change you. You're not used to considering other people's feelings. It's not that you're rude. You're—'

'I get it,' Ari interposed before she could expand more on the topic. 'Now can we eat something? That crack about sultans and harems killed my appetite earlier.'

'Show me the kitchen,' Cleo told him with a relieved grin that lit up her delicate face like sunshine.

For a split second, Ari wanted to grab her, flatten her to the nearest horizontal surface or plaster her up against a wall and sink into the warm, wet heat of her curvy, sexy little body, but that kind of impetuosity could be deemed inconsiderate, he calculated, and he desisted from that libidinous urge with the greatest difficulty.

'I have quite a hot temper,' he muttered between bites of the snacks she piled in front of him. 'But I didn't want to argue with you on our wedding day or say anything that might upset you more.'

'So instead you simmered like a cauldron of oil on a fire and went silent on me. Good to know,' Cleo teased.

Ari snaked out a long arm and drew her between his spread thighs. 'Mrs Stefanos, you are sassy.'

Her blue eyes danced. 'You're only just noticing?'

He leant forward and claimed her parted lips with unashamed hunger. 'Last night, I would've killed to have you here with me.' He breathed that frank admission rawly.

'Last night,' Cleo whispered, drinking in the warm, wonderfully familiar scent of him like an addict as her hands wound round his neck, 'I said no when I really wanted to say yes...'

With a growl of response, Ari vaulted upright and grabbed her hand to lead her into the hall. 'Time to give you a tour of the upstairs.'

A wicked little spark of anticipation curled low in her pelvis.

He walked her up into a huge bedroom with patio doors opening out onto a balcony. The room was decorated in pale aqua colours, providing a fitting frame for the glorious panoramic view of the starry night sky above the dark shadowy ocean below while the white sandy beach glowed even in moonlight.

'Help me with the hooks,' she urged him, shifting her slight shoulders.

Ari undid the dress and she shifted her arms and let it drop to the rug beneath her. Hearing the catch in his breath, she smiled and turned round, refusing to allow herself to be self-conscious in a lingerie set she had chosen to wear.

Ari took a step back to fully appreciate the short peacock-blue corset cupping her plump breasts, the silk panties lovingly moulding the rounded swell of her derrière and the suspenders adorning her slender thighs.

'You were worth waiting for...the perfect wedding present to unwrap,' Ari husked. 'No sultan could greet his harem favourite with greater appreciation than I at this moment, *glykia mou*.'

Cleo sent him a speaking glance, amused and not at all surprised at the way he was throwing her crack back in her teeth like a challenge. He cast off his jacket, jerked loose his cravat and began unbuttoning his dress shirt, a sliver of bronzed muscular torso catching her eye as he shifted his lean hips to kick off his shoes. His exotic eyes connected with hers and he grinned. 'I love the way you watch me.'

Cleo went red as fire. 'I can hardly avoid watching you when you're right in front of me…'

'You watch me the way I watch you. With desire,' Ari contradicted, dropping down to his knees in front of her. 'I like it.'

He made that confession as he gently tugged her panties down her slender legs and her breath caught in her throat as she stood there, willing herself not to go into embarrassed retreat. There was nothing to hide, she reminded herself irritably, when he was already familiar with her body and all its flaws. He had none of her innate inhibitions.

'I'd take off your shoes, but that would make you too short for me to appreciate like this,' Ari muttered intently.

'It's all right,' she said in a voice that sounded as though her vocal cords were being squeezed, even though her fancy bridal shoes were torturing her toes, because when Ari smiled up at her, she was as much *his* as if he had branded her. She was discovering that she really liked being needed and wanted. His hunger for her made her feel empowered, *necessary*.

He ran his hands lightly up and down her thighs, gently spreading them, and she quivered. His lips grazed her heated core and she jerked, suddenly the party most wanting, most needing, and as he ran his tongue through that honeyed heat, she moaned his name. A jolt of feverish pleasure gripped her as he flicked her sensitive bud. Her hips bucked as he continued his sensual assault. Her legs trembled as the flaming heat at the juncture of her thighs roared higher. Her hands lifted in a silent seeking gesture of unbearable arousal and then her body detonated in an explosion of wild, seething delight.

Catching her up in his arms while she was still quivering, Ari spread her on the bed, flipping off the shoes and the stockings, unzipping the corset and then bending over her to capture a straining bullet-hard nipple in his mouth. She gasped out loud, liquid and boneless. He paused only to strip off what remained of his clothes, leaving them lying where they fell with uncharacteristic untidiness.

He came down to her hungry and urgent, tipping her legs over his shoulders, rising above her to penetrate her with one fluid stroke. She cried out in response to that sudden fullness, hips writhing as heavenly longed-for sensation shimmied through her pelvis, bringing a wash of heated excitement in its wake. He tilted her back even further, thrusting deep and sending her pleasure to an unholy height. Her body surged with the sheer thrill of it, and in the passionate minutes that followed, she finally plunged over the edge into another climax.

'I'm never going to move again,' she mumbled weakly as he hauled her with him under the sheet.

Ari leant over her and dropped a careless kiss on her cheekbone, tawny eyes smouldering over her with immense masculine satisfaction. 'You're my personal kryptonite.'

'Not feeling too much like a superhero right now… but my goodness, I'm starving,' she confided.

Stark naked, Ari sprang out of bed within seconds of that announcement. 'I'll go and fill a tray.'

'You're in a helpful mood,' she remarked in surprise.

'Maybe I don't want you flagging in energy this early in the evening,' Ari contended.

Sitting up, Cleo swallowed a yawn. 'Weddings are incredibly exhausting,' she warned him.

'I'm as hungry for you as you are for food,' Ari explained almost apologetically.

He knew she was tired. She was pale and her eyes were shadowed. But he had told her the truth. He had a hunger for her that seemed to have no limits and it had made him a little uneasy before he married her. Now, however, that he had acquired Cleo on a permanent basis, that amazing hunger for her no longer bothered him in the same way. There was nothing dangerous or worrying about lusting after his wife. In fact, he now thought it was healthy.

That comment of hers about harems had hit him harder than she could even appreciate. His sex life *had* been highly organised, he acknowledged grimly. He had been careful not to spend too much time with any one woman, not to favour one over another, and for years that cool, logical approach had paid dividends by keeping his life smooth and free of strife. Of course, there was always the occasional hiccup in even the smoothest, slickest schedule, he reflected wryly, recalling Galina, the gorgeous but slightly unhinged Russian supermodel, who had revealed stalking tendencies after only one dinner date.

He had backed off fast, blocked the woman's repeated phone calls and ignored her appearances in his favourite haunts. To the best of his ability, he had protected himself from that kind of nuisance. And now he was married, and he felt remarkably content with the bargain he had struck with Cleo, but possibly rather more aware now that his niece, Lucy, would not be the only party to benefit from their official status as a couple. A wife who attracted him as much as Cleo did was a find, a huge and wonderful *find*...

Thinking that he was now a married man still shook him. In a matter of weeks his life had changed course to an extraordinary degree. Lucy had come along, of course, a totally unexpected but decidedly cute development in his world, but before her had come *Cleo*. Ari struggled to choose food and concentrate at the same time as he thought about Cleo.

Two weeks later, the afternoon before their return to London, Cleo stretched in the warmth of the shade.

She was reclining on a shaded and padded lounger in more comfort than she had ever known, and she had a wonderful view of the beach in front of her.

After the first couple of days of their honeymoon on Spinos, Cleo and Ari had reached an agreement that covered their radically different approaches to what constituted a break. Ari always had to be *doing* something, while Cleo liked to sunbathe with a good thriller or go for a not-too-strenuous stroll. It had had to work after Ari had dragged her huffing and puffing in the heat to see the remains of the Greek shrine at the top of the island's only hill. She had been on the brink of expiring on the peak of that hill, while Ari had barely broken a sweat. Now, one day they went out and did *physical stuff*—as she termed it—and the next she got to be lazier, aside of the daily swimming lessons he insisted on, and that combination worked. She had finally learned how to swim and she was hugely proud of herself for conquering her former fear of deep water.

Today, Ari was out diving in the bay.

'Isn't that dangerous?' she had said to him anxiously.

And he had laughed, but he had also liked that she was worried about him. He had confessed that it felt like a very long time since anyone had worried about him, and with prudent probing, she had gained a view of his childhood that she didn't like and which he would probably dispute out of loyalty to his mother and father.

There was no doubt that his sister's death had

ripped the heart out of Ari's family. Instead of cherishing the child who had survived, however, his parents had retired to separate corners to grieve for the child they had lost. Ari had been left very much to his own devices after he lost his twin, yet his involvement in that tragedy had damaged him as well. Even so, his parents had spent little subsequent time with their son and had sent him off to boarding school at eight years old. That detachment and distance had influenced Ari, making him too much of a loner who lacked understanding of normal relationships either in or outside the family circle.

On her family's last night on the island, they had enjoyed a dinner together at the resort. Ari had emerged shell-shocked from the chattering closeness of her mother and stepfamily, with everybody talking at once and the children alternately playing and then squabbling. The relaxed and yet warm informality he had witnessed had surprised Ari, but, ultimately, charmed him.

Only the day before, she and Ari had flown to Corfu for a day of sightseeing that had ended with dinner on the beach and a late night at a fancy club. Cleo fingered the diamond platinum pendant Ari had casually handed her over the meal, touched the diamonds in her ears, glanced at the delicate watch on her wrist and smiled, dazed by the heat and a growing sense of security. Ari liked giving her stuff. He liked giving her stuff so much that it got embarrassing. She knew he would go out of his way to spoil Lucy as well.

Lucy. Briefly, her smile dipped. She missed that baby so much, and occasional bulletins from her caseworker didn't replace actual bodily contact. Ari's lawyer was working on their fostering application but had warned them to be patient because the authorities dealt slowly with such matters. She watched as a motorboat came to shore and Ari vaulted out into the shallow water. Clad only in swim shorts, he was stunning, tall, bronzed and muscular as he strode up onto the beach, dripping wet and gorgeous.

You watch me the way I watch you.

He had nailed that observation to perfection.

But then, Cleo conceded ruefully, she had watched Ari from the very first day she saw him. The attraction for her had been instant, visceral, while with Ari she had proved to be more of an acquired taste. Fortunately for her, he *had* acquired that taste, but she didn't kid herself that that was anything deeper than sexual chemistry. Yet, in comparison, she had become very conscious that she was in love with the man she had married. Indeed, she had probably taken the first crucial steps along that path that first evening together, when he had chosen to confide in her about his father's second family. Now he was her obsession, she allowed, her mouth running dry and a zing of excitement curling between her thighs as he strode up the beach path with her firmly in his sights and a wolfish smile curving his sensual mouth.

'Were you waiting for me?' Ari intoned huskily.

'Don't you just wish?' Cleo mocked, insanely conscious of his gaze welded to her lips and straying down to the full breasts moulded by the rather brief bikini she wore. 'No, I was just reading and lazing—

'You're wet!' she shrieked as he grabbed her.

'You should've lied and said you were waiting for me this *once*!' Ari complained. 'You're bad for my ego.'

'You don't need any more compliments,' Cleo told him, running a small hand down over his washboard-flat abdomen and feeling him shiver in response, noting the thrust of the erection the shorts couldn't hide. 'Can we be seen from here?'

'No,' Ari confirmed, coming down over her with hungry sexual intent etched in every angle of his lean, darkly handsome features and his strong, muscular body. 'I wouldn't risk any other man seeing you naked, *kardoula mou*.'

Some minutes later, they were both naked and intent on each other. Cleo went up in sensual flames as he surged into her and sated the fierce craving he had lit inside her. In the aftermath, she lay limp in his arms, blissfully at peace and not a single shadow in her world, barring the absence of Lucy. She was incredibly happy, happier, she acknowledged, than she had ever known she even could be.

Ari ran a hand down over her spine, pure satisfaction engulfing him. He found the strangest sort of peace when he was with Cleo, rather as if she were the missing puzzle piece that made him whole or, at the very least, he adjusted, somehow *more* than he had been without her. She made him see the world and the people who surrounded him in a different light. She *wasn't* changing him, though.

'Tell me about your ex, Dominic,' Ari murmured, startling Cleo, who had not expected that question. 'You mentioned him in passing but never told me why you broke up.'

With a recollective wince of her generous mouth, Cleo explained about Dominic's girlfriend and child showing up at her door.

'What did he say when you confronted him?' Ari prompted with interest.

'I didn't confront him. I just cut all contact with him, and I was moving on to work at another office, so I didn't run into him again,' Cleo confided, wondering what he was getting at and why in his estimation she would have put herself through such a humiliating confrontation.

'Didn't it occur to you that *she* might have been the liar?' Ari pressed with a frown of bemusement as he stared down at her, his extraordinary eyes holding her full attention. 'Easy enough to borrow a child to make such a visit on a rival and see her off.'

Cleo blinked rapidly. 'I never thought of that… I have to admit that that suspicion never once crossed my mind—'

'You didn't do *anything* to check out her contention that she was living with him?' Ari stressed in wonderment, and he shook his tousled dark head slowly. 'You just condemned him out of hand on her word.

Maybe she was telling the truth, but maybe she wasn't. Whichever, you should have checked it out, not simply assumed that he was guilty as charged. Please be a little more thorough in your approach if I ever get on your wrong side.'

Cleo swallowed hard, taken aback by his very different reading of the situation while seeing her own skewed reasoning process at the time. Her innate distrust of the opposite sex had fuelled her willingness to believe that Dominic had been lying to her and she had never given him the chance to defend himself, which really hadn't been fair, she belatedly acknowledged.

Ari's mobile phone rang as he was pulling on his shorts. It was his London lawyer, a stuffy old-fashioned sort of man, who tended to talk in a confidential murmur and preferred face-to-face meetings to phone consultations, but he was very wily and knowledgeable, which was why Ari retained his services.

'I'll be back in London tomorrow,' Ari confirmed. 'What sort of news?'

Regrettably, the sort of news that Oliver Matthews didn't wish to discuss on the phone. Ari suppressed a groan and mastered his impatience as he agreed to see the lawyer the following afternoon.

'Oliver's being cagey as usual, which means that what he has to tell me is unlikely to be good.' Ari sighed, his lean, dark face shadowing as Cleo asked him what was happening. 'It can only relate to my sisters. *Thee mou*, surely one of them can't be deceased as well—not at their age!'

Cleo closed a hand over the clenched fist that betrayed his tension. 'I'm coming with you to see the lawyer,' she said soothingly. 'Don't be such a pessimist.'

CHAPTER NINE

'LUCY REMEMBERS YOU,' the caseworker commented.

'Thank goodness,' Cleo responded cheerfully. 'I was worried she would forget our faces after two weeks.'

Lucy was smiling widely at her, showing the tooth that had finally emerged during their absence and which had, apparently, given her foster carer some sleepless nights. She lifted her hand to Ari's jaw and giggled.

'He feels just like a hedgehog, doesn't he?' Cleo quipped, because they had come straight from the airport and Ari hadn't yet shaved. A shadow of dark stubble surrounded his wildly sensual mouth.

'But it's sexy,' Ari informed her with all-male confidence.

And Cleo smiled as widely at him as his niece did. She was hoping the lawyer had some encouraging news for him, rather than the kind of depressing information he had received about the brother he had never met and now never would meet. Instead, he was hoping to raise his brother's child, striving to make up for what he viewed as his late father's neglect. Ari had a lot of heart. He mightn't like to show the fact, but his search for his father's second family was the proof of his compassion.

When they entered the senior lawyer's imposing office, Cleo immediately saw that the older man was disconcerted by her arrival with his client.

'Mrs Stefanos may—' he began tightly.

'Cleo and I have no secrets from each other,' Ari imparted with scorching assurance.

Feeling embarrassed by the suspicion that she was unwelcome at the consultation, Cleo took a seat beside Ari, and only moments later she had to battle to keep her face composed because the older man plunged straight into the matter he wished to discuss. Sadly, Cleo would very much have preferred *not* to be present once she realised what the issue encompassed.

'A *paternity* claim?' Ari repeated in a flat tone of emphasis in which no discernible emotional expression could have been read. 'From whom?'

Cleo had gone rigid in her seat, her spine straight, her hands clasped tight on her lap, not a muscle moving in her small face. She had insisted on accompanying Ari to the appointment and pride would not allow her to show how distressed she was by the very idea of another woman giving birth to Ari's first child.

They had discussed having children but had decided it would be a year or two before they did because, at present, Lucy had needs that could well demand a lot of time and attention and she had to be their priority. Furthermore, they needed to adjust to being Lucy's parents before they could consider extending the family. But that Ari could still become a father *without* Cleo had never once struck Cleo as even a possibility! And now she was deep in shock at the discovery that the sex life prior to his marriage, which Ari had dared to say was none of her business, was promising to impact on both their lives in a way neither of them could have foreseen.

She sat in silence while Ari and his lawyer discussed prenatal DNA testing and the necessity of obtaining the birth mother's agreement to the non-invasive procedure. It only required a cheek swab from Ari and a blood test for the expectant mother. Ari sounded so calm and yet she felt sick to the stomach! How could he be so *calm*? Had he suspected that there could be a potential pregnancy risk with some woman? Was he one of those men who could occasionally be careless with precautions? He had not been irresponsible with her. But how was she to know how he had behaved with other women in his bed? That thought made her feel even more nauseous and distanced from him because Cleo was now at a stage where she could not bear even to *think* of Ari having bedded other women, and now she was being faced with the prospect of having to deal with the evidence of that fact for the next twenty years.

Forget twenty years, she thought almost hysterically. Any child would be around and part of her life as well for the whole of their marriage and lives. Children grew up but they did not go away. Ari was very responsible. He would be a supportive father to *any* child that was *his*. Such devastating news was a huge and cruel blow to receive in the very first weeks of their marriage.

Ari glanced at Cleo by his side, registering that she had not said a single word since her arrival. But then what did he expect after such an announcement? A paternity claim, his first. He was in shock, striving to hide it because Cleo was silently freaking out and he did not want to encourage her to feel that way. But he knew that, no matter how careful any male was, there was always the risk that a baby could be conceived. But to have a baby with that *particular* woman? Ari gritted his teeth while acknowledging that thinking negative stuff about his potential baby's mother was a very bad idea. He needed to stay off that fence until he knew more.

'Ready?' Ari was standing, looking down at her with an enquiring gaze because the appointment was over.

Cleo blinked rapidly, struggling to come out of the turmoil of her anguished thoughts and her sense of betrayal, but it was a serious struggle to pull herself together again. Shock, panic and dismay were all pulling at her simultaneously. Her image of Ari with a child who was not hers clawed at her like salt scattered on an open wound…

Yet Lucy was not her child, she reminded herself, sanity attempting to intrude on her intense mental upheaval. But Lucy *was* different, she reasoned. Ari had not been involved with Lucy's mother and Cleo was as much in love with tiny smiley Lucy as Ari was.

If only Ari had not been such an unrepentant man whore, she found herself thinking helplessly, angry resentment assailing her because suddenly her shiny new marriage no longer seemed half as appealing as it had only hours earlier.

Not that that mattered, Cleo conceded unhappily. She loved Ari, flaws and all, and she was growing to love Lucy as well, and no way could she consider walking away from either of them for good. At the same time, however, she felt that she had to have some space to come to terms with what she had just learned. As it was, she felt utterly trapped by undesirable circumstances that couldn't be changed. It was painful too to be forced to accept that, although she would suffer much from the development, she had no rights whatsoever in such a situation.

'Just say what you're thinking,' Ari urged in a raw undertone in the back of the limousine, stunned by Cleo's ongoing lack of either questions or comment about a development that had knocked him for six.

Nor did it help that the prospective mother was Galina Ivanova, who could quite correctly declare that he had refused to have anything more to do with her. Had the woman truly been chasing him in an effort to tell him that she had fallen pregnant? Had he so misread the situation *and* the woman involved that he had inadvertently put himself very much in the wrong? He was appalled by the suspicion and determined to play his every next step by the book.

Cleo swallowed hard and breathed in deep. 'I

didn't sign up for this,' she mumbled bitterly, half under her breath.

'Neither did I, but we're married now. Difficult issues must be faced together and dealt with together,' Ari murmured with a cool distance that she was painfully aware of. 'Are you with me or against me on this?'

The silence stretched because Cleo truly didn't know how to respond to that question in the state she was in at that precise moment.

'In this instance, silence is not golden,' Ari said very drily.

'Who *is* this woman?' Cleo asked tightly, having to force the question past her lips because she knew that she didn't really want the answer. She didn't want any image inside her head, particularly when she was thinking that it could be one of the bitchy wedding guests.

Ari frowned in astonishment. 'You weren't listening to what Oliver told us?'

'I sort of zoned out,' Cleo admitted grudgingly.

'Galina Ivanova, the woman you let into my office on your first day...and I censured you for it,' Ari reminded her doggedly. 'It sounds as though that was, very much, my mistake.'

'That brunette?' Cleo was horrified because the woman had possibly been the most stunning woman Cleo had ever seen, with a mass of tumbling silky black hair, cut-glass cheekbones, huge sultry brown eyes and a slender figure straight out of a fashion magazine adorned with legs as long as rail tracks.

'Yes,' Ari confirmed. 'If her claim is true, I will have to make amends for having asked her to leave my office. I cannot risk being on poor terms with her now.'

'No…of course not,' Cleo muttered sickly, sick to the stomach at the prospect of his having an ongoing relationship with the woman and merely reaching a new high of misery at his explanation.

'It was only one night—' Ari gritted with startling abruptness.

Cleo jerked up a hand to silence any such recollections and directed a blazing glance of reproach at him. 'No, no details, *please*!' she slung back at him in condemnation.

'You are not handling this in an adult way,' Ari rebuked her.

'I wonder how adult you would feel were I to tell you that I was pregnant by another man a few weeks after we had married. That is the *nearest* approximation I can make to your current position,' Cleo framed bitterly.

'In no way would that be the same, but I would accept it because you are my wife. Such things happen, Cleo, whether we want them to or not. Sometimes, nature or fate is in control, not us. Anyone who has sex must recognise such contingencies,' he bit out in a savage undertone.

Contingencies—the same word the lawyer had used at one point, Cleo dimly recalled, nicely sidestepping all more personal and intimate references to the child that was to be born. She recognised that Ari was now furious with her, as though she were the one who had brought this nightmare down on them, and that infuriated her. But it also scared her because she knew she loved him, and she didn't want this child to fatally damage their relationship. He expected her to stand by him and she *would* stand by him because she loved him...but that didn't mean she had to *like* it.

Still in a state of passionately rejecting their plight, Cleo resolved to go home for a visit. A trip to Scotland made sense, she reasoned. Her mother would talk sense to her and calm her down, drag her out of the turbulent feelings and urges that she could not afford to direct at Ari.

She needed time away from him to deal with the situation and come to terms with their altered future. *Stand up and grow up*, she told herself irritably, thoroughly ashamed of the emotions she was drowning in. She was so jealous, so bitter at the concept of another woman carrying Ari's child, particularly a woman as very beautiful as Galina was. No normal woman, she consoled herself, would want a Galina on the sidelines of their life, particularly not as the mother of an all-important eldest child.

Ari would be in regular contact with Galina from now on. He would be looking after the mother of his child, being supportive...and how could she fault him for that? Wasn't that what a decent man was supposed to do? Step up and accept full responsibility? Do whatever was in his power to support the expectant mother?

Gripped by yet another wave of anguish, Cleo fled upstairs to their bedroom to pack an overnight bag.

She didn't pack anything more than jeans and tops. She wanted to be anonymous.

Ari filled the doorway. 'What the hell are you doing?' he gritted incredulously.

'I'm going to visit Mum…only for a few days,' Cleo responded stiffly. 'I think it would be the best thing for us both to have some space from each other for a *little* while.'

'The first bump on the road that we hit, you abandon ship and run!' Ari slashed back at her furiously.

He was losing his English. He would never have mixed up clichés like that in a normal mood. His beautiful eyes were scorching gold with anger and her tummy flipped and the breath shortened in her throat, making her chest feel tight. 'It's not like that,' she argued vehemently. 'I have to have some time alone, but I'm coming back.'

'Bully for you!' Ari bit out angrily. 'That makes me feel a whole lot better!'

'I'll get the train—'

'No, you won't. You'll fly there,' Ari countered squarely. 'As my wife, you have security needs. When are you planning to return?'

'Just the rest of this week…back Sunday,' Cleo promised, thinking fast because they had a visit scheduled with Lucy only a day later.

Ari dealt her an angry fulminating appraisal. 'I don't agree with this tack. Walking away doesn't deal with this… It's *running* away,' he condemned.

'No, it's not,' Cleo protested, turning away from the disturbing image of him in the doorway, all lean and dark and beautiful and absolutely everything that she loved. Tears prickled her eyes in a stinging lash. She didn't want to go, but she didn't want to stay either and say the wrong things, and she was terribly afraid that, in the resentful frame of mind she was in, she would totally say the *wrong* things to him. And he definitely did not deserve that, she reckoned wretchedly.

Nothing more was said. Cleo went to the airport, climbed on board the jet for the short flight and worked at drying the tears trickling down her face. She felt betrayed...but was that *his* fault? Or the fault of her ingrained habit of distrusting men? She supposed it had begun when her mother first poisoned her view of her father and had settled in hard after her infatuation with Dominic had been destroyed by his seeming lies. But then Ari had come along, and Ari was very honest and just about perfect, she reflected miserably. He hadn't pretended that he had fallen miraculously in love with her. He had asked her to marry him for Lucy's benefit. That was a praiseworthy act for his niece's welfare, but it was also an act and a level of honesty that increasingly cut Cleo to the quick. Loving Ari had made her more sensitive.

How did one trust a man with a woman like Galina when he didn't love his wife? Galina was ten times more beautiful and sexier than Cleo would ever be, and once she had Ari's child, she would have magnetic appeal for him. Cleo knew that. Ari set a deep value on blood ties and he would be very keen to spend time with his child. Only witness what he was willing to do for his half-brother's daughter! What might he wish to do for his *own* child with Galina? Wasn't there a very strong chance that what had initially attracted him to Galina would revive once he saw her with his child? And wouldn't it make sense that he could want to eventually marry Galina for the sake of his own flesh and blood?

And where would Cleo be then? His *practical* choice? Not the woman he loved, who could at least have felt secure in that love at such a testing time. Cleo didn't have that stability, that sense of safety, to ground her in their relationship. As a result, that first bump in the road that he had mentioned had been a complete car crash for her…

'Cleo…nothing's perfect.' Lisa Brown sighed at the kitchen island of the house attached to the pub that she and Cleo's stepfather ran. 'Not life, not people, not marriage. You can't blame Ari because he burst your fantasy bubble… He's right. These things do happen, whether we want them to or not. I thought you loved him—'

'I do!' Cleo proclaimed uncomfortably.

'Then why are you here with me?' the older woman prompted gently. 'He must be upset about this as well and you have to sort this out with him. Can you live with this child being a part of your life as well? It's that basic.'

'Maybe the DNA test will reveal that it isn't his kid,' Cleo opined, looking hopeful.

'Do you have cause to suspect that it may not be his?'

'No. I don't know anything about the woman, don't

want to either!' Cleo confided in a distressed rush of honesty.

'In this scenario, you can't afford to take that attitude.' Lisa sighed. 'If you can't learn to cope with this, it could mean the end of your marriage—'

In receipt of that warning, Cleo lost colour. 'I don't want that.'

'Learn to cope with it, then,' her mother advised ruefully, sliding off her bar stool. 'Sorry, love, I have to get back to work.'

'That's fine. Just forget I'm here,' Cleo urged guiltily.

It was Sunday and she was due to fly home that evening. She had had several days and several sleepless nights to think stuff through. The blinding resentment, anger and turmoil *had* receded somewhat, leaving her facing the reality that she had to handle the situation as it was, not as she wished it could be. Pessimism had already convinced her that, of course, the baby would prove to be a Stefanos baby.

The doorbell buzzed and she slid off her stool, glimpsing her reflection in the hall mirror as she passed and grimacing because she hadn't bothered to put on any make-up and she was wearing 'comfort' clothes from her teenage years that consisted of a pair of lounge pants, a stretched, already oversized pullover and slippers.

To say that she was shattered to open the door and find Ari standing there would have been an understatement. One glimpse of his familiar tall, lean and powerful figure and a complex tumble of emotions washed over her. Joy, consternation and annoyance that he had taken her by surprise and found her clad in her rattiest, oldest clothes.

'Ari…' she whispered shakily once she had found her voice again.

'We have some serious talking to do,' Ari intoned coolly, his gaze raking over every inch of her, noting the tender valley of smooth skin visible at the neck of her jersey, the curve of her hip as she turned towards him, blue eyes widening, golden curls tangled.

And both that announcement in that tone and the forbidding expression on his lean, darkly handsome features made Cleo's heart sink to her very toes.

CHAPTER TEN

'WE'LL TAKE THIS discussion to the hotel I'm staying in locally,' Ari decreed.

'I'm not going anywhere dressed like this.' Cleo sighed. 'Give me twenty minutes to change.'

His beautifully moulded mouth firmed. 'I'll wait in the car.'

Cleo fled back to the bedroom she had been using and stripped at the speed of a maniac before rushing into the shower. The whole time her brain was crackling with frantic frightened thoughts. Perhaps Ari had already decided that a divorce was the best way forward. Would he risk such a move in the midst of their application to foster Lucy? Or was it possible that the news of the baby that had been conceived with Galina could now take precedence over his niece? She supposed anything could be possible because she had run away rather than talk about that baby with him. Shame filled her as she frantically dried her hair and dabbed on some make-up to conceal her reddened eyelids. She *had* run home like a little girl rather than stand her ground and act like a grown woman, she conceded in mortification.

Clad in jeans, a stylish red top and sneakers, Cleo walked out to the car with her heart pounding very fast in her chest.

'I wasn't expecting you,' she admitted, filling the silence when she joined him.

Ari said nothing. A fierce rage had settled inside him as the days of her absence crept past on leaden feet. He couldn't initially credit that Cleo had run home to her mother until common sense kicked in and he contrived to imagine how he might have reacted to such a situation at her age. His bride was still very young, and if she did not have his life experience and greater maturity, that rested on *his* shoulders, because he had married her, hadn't he? In any case, none of that mattered when he was so hopelessly relieved to be back with Cleo again. At that moment nothing else really seemed to matter.

Predictably, Ari was staying at a madly grand country-house hotel with turrets, luxury suites and awesome service. Too twitchy to stand still or sit down, Cleo crossed the vast reception room with its ornate antique furniture and elaborate curtains and stood at one of the windows, which overlooked an immaculately kept lawn and trees. Ari offered her a drink and she asked for water.

As he slotted the glass between her fingers, she glanced up at him mutinously. 'I *was* planning to catch that flight tonight and come back to London,' she told him squarely.

'I wasn't prepared to wait that long,' Ari parried without skipping a beat.

The gleam of his dark golden eyes below curling black lashes ensnared her and the heat rose in her pale cheeks. 'I shouldn't have left in the first place,' she muttered reluctantly. 'But I… I just didn't know how to handle it—'

Ari lifted a straight ebony brow in challenge. 'And you think that *I* did?'

Cleo reddened even more, her discomfiture pronounced.

'I was as shocked by the information as you were,' he admitted quietly. 'But it also bothers me to see a pattern in your behaviour…'

Her brow indented as she shifted from one foot to the other. 'What pattern?'

'It worries me that we're in conflict again over a past that I cannot change,' Ari confessed levelly. 'We had an argument on our wedding day about my exes—'

'Not about their existence,' Cleo disagreed, lifting her head high. 'About you inviting them all to our wedding! As for this baby—'

'I had a normal sex life in which I took every possible precaution to ensure that there were no accidental conceptions,' Ari slotted in, his lean, darkly handsome face grave. 'No male can do more than that. Yet I feel that you are *blaming* me—'

'That's…that's just human nature in a tight and unpleasant corner,' Cleo protested uncomfortably, taking his point but not admitting the fact. 'And our wedding did make it rather obvious that your…er…past is rather extensive in comparison to mine.'

'Unfortunately for me, I didn't appreciate that I would end up married to a woman who would find my past so distasteful,' Ari breathed harshly.

'That's not fair. I'm not judging you. In fact, I would never have thought about your past sex life at all had it not been for all those women at our wedding,' Cleo pointed out truthfully, standing her ground. 'You're the one who put a spotlight on your past for my benefit.'

Ari felt rather less certain of his position than he had once been. A married friend had remarked after the wedding on *his* wife's comments concerning that inconsiderate guest list. He had shot himself in the foot, Ari recognised, owning his mistake but typically reluctant to acknowledge it.

'I'm not remotely concerned about your past history with other women unless it impinges on our marriage,' Cleo declared steadily, meeting his gorgeous eyes calmly. 'And sadly, this baby does, and it threw me for a loop, I'm afraid. You need to try and view this development from my point of view—'

'I have—'

'No, you haven't,' Cleo responded, with bitter certainty in that accusation. 'This isn't a *real* marriage, not the way others are. You married me for Lucy's sake. I don't have the security of knowing that you love me, so I felt more threatened than many women would by the idea of a former lover having your child and the constant contact between you that will obviously follow on from that continuing relationship.'

'I'm possibly not the most emotionally intelligent guy you will ever meet,' Ari breathed tautly. 'Well, we already know that from the wedding guest list...but I'm not totally stupid. When I wake up in the morning and you're not there and I miss you. Well, that's never happened to me before with a woman—'

'You missed me?' Cleo slotted in brightly.

'And I'm not used either to thinking about a woman all day, because that *seriously* interferes with my concentration, but I can't get you out of my head,' Ari complained. 'I look at you, and as far as I'm concerned, you're the most beautiful and sexy woman in the world, which means that I truly don't see anyone but you now...'

By that stage, Cleo was simply staring back at him in shock at that unexpected rambling speech.

Ari sent her a wolfish smile of achievement. 'I believe it's called love. So, yes, you do have the security of knowing that I love you and that, as far as I'm concerned, this is a *very* real marriage.'

Not quite able to jump that fast from her assumptions to what appeared to be her new reality, Cleo trembled and frowned. 'Do you mean that?'

'Hey, I'm the guy who couldn't wait until tonight to see you,' Ari pointed out without hesitation. 'And no, I don't know when exactly I fell in love with you or how it happened in the first place. I only know that we forged bonds at the very beginning that first night, and the minute I had you in my bed, I wanted you back there again in the worst way. And absolutely nobody else would do as a substitute.'

'Is that so?' Cleo queried as she finally shook free of her paralysis with the craziest, fiercest happiness circulating through her in an enervating surge. Nothing at all mattered at that moment but that he loved her. Everything else, she thought warmly, would just fall naturally into place. She was no longer second-best, no longer the practical choice of wife. In fact, she found herself suspecting that Ari would have married her anyway once he understood how he felt about her.

'That is so,' Ari confirmed, resting both hands on her slight shoulders, flexing possessive fingers over her fine bones, dark golden eyes aglow with more emotion than she had ever hoped to see there.

'Well, you were way behind me,' Cleo informed him teasingly. 'The first time I laid eyes on you, I wanted you. That's how I ended up in bed with you that first time. You were my fantasy.'

'I like being your fantasy, *kardia mou*. But I did notice you from the start. I thought it was because your clothes were too colourful for me,' he admitted. 'Only I think it was because you were so different from my usual type...and now I only have one type and it's you.'

'I like that,' Cleo confided sunnily. 'You do realise that I fell for you on our honeymoon?'

'I was ahead of you there,' Ari asserted with pride. 'I knew when you walked down the aisle towards me in the church. You looked magical and I was so excited that you were mine.'

Cleo frowned. 'But you never said that you loved me!' she censured.

'I'd made all those speeches about Lucy, and changing tack that fast made me feel a little lame,' he explained. 'But the way I was behaving, I think you should have guessed how I felt about you. I was jealous of every man that looked at you, possessive beyond reason, and I couldn't get enough of you in bed or out of it. If that's not love, what is?'

Cleo rested tender fingers against his hard jawline. 'I do love you very much and I'm so sorry I ran away. I always knew I was coming back, though—I should get points for that, shouldn't I?'

'I was worried you wouldn't come back,' Ari confessed in a driven undertone as he closed both strong arms round her and literally lifted her into close contact with his lean, powerful body. 'Do you think I didn't appreciate that that news from Galina Ivanova was a body blow?'

'I don't have much to say about that yet,' Cleo admitted honestly. 'I'll get used to the idea, though. Time will help—'

Ari froze and looked down at her with a sudden grimace. 'It's *not* my baby she's carrying,' he told her bluntly.

'*Not* your baby?' Cleo whispered in shock.

'No. The DNA test proved that the child isn't mine. I think I was the richest bet Galina had and she just hoped that I would turn out to be the father, but obviously I wasn't her only lover at the time—'

'You should've told me it wasn't your child *first*!' Cleo exclaimed in rampant disbelief at that oversight.

'No. I wanted to wait. I needed to know that you

were willing to accept me as I am, flaws and all…because it *could've* been my kid. I'm very grateful that it's not. It's not how I would want to have my first child, but if it had been mine, I would have stood by her, and that would have been a major challenge because I don't like her—'

Her brow furrowed. 'You don't like her?'

'Not when she was behaving like a stalker. She was a little weird with me,' he confided, his mouth tightening. 'I was with her once and never again. Then she began constantly phoning, turning up places I went, showing up at the office uninvited. It was all too much.'

'But you're safe now from those kinds of mistakes,' Cleo said with a wicked grin. 'I won't let you out of my sight very often. You are truly off the market now, Mr Stefanos.'

'Is that supposed to be a threat?' Ari husked, running his hands up below her top and levering it off her with the slick skill that only he could contrive. Her bra followed. He lifted his hands to cup her ripe curves and backed her towards the bedroom next door. 'Right now, seeing more of you feels more like a very exciting promise.'

With thrilling impatience, he bent down and swept her up into his arms to carry her into the bedroom and lay her down on the wide, comfortable bed. Clothes were tossed aside and silence fell, broken only by little moans and mutters as they made love, satisfying the gnawing sense of insecurity that had attacked them both when they were apart. In the aftermath of all that excitement, Cleo lay in the circle of Ari's arms, feeling gloriously content and safe at last.

'I wanted my baby to be your first child. I suppose that was sort of childish and mean,' she conceded ruefully.

'I don't think so. I wanted the same thing, but I also knew that, even if you stood by me, it would damage our relationship. How could a child with another woman do anything else when we were so newly married?' Ari murmured grimly, his arms tightening their hold on her slight body. 'We'll go and pack your clothes and catch up with your mother. Since I assume you told her about the baby that isn't mine, we'll have to explain that it was simply a con. And when we get back to London tomorrow morning, I have a surprise for you...'

'What sort of a surprise?' Cleo prompted, twisting her head to look at him, loving those gorgeous tawny eyes of his.

'Something unexpected. It's up to you to decide whether it's a positive or negative development,' he framed mysteriously.

'I don't like mysteries.'

'It won't be a mystery for long.' Ari ran a soothing hand down over her spine and grabbed her to kiss her again, and all thought of the surprise vanished under the sensual onslaught of his mouth on hers.

On the flight back to London the next day, he explained that her father had seen a picture of their wedding in a newspaper and had contacted him to ask if they could meet.

'I told him that you were away and I suggested we meet for coffee,' Ari explained. 'You may think that was interfering of me, but I wanted to *vet* him for you lest he was only getting in touch because you had married a rich man.'

In shock, Cleo gazed back at him. 'My father?' she gasped. 'Why would he get in touch?'

'Because he would like the chance to get to know you. He parted from the woman he was originally with several years ago and tried to track you down then. He was unable to find you because of course your mother has moved on, married and changed her name. He is in regular contact with the son and daughter he has and he has now told them about you. He seems pleasant enough and genuine in his interest in you and a little nervous as to his reception with you,' Ari told her levelly. 'But it's up to you what you choose to do.'

'Do we look alike?' Cleo demanded curiously.

'You're almost a doppelganger for your mother,' he reminded her with amusement. 'But you do definitely have your father's big wide smile. Would it bother your mother if you had contact with him?'

'No. He's old history, as far as she's concerned.'

Cleo smiled sunnily and looked at Ari. 'I will see him. Our contact may not amount to anything more than a couple of meetings, but I would like the chance to get to know him. It's a chance I never thought I'd have.'

'As long as it doesn't cause you distress,' Ari commented, his protectiveness touching her heart. 'You've got by without him all these years and I don't want you upset.'

'I've got you now...and hopefully Lucy some day soon,' Cleo pointed out gently. 'My world is a secure one. I'm very curious about my half-brother and sister as well. I would like the opportunity to meet them if...if I like him and, of course, if they want to meet me. Now that we're all grown up, it doesn't seem as controversial as it seemed when I was a teenager.'

'It struck me the very first time we met that we had a lot in common.' Ari curved her into his arms as the limo wafted them through the traffic on their homeward journey. 'And it really is a challenge to keep my hands off you...'

'*So* romantic, Ari,' she whispered cheekily.

'I've organised a special dinner for your homecoming,' he announced with a smile of pure one-upmanship. 'And a gift.'

'And you're such a trier,' Cleo pronounced with a helpless giggle and sheer joy bubbling up through her. 'Always determined to take top billing...'

EPILOGUE

Two years after that conversation took place, Cleo was on the island of Spinos in Greece. It was summer and a bunch of young children were playing a noisy game on the grassy space in front of the terrace where Cleo was enjoying tea with her mother.

'I love staying at the resort. Tell Ari thanks,' Lisa said happily. 'You know he won't let me thank him for all the free luxury holidays we get here.'

'We enjoy the company,' Cleo responded lightly, and it was true. Her stepfamily were lively company for her own little family and she got to enjoy spending time with her mother at the same time.

Lisa snorted with laughter. 'Like you couldn't find company with this place and Ari behind you! You're living the dream, my love. You and those babies of yours are going to have a wonderful life.'

'I certainly hope so.' Cleo contemplated the huge mound of her pregnant tummy, being at that stage of pregnancy where she could no longer see her feet and when she felt as though she had been pregnant for ever, rather than a mere seven months.

She was carrying twins: two little boys she couldn't wait to meet. And considering the fuss she had made about the unplanned conception Ari's ex had tried to lay at his door, she did not have a leg to stand on when it came to her own. They had decided to wait for two years before starting a family, and then, over a year into their marriage, they had had a romp late one hot night in the swimming pool when Cleo had been ready to expire from the heat and… *Boom.* Cleo had conceived and twins were on their way, with Ari claiming that he was delighted, regardless of that conception having been an accident.

Ari might continue to insist that he hadn't changed, but he had definitely mellowed. His wardrobe was no longer colour-coded, and he had learned to live with the clutter of a toddler's life, not to mention a wife who was infinitely less organised and tidy than he was, Cleo reflected fondly.

And having observed her husband with Lucy, who was almost three years old now, for they had picked her birthday as the date she had been found and rescued, Cleo was pretty sure Ari *was* delighted about the little boys soon to join their family. He was brilliant with Lucy, who had recovered from her poor start in life slowly, reaching the milestones other children took for granted at her own pace. Luckily for her, Lucy had no lingering medical issues. Now she was a happy, healthy toddler with a shock of black hair and she still had Ari's eyes, except hers were full of mischief most of the time. Those dancing dark eyes full of love and trust had walked so easily into Cleo's and Ari's hearts. Lucy had finally become officially their adoptive daughter only a couple of months earlier, but they had become her foster parents within a few months of that first meeting.

Now watching Lucy walk up from the beach with her little fingers possessively clinging to the leg of Ari's denim shorts, Cleo smiled because father and daughter, uncle and niece, however you wanted to look at them, were very close. And Lucy couldn't wait for the babies to come, the little brothers she would undoubtedly fuss over and boss around.

'It's idyllic here,' her mother sighed happily.

She watched Ari come to a halt to answer his mobile phone. Lucy abandoned him and ran up to the house, ducking the other children, who were all older than her, and rushing up the steps to Cleo to climb straight onto her lap. Unfortunately, it was a lap no longer in existence since pregnancy had altered Cleo's shape, and she sat up to accommodate the little girl more comfortably.

'Sleepy,' Lucy grumbled, slotting her thumb into her mouth.

'I'll take you upstairs for a nap,' Cleo promised.

'Love you, Mum-mum,' Lucy sighed.

Cleo's mother stood up and lifted the little girl. 'I'll take her up. You're supposed to be staying off your feet in the afternoon,' she reminded her daughter as Lucy snuggled her head into her grandmother's shoulder. 'And I'll be a while. I like reading her a story.'

'I only do that at night.'

'Well, when Granny's here, it's naps as well,' Lisa said cheerfully.

'Thanks, Mum,' Cleo murmured, thinking about how grateful she had been for her mother's laid-back attitude towards her getting to know her long-lost father.

Gregory Stevens was not the selfish, uncaring man Cleo had once imagined he would be. She saw her father when she was in London and she liked him, although she doubted that they would ever develop a truly close relationship. She had also met her half-brother, Peter, who was a medical student and very down to earth. Her half-sister, Gwen, hadn't yet agreed to meet up with Cleo and clearly wasn't sure she wanted the connection, and that was fine with Cleo. She had no desire to upset anybody and thought it was sad that Gwen's loyalty to her mother should have made meeting Cleo contentious. But Cleo was so happy in her own life that she had no need to put pressure on anyone.

Ari, having been cornered to settle a dispute in the kids' ball game, mounted the steps into the shade. He scrutinised Cleo, lying there all golden and ripe and so damned sexy it made him smile, because he knew that if he told her she looked like some sensual fertility goddess in her current condition, she would threaten to slap him. Unlike her husband, Cleo was way *past* finding pregnancy sexy.

He sat down in the seat his mother-in-law had vacated. 'Oliver's got information on the whereabouts of Lucas's twin sister,' he told her in an excited surge, his gorgeous dark eyes golden and bright with satisfaction, for he had been chasing dead ends in his search for his siblings for the whole of their marriage.

Cleo sat up. 'No bad news?' she checked.

'Well, Oliver said it's a mix. She's healthy, not an addict or anything like that. Clever girl, has a business degree, but, as Oliver put it and, no, I don't know what he means by it, she's had a lot of bad luck.'

'Oh, dear… You'll have to be careful about how you deal with her,' Cleo warned him. 'No bull-in-the-china-shop approach. You've seen how differently my siblings have reacted, so you have to accept that you may not be a welcome arrival in her life.'

Ari raised a cynical ebony brow and said drily, 'Beware Greeks offering you a small fortune?'

'Ari! There's much more to it than the bottom line of an inheritance!' Cleo framed worriedly, fearful that he would be tactless and would destroy the potential relationship before he even got the opportunity to have one.

Ari just laughed, all sun-bronzed and gorgeous and smiling, his spectacular eyes glittering. 'I was only teasing you. I'll find out what Oliver has to tell me about her "bad luck".' His handsome mouth took on a sardonic twist at that phrase. 'And I will act accordingly, but you have no idea how relieved I am just to find her and know she's alive and healthy.'

'I do understand,' Cleo protested, linking her fingers with his to tug him down to her. 'Now, just one kiss…'

'Just one kiss could lead to more,' Ari warned her

thickly, leaning down, closing his beautifully moulded mouth to hers and saying huskily, 'Do you have any idea how much I love you?'

'Possibly just as much as I love you,' Cleo whispered as she gave herself up to that passionate kiss.

* * * * *

THE SCANDAL THAT MADE HER HIS QUEEN

CAITLIN CREWS

MILLS & BOON

For Nina Pépin, because she asked.

CHAPTER ONE

CASTLES AND PALACES and all such trappings of royalty, Nina Graine reflected dryly, were much better in theory than in practice.

She would know, having had far too much of that practice.

In theory, castles were all about fairy tales. She'd thought so herself while growing up in the orphanage. Think of castles and it was all happy, merry songs dancing gracefully on a sweet breeze. Happy-ever-afters sounding from on high, possibly with the help of fleets of cantering unicorns.

Nina was pretty sure she'd had that dream at least a thousand times.

But then she'd learned the truth.

In practice, castles were dark and drafty old things. Most of them had been fortresses first and were therefore built in places where ransacking armies and the odd barbarian could be turned away with a minimum of fuss. They were filled with musty tapestries and bristling with trophies of battles past. No matter how modernized they claimed to be, there were always too many ghosts in the fortified walls.

Palaces, meanwhile, were less about defense and more about drama. *Look at me*, a palace cried. *I'm better than everything and especially you.*

Like the one she was currently visiting in the island kingdom of Theosia, sitting pretty in the Mediterranean Sea. The Kings of Theosia had called this place the Palace of the Gods, clearly not suffering from any form of impostor syndrome.

She *almost* started thinking about the palace's current occupants, the unwell, old King Cronos and his only son and heir, the wicked, scandalous, upsettingly beautiful Prince Zeus. *Almost.*

But there would be time enough for that.

Instead, Nina focused her attention on the stuffy little room she'd been left in. It could have been in any palace, an afterthought of a space tucked away in the administrative wing where royal feet seldom trod. Nina had been marched here after she'd pleaded her case to a succession of palace guards, starting with the ones at the looming gate. They had finally transferred her into the care of the palace staff and she had been brought here by the sniffiest, most disdainful butler she had ever encountered.

But that was par for the course in the underbelly of a royal household. Nina tried to make herself comfortable on a settee that had likely been built for the express purpose of making interlopers squirm. No wonder it was down here in the basement, the domain of all manner of petty cruelties and intense jockeying for position. Down here—and it was always the same, no matter what kingdom or huffy principality—it was really more the palace of gorgons than gods.

Because the royals were bad enough. Kings and queens with their reigns and their wars and their commandments were all very well, though they did tend to litter princes and princesses about—all primed by lives of excess to behave as atrociously as possible.

They almost couldn't help themselves, what with all that blue blood making them so constitutionally obnoxious.

It was the people who trailed about after royalty, obsequious and scheming, that Nina truly couldn't stand. The palace courtiers and uppity staff. They *could* have helped themselves but chose not to. However subservient they were when faced with the royalty they served, that was exactly how cutthroat they were behind the scenes. It might as well still be the Dark Ages, when the wrong whisper in the right ear led straight to beheadings.

There might not be too many beheadings with a blade these days, because monarchies were ever more concerned with their images. These days, beheadings were performed in the press, reputations were slashed with a single headline, and on and on the courtiers whispered gleefully, as if actual lives weren't ruined because of their games.

Why swing a blade when you could gossip to the same end?

Nina knew all of this entirely too well, and too personally. She'd been the primary lady-in-waiting to Her Royal Highness, Princess Isabeau of Haught Montagne, a small kingdom high in the Alps, since the day before her sixteenth birthday. A role she had not wanted, had not liked, and should have been overjoyed to lose six months ago.

Alas, her exit had been…complicated.

She was brooding about those complications as she fidgeted in her uncomfortable seat. The palace guards had confiscated her personal effects, so she couldn't distract herself from what she was doing. No mobile. No snacks.

It really was torture.

And then her baby kicked inside her, no doubt as cranky without a snack as Nina was—but the sensation made her smile. She smoothed her hands over her belly, murmuring a little to soothe them both.

Soon enough, someone would come and get her. And then, at some point or another, she would be face-to-face with the creature responsible for the state she was in—a state that required, once again, that she concern herself with the doings of royalty when that was the last thing she wanted.

Some people went their whole lives without encountering a person of royal blood. Nina couldn't seem to stop tripping over them. Though tripping was not how she would describe her last encounter with the arrogantly named Zeus.

Prince Zeus.

Even thinking that name made her…determined.

Nina clung to that word. She was determined, that was all. To see this through. To acquit herself appropriately. To handle this situation as well as possible, for the sake of her child.

To do the right thing—without going down the rabbit hole of blame. She was determined, and that was enough. Because she didn't like any of the other words she could have chosen to describe her current state.

She sighed and returned her attention to this palace and her officious little waiting room. All the furnishings here were too big, too formal, for a palace made all in glorious white—the better to beckon the sea, the guidebooks simpered.

When, once upon a time, the always overconfident Theosian monarchs had been far more concerned with commanding the sea than beckoning it.

The original Theosian castle lay in ruins at the far end of the island that made up the kingdom. Nina had seen it out her window as she'd flown in today from Athens. The parts that were still standing looked suitably cramped and dark, unlike the high ceilings and open archways that made the Palace of the Gods such a pageant of neoclassical eighteenth-century drama.

She'd spent the past few months studying this place as she'd slowly come to terms with what she was going to have to do. And that it was inevitable that she would actually have to come here. Sometimes she'd managed to lose herself a little in the studying, the way she had when she'd first found herself with Isabeau—and would have given anything to escape.

Nina had not had the opportunity to go off to university. Had Isabeau not chosen Nina on her desperate orphanage campaign—the Princess's attempt to show that she was benevolent in the wake of one of her many scandals—Nina would have woken up the next day released from the hold of the state at last. She would have gone out into the world, found her own way, and been marvelously free—but likely would not have studied anything. She'd always tried to remind herself of that.

Isabeau could not have cared less about the private tutoring sessions her father insisted she take. Half the time she hadn't bothered to turn up.

That had left Nina with the very finest tutors in Europe at her disposal. She'd loved every moment of her education, and she'd taken the overarching lesson with her through the years since. If she was to be forced to trail about after Isabeau, she might as well make something of the experience. She'd studied, therefore, every castle, palace, private island, and other such glorious place she found herself, dragged along with Isabeau's catty entourage wherever the Princess went. She'd studied the places and all the contents therein as if she expected she might have to sit an exam on the material.

What Nina really loved was the art all these noble-blooded people tended to hoard. Museums were lovely, but the real collections were in the private homes of collectors with bloodlines—and fortunes—that soared back through the ages. Nina had loved nothing more than sneaking away while Isabeau was entertaining one of her many lovers to take a turn about the gallery of whatever stately place they were trysting in.

That was how she knew that the painting that took up most of the wall opposite her, rather ferociously, was a satirical take on a courtier type some three hundred years ago. And it was comforting, almost, to think that those sorts had always been appalling. It made sense. As long as there were kings, courtiers swarmed.

She was telling her unborn baby about the history of Theosia—ancient Macedonians this, ancient Venetians that—when, finally, the door to her chamber opened.

Nina braced herself, but, of course, it wasn't Prince Zeus who stood there. She doubted the Prince knew this part of the palace existed. Instead, it was the starchy-looking butler who managed to give her the impression that he was curling his thin lip at her without actually moving a single muscle in his face.

It was impressive, Nina thought. Truly.

"Were you speaking with someone?" he asked, each syllable dripping with scorn. He had introduced himself the same way when he'd brought her here. *I am Thaddeus*, he had intoned.

"Yes," Nina said. They stared at each other, and she patted her bump. With, admittedly, some theatrical flair. "The royal child currently occupying my womb, of course."

She might have drawn out the word *womb.*

And it was worth it, because she had the very great pleasure of sitting there, smiling serenely, as the man battled to conceal his distaste. Not because he was trying to spare her feelings, she knew. But because it had no doubt occurred to him that said occupant of her womb might, in fact, turn out to be the heir to the kingdom, and a good servant never burned a bridge if he could help it.

She was all too aware of how these people thought.

After all, she'd been one of them. Not quite staff, not quite a courtier, and therefore condescended to on all sides.

Nina had not missed it.

"If you'll follow me, miss," said the man, all cool disdain and not-quite-repressed horror. Not to mention a subtle emphasis on *miss*, to remind her she had no title or people or, in his view, any reason whatsoever to be here. *I have seen a great many tarts*, his tone assured her, *and vanquished them all.* "His Royal Highness has deigned to grant you an audience after all."

Nina had been told repeatedly that it would not be possible to see the Prince. If indeed Zeus was even here, which perhaps he was not, none could say—despite the standard that flew today, high above the palace, which was how the Prince informed his people he was in residence. She had only smiled calmly, explained and reexplained the situation, and waited.

And, when necessary, shared both her unmistakable belly as well as photographic evidence of the fact that, yes, she knew the Prince. Yes, in *that* way.

Because while it was probably not helpful to any palace staff to ask them to think back to a scandal six months ago—given how many scandals Prince Zeus was involved in on a daily basis—not all of them had been splashed about in all the international papers. Apparently, she really was special.

Nina ignored the little tug of an emotion she did not care to recognize, smiling the sharp little smile she'd learned in the Haught Montagne court.

"How gracious of the Prince to attend to his mistakes," she murmured. "How accommodating."

Then she took her time standing up, a basic sort of movement she had never given any thought to before. But it was different at six months pregnant.

Everything was different at six months pregnant.

She found she rather enjoyed seeing the faintest hint of a crack in the butler's facade as he watched her ungainly attempts to rise. More ungainly than necessary, to be sure, but she was the pregnant woman here. They were treating her like she'd done it to herself.

When she most certainly had not—but it would help no one, least of all her child, if she let herself get lost in images that served no one. She already knew how little it served *her*, because she dreamed about that night all the time already, and always woke alone and too hot and riddled with that *longing*—

Stop it, Nina ordered herself crossly.

She kept her expression placid with the aid of years of practice, having had to hide herself in the orphanage and Princess Isabeau's entourage alike. Then she followed the snooty butler out of the antechamber, up from the bowels of the palace, and through the hushed, gleaming halls that were all about airiness and timeless glory, as if gods truly did walk here.

Nina was impressed despite herself.

She kept catching sight of herself in this or that gleaming surface. As ever, she was taken aback by the fact that her belly preceded her. But she was perfectly well acquainted with the rest of the package. *Here comes our Dumpy!* Isabeau would trill, pretending that it was an affectionate nickname. *Hurry, little hen*, she would say as Nina trailed along behind her, forced to keep a smile on her face and her thoughts on such nicknames to herself.

Isabeau had believed that she was being hurtful. And given that being hurtful was one of the main joys in Princess Isabeau's pampered life, it had taken everything Nina had to keep the fact that she was in no way hurt to herself. Snide remarks from a royal princess really didn't hold a candle to daily life in the orphanage, but Isabeau didn't have to know that.

But Isabeau saw her as a hen, so a hen Nina became. She dressed as frumpily as possible, because it annoyed the Princess, herself a fashion icon. Not only were the clothes she chose not quite right, she made sure they never fit her correctly. She made a grand mess of her hair and pretended she didn't understand what was the matter with it.

And she took particular pleasure in forever eating sweets and cakes *at* Isabeau, whose strident dedication to her figure bordered on fanatical.

Nina found she rather liked the hennishness of it all today, though. There were many ways she could have dressed for this encounter, but she'd chosen the maternity outfit that most made her look like the side of a barn. She could have done her hair, or at least brushed it. Instead, she'd opted to let it do as it would, frizzing about of its own accord. Like a rather unkempt blond halo, she thought, pleased, when she saw herself in the polished surface of an ancient mask—hanging there on the wall in bronze disapproval.

Thaddeus was striding forth briskly, clearly trying to hasten their pace, so she slowed her walk to an ungainly waddle. Then only smiled blandly when the man tried to hurry her along. And went even slower.

She was determined to do what was right, or she wouldn't have come here.

But that didn't mean she couldn't enjoy herself in the process.

That had been her philosophy throughout her indentured servitude to the Princess. She was the little orphan girl plucked from obscurity and expected to live in perpetual cringing gratitude for every scrap thrown her way, when she would have been perfectly happy to be left to her own devices in her gutter, thank you. She had perfected the downcast look, with an unreadable curve of her lips that fell somewhere between possible sainthood and the expected servility. Depending on who was looking at her.

But she made her own fun all the same. Her clothes. Her constant sweet and cake consumption, leaving her forever covered in crumbs, which had sent Isabeau into rages. She'd often pretended not to understand the things Isabeau asked of her, forcing her to ask repeatedly. And she had been known to affect deafness when most likely to make the Princess go spare.

A subject of the house of Haught Montagne could not openly defy her Princess, of course. That was unthinkable.

But there were always ways.

Nina reminded herself that she'd found those ways once and could do it again, as she walked through another set of gilded arches. More gilded than before, in fact. Her hands crept over her belly, where the baby was moving around, making itself known. She had not actually intended for this last, final act of rebellion, she could admit, if only to herself. She'd thought that she was perfectly all right with the consequences as they were.

But that was when the consequences were being ejected from Isabeau's service and called a national disgrace, among a great many other, less polite names, in an endless slew of articles that were always sourced from unnamed people in Isabeau's circle—the curse of the courtiers.

These consequences were a bit different than a bit of scandal and being called mean names by terrible people, she thought, leaving one hand on her belly as she walked.

And that same fierce, mad love blazed through her again, the way it did so often these days. Maybe she hadn't planned this baby, but she wanted it. She had never loved anything the way she loved the tiny human inside her. The little gift she couldn't wait to meet.

She reminded herself that today was all about determination. Nothing more.

Thaddeus flung open a suitably impressive set of doors with all attendant fanfare, then led Nina inside.

"Your Royal Highness," he intoned, "may I present Miss Nina Graine. Your…guest."

Nina blinked as she looked around, and it took her a moment to get her bearings. She found herself in a vast room flooded with light that poured in from exquisitely arched openings on three sides. They were not so much windows as graceful doors that let in all that Mediterranean blue, the boundless sun, and the far-off call of wheeling seabirds. There was the hint of riotous bougainvillea on the terrace outside, and the breeze brought in the scent of honeysuckle and jasmine.

She knew she was standing in a room in the palace

—very likely the royal version of a lounge—but it seemed more like some kind of temple.

And as if summoned by that thought alone, there was suddenly a far brighter gleam where the sun was brightest, until it detached itself from such lesser light and became a man.

Not just any man.

Zeus.

Bathed in light as if he'd conjured it and wearing nothing but a pair of flowing white trousers that clung low on his hips.

Nina hated herself, but that didn't stop the way the sight of him rolled through her, like a song from on high. Except this song came with heat and licked over her. Her breasts. Her belly. The softness between her legs.

Focus, she ordered herself. He was magnificent, but as a person saddled with the name Zeus, he would have to be. He had clearly taken his name as a lifelong challenge.

A challenge he had met, if not exceeded.

And Nina couldn't help but remember, with an unhelpful vividness, that she knew every inch of him.

Zeus moved closer, somehow looking regal and glorious when he was barefoot and wearing the princely version of pajama bottoms. She tried her best to find him ridiculous, with that dark blond hair that looked forever tousled and the half smile that appeared welded to his lips, but she couldn't quite get there. Instead, she was struck by the similarity between him and that bronze mask she'd seen out in the palace halls.

He looked ancient. Almost forbidding, so severely

drawn were his features. If she hadn't known better, she would have sworn that he could only have been carved from stone or forged from metal. There was no possibility he could be a man of flesh and blood.

But Nina knew better.

Still he came toward her, until she could see the green of his wicked eyes. And then, sure enough, that slow, edgy curve of his sculpted lips.

She braced herself for that inescapable magnetism of his that she had always thought ought to be bottled, so it could be used as a weapon. It was that fierce. That intense. It seemed to fill the room, closing around her so it was impossible to pretend that she was anything but captivated, no matter how little she wished to be. Her pulse was a racket inside her veins. Her heart thudded.

Even her baby stopped kicking, as if awed.

But far more concerning was the melting sensation that swept over her, making the fire in her burn hotter. Brighter.

As if she hadn't already gotten into enough trouble with this man.

Prince Zeus of Theosia did not say a word. He put his hands on his lean hips, still with that half smile, as if this was all deeply entertaining, and took a long, slow circle around her. Studying her like she was a cow on a market block in the kind of medieval keeps this man's relatives had ruled over when the earth was young.

When he made it back around to her front, his face was transformed with laughter.

Her heart stopped. Then kicked back into gear, so hard it was painful.

Nina had prepared a brief, informative little speech so she could get the practicalities out of the way and then get back to her life. And she would have told anyone who asked—though no one ever had—that she was not the least bit intimidated by royalty of any stripe. In her case, familiarity really had bred contempt. She wanted no part of hereditary laziness, ceremonial scepters in place of any hint of kindness, or too many thrones instead of thoughtfulness.

And yet she couldn't seem to make her mouth work the way it should.

"I remember you," Zeus said after a long moment of that face of his, far too beautiful for any mortal man.

But he said it as if that surprised him. That it was not that she was in any way memorable, but it was deeply amusing to him that he should recognize her.

As if it was a great compliment to a woman who stood before him, her reason for being here clear enough, as she was swollen with his child.

Nina was sick to death of these royals.

"Are you certain?" she asked crisply, ignoring all that stunning male beauty. Not to mention her memories and the chaos inside. She also ignored the way his brows rose at her tone. "You've had more than a legion or two, I imagine, and there's no telling how many have turned up with claims like mine. Easy to get them all mixed up. You should take a closer look, surely. I could be anyone."

CHAPTER TWO

THE LITTLE BROWN hen clucking at him was…unexpected.

Yet unexpected was not boring.

And His Royal Highness, Crown Prince Zeus of Theosia, had been bored beyond all reason for entirely too long. Since the last time he'd seen her, not that he cared to think too closely about his curious reactions to that night. He'd put them aside and had quickly returned to his usual state of tedium. That was the trouble with declaring oneself rebellious at a young age and then pursuing each and every potential rebellion that arose thereafter with intensity and commitment.

It turned out that a man could not live on sin alone.

Zeus had certainly tried.

"A legion or two, perhaps," he agreed, moving toward the bizarre apparition in the vague shape of a woman who had somehow braved the palace gates and found her way here. A task many had tried, but most had failed. Resoundingly. He received weekly reports on the women who attempted to skirt security and chase him down. That she had succeeded was…

not boring at all. "A gentleman does not count such things."

"No need when the tabloids count for you."

He stopped before her, taking in this strange little creature who had scurried around in the wake of Princess Isabeau for all these years. She looked much as she had during the years of his irksome arranged engagement. Dressed to accentuate every possible flaw on her body. Her hair an obvious afterthought. Isabeau had always cultivated glamour, and yet in the background of too many of her photos had lurked her little pet.

Impervious to criticism. Unmoved by commentary.

Zeus had come to see Miss Nina Graine as a kind of symbol. Perhaps, particularly last summer, he had ascribed to her a great many motivations and inner thoughts she did not possess. He had spent more time than he liked to admit conjuring her into an unlikely heroine, the better to suit his schemes.

Then he'd discovered the truth. Beneath all the stories he'd told himself and more, beneath each and every one of the masks she'd ever worn. And the truth had nearly burned him alive.

He didn't like to think about that too much.

Or the fact that her disappearance after their night together had...bothered him.

Zeus allowed himself a smile now as he gazed down at her, returned to all her frumpy splendor. "Most women who claw their way past the palace guard for an audience with me are of a certain stripe. They are not you, however. They do not *actually* convince poor Thaddeus to bring them before me."

Isabeau's hen did not smile. She did not flutter, as women so often did in his presence, like so many small and hapless birds in need of a strong hand to perch upon. She only gripped her enormous, pregnant belly—a development Zeus doubted very much was unrelated to her appearance in his rooms, yet did not wish to consider too closely just yet—and glared at him.

Glared, when he was used to obliging sighs and simpering calf's eyes.

How novel.

"Is that meant to be flattering?" Nina demanded.

When, as a rule, no one dared make demands of him. Unless they were his perpetually unamused father, who never did anything but. And was eternally disappointed at Zeus's refusal to meet them.

His fondest rebellion yet.

"Your memory losses are your own business," Nina was saying in that same distinctly unsimpering manner. "But you must have me confused for one of those women you can't remember if you think I'd find your inability to recall the faces of the women you've slept with to be anything but sad. For you."

Zeus was unrepentant. "I always remember *some* part of the women gracious enough to share themselves with me. It is not always their faces, I grant you. Shall I tell you what I recall of you?"

"I think not. My memory is not clouded with excess. *I* know what happened that night."

She did not exactly *thrust* her belly at him, but Zeus eyed it like it was a weapon all the same. Still, he wasn't ready to go there. He was intrigued for the first time in as long as he could remember—*six months, perhaps*, a voice in him suggested slyly—and besides, he was perfectly capable of plotting his next move while appearing to be nothing more than the sybaritic fool he'd been playing too well for too long.

He lived in that space. Owned it, even.

Zeus shoved his hands in his trouser pockets and endeavored to look as if, given the faintest push, he might actually lounge about in midair.

"If you mean you did me a great service, I certainly remember that," he said lazily. "Have you gone to all this trouble so that I might thank you? Perhaps an investiture of some kind? I do wish I'd known to dig out the ceremonial swords."

"I shouldn't be at all surprised that you've rewritten what happened to suit yourself." She rolled her eyes—another gesture that Zeus did not usually see before him. Who would dare? No matter how little he seemed to stand upon ceremony, he was still the Crown Prince of Theosia. "I think we both know that you used me."

"I?" Zeus laughed then. He had wanted something novel, something more than this morbid waiting game he had no choice but to be mired in. He hadn't thought to specify what it was he wanted, and lo, she had appeared. "*I* used *you*? I was under the impression it was the other way around. I have long felt that my primary function is to provide scandals on command, the better for a certain kind of woman to be forced to leave a life she secretly never liked in the first place."

The creature before him scowled, her wild blond hair bobbing slightly from where it was inadequately knotted atop her head. "That is not a *function.* You say it like you've made toying with sad women your own cottage industry."

"I do what I can," Zeus murmured, as if attempting to be humble. A state of being he did not recognize, personally. What purpose could it serve? "No, no, your gratitude alone is my reward."

"Don't be ridiculous," huffed the little brown hen. "I was nothing but a servant. You, on the other hand, were not only a royal prince, destined for a throne—"

"Not just any throne," he added helpfully. "The humbly named Throne of Ages. It's right down the hall if you want to take a peek. Maybe snap a few pictures? I hear that's all the rage."

"You were also engaged," Nina continued doggedly. "To be married. Since the very day of her birth, if I remember it rightly, as set up by your fathers in an agreement that all of Europe knows inside and out. Given how many times it's been trotted out in the tabloids while one or the other of you was caught entertaining someone outside the bonds of your arrangement."

"Such busybodies, fathers," Zeus murmured. "Don't you think? Forever arranging things on their own and then acting surprised that no one wishes to be an *arrangement.*"

"I wouldn't know," she replied coolly. Censoriously, even. "My father died when I was five, and the only arrangements that were ever made for me involved orphanages or princesses."

"Neither of which you liked all that much, if memory serves."

"We have already established that you have pervasive memory issues," she shot back, her chin tilting up. "I will remind you that you were not only the Crown Prince of Theosia that night. You were not only engaged. You were engaged *to my mistress.*"

That had rather been the point.

Though, admittedly, Zeus had gotten sidetracked. How could he have known that Isabeau's little hen was hiding the curves of a goddess beneath the outlandish and unflattering things she wore?

And Zeus was, at heart, a connoisseur of the female form.

He had spent six months assuring himself that was all he was, especially when it came to her.

"Darling Isabeau, the most poisonous viper in all of Europe," he said now with a sigh, fairly certain that Nina would not care for any rhapsodizing about her charms. She looked as if she might bite him. "Such a tender union that would have been."

The fact that Isabeau was fake and unpleasant, at best, had not been the reason Zeus hadn't wanted to marry her. Zeus didn't want to marry anyone. He had been making his sentiments known for years and had questioned the arrangement he'd had no hand in making—but his royal fiancée had been nothing if not ambitious. Her kingdom was little more than an uppity ski slope, and that wasn't enough for Isabeau. She'd had big dreams of what it would mean to be the Theosian Queen.

Fidelity hadn't factored in.

Zeus had needed to find a way to make her break things off before her thirtieth birthday, as stipulated in the contracts his father had signed a lifetime ago. It was that or pay outrageous penalties. Like ransoming off one of the outlying Theosian islands, which even Zeus, for all his game playing, could not justify. Or countenance.

His ancestors would have risen from the dead in protest. And really, his father was quite enough. Zeus couldn't imagine having more family around to shout at him about bloodlines and duties and the debt he owed to history.

The perfect solution had come to him in a blast of inspiration during a deathly boring dinner engagement on one of his trips to Haught Montagne—the trips he put off as long as possible, until Isabeau's father began to make threats of violence. Which in their world could lead to war—whether in the markets or the streets. Neither was acceptable, for obvious reasons.

Or so Zeus had been constantly told by his father for the whole of his life.

Though Zeus had been entertaining himself by imagining otherwise at that dinner. Then he'd spied Isabeau's pet and his plotting had gone off in an entirely different direction. Zeus had been deeply pleased with himself.

But that night had not gone according to plan.

He was blessed with the ability to see the beauty in any woman he encountered. And so he did, and had. Yet what he had not anticipated was that Nina was wholly unlike the other courtiers and ladies who circled his unwanted bride-to-be. Her innocence had awed him. Her enthusiasm had left a permanent mark.

And it turned out a man did not have to look hard

for the beauty in Nina. She was hiding it. Deliberately. But he'd found her out.

The truth he did not intend to share was that he, Zeus of Theosia, had actually thought about her in the months since that night.

More than once.

And at the start, he had done more than *think* about her—

But he barely admitted that to himself.

"You are welcome, Your Royal Highness," Nina was saying in that sharp way he remembered from that evening in Haught Montagne, when he'd found his way beneath all those layers she wore. So deliciously sharp up close when she seemed so soft from a distance. "What a pleasure it was to break off your engagement for you, since you were apparently unable to do it yourself."

But Zeus could not be shamed. Many had attempted it. All had fallen short. He merely lifted a shoulder. "If I had broken it myself, there would have been too many unpleasant consequences. Monies to be paid. Kings to placate. Wars to avert. Far better all round to make Isabeau break it herself." He inclined his head in her direction. "You, apparently, were the bridge too far."

Nina made a noise of frustration. He found it cute.

Yes. *Cute.*

More unforeseen reactions. Zeus hardly knew what to do with himself.

"Your assorted scandals never bothered her." Nina scowled up at him. "Why should they? She always enjoyed her own fun. It was that it was me, her dumpy charity case that she was saddled with because the palace worried she seemed too unlikable. But then, you know this. It's why you chose me."

"Surely lightning struck us both. That is how I recall it."

"It was a clear night in summer." She shook her head. "We were not engaged in the same enterprise, I think."

"Little hen," he chided her. "You break my heart, which is nothing, as anyone will tell you. It is but a cheap little trinket. But you also poke at my pride. A dangerous game. I am not only certain that we were, both of us, very much engaged in the same glorious enterprise that night. But that you enjoyed yourself thoroughly."

Zeus remembered more about that night than he wanted to. He remembered the heat, the unexpected longing, the blast of unconquerable desire. He remembered the way his lips had moved over hers and the responses he had coaxed from her.

How it had all become need and flame—then burned out of control. So bright and greedy that instead of the happy, carefree seduction he'd intended, all charm and release, he'd had no choice but to throw himself into it.

Headfirst.

And he might have spent the past six months telling himself he remembered very little about that night, but that was a lie.

He remembered everything.

Her taste. Her scent.

The small sounds she'd made in the back of her throat.

"I'm afraid the night dims a bit in my memory," she said now, her brown eyes glittering. And she was lying. He could see that she was lying, but in a way, that was more fascinating. "Given what happened the next morning."

She looked at him as if she expected he might collapse in paroxysms of shame at that. Sadly for her, he was still…himself.

"Desperate times," he said, with the grin that had gotten him out of more scrapes than he could count.

And he could see that she was not unaffected.

But she did not giggle or melt. She frowned.

"I'm embarrassed to say that it took me some time to work out what had actually happened," she said. Without the faintest hint of a giggle. "Then I realized. You called them. You *personally invited* the paparazzi in that morning."

"I am devastated to discover that you were so misled in your assessment of my character." Zeus enjoyed watching her brow furrow all the more. "Were you truly under the impression that I was or am a good man?"

Though he remembered, little as he might wish to, that making love to this woman had made him wish he was. If only because the gift of her sweet innocence had demanded it.

But it had been too late.

"I have never thought you were anything but you." And that was what made her smile at last, edgy as that smile was. At least it looked like a real one. "If anything, understanding the role you played in this has helped make my course of action clear."

She looked down at the belly between them. He did the same.

But luckily, he'd now had some time to think about the opportunity she presented.

Zeus always had liked an opportunity.

Especially if it helped stick the knife in deeper.

"I do hate to be indelicate," he began. She let out a laugh, and he grinned. "You're quite right. I don't. But you must know that there's almost no purpose to this confrontation scene you have planned, all tears and recriminations followed swiftly by demands—"

"You've had this conversation often, have you?"

He offered her a bland smile. "A great many women assume they must be carrying my child, simply because they wish it to be so."

Her brows lifted. "You being such a paragon of fatherhood and all."

"I'm sure that's the draw." He inclined his head. "Unless and until a DNA test proves that you're carrying my child, this can only be a theoretical conversation. A parade of what-ifs, all destined to end in nothing." Zeus shrugged with a wholly unaffected lack of concern. "I have always enjoyed these things."

She eyed him. "How many children do you have, then?"

"Theoretical children any number of distraught women have claimed must be mine? Pick a number, then multiply it. Real children? Not a one." He allowed himself a smile, perhaps a little more real than necessary. When he usually preferred to hide anything real. There was something about this woman—but he brushed that off. "Perhaps that has something to do with the fact that I do not partake in unprotected sex."

Yet even as he said that, hadn't he gotten a little too enthusiastic with Nina? He remembered that he had been…a little too intense. All of that fire had been such an unexpected wallop. There had been a little too much bathing in it. A little too much wishing that he hadn't already set the wheels in motion that would end their encounter with a shower of flashbulbs.

Something in him seemed to roll over, then hum.

Almost like…anticipation.

He hardly recognized it.

"You may give me any tests you like," she was saying with a dismissive wave of her hand. No tears. No caterwauling. None of the performance of pregnancy that he'd come to expect from this scene. "I've come to inform you of your impending fatherhood, and you may do with that information anything you wish. Summon your doctors and lab technicians at will. Oh, and congratulations."

Zeus wondered if his mask had slipped a little when she paused a moment, that dent between her brows returning. He made sure to look as bored as possible until she cleared her throat and carried on.

"I'll catch you up on what happened after you invited the tabloids in." She paused as if waiting for him to toss in an apology. He didn't, of course. But something in him almost wanted to, and that was unnerving enough. "I was cast out of all royal circles. As this was, in fact, the goal I've been striving toward since

Isabeau first took it upon herself to force me under her wing, I was quite pleased. Until…"

She only lifted a hand, indicating her belly. "I thought I was ill. Or perhaps detoxing from too long in Isabeau's presence. Either way, it took me quite some time to understand what had happened to me. And even longer to accept it."

"So long that any other alternatives were no longer available to you," he said, smoothly enough, though he found—to his great surprise—that he had a certain distaste for the notion, as it involved this woman and this baby.

But Nina jerked back as if he'd slapped her.

"I'm an orphan," she said matter-of-factly, though he could see far more emotion in her brown gaze, gone as dark as the bitterest coffee now. His favorite. "This baby is the only family I have."

Something seemed to roar inside him then, shocking Zeus. And he had not been shocked by anything in…six long months. It reminded him a little too closely of that night they'd shared, the shock of all that heat where he'd expected an easy, forgettable pleasure.

Nina had come out of nowhere with a sucker punch yet again.

"I can't say I had any particular intention of sharing this news with you," Nina was saying. "I thought that perhaps I could simply live my life, as I always wanted, with no royal nonsense to consider." She shrugged. "I'm afraid I know too much."

"About royalty?" He nodded sagely. "A tragedy indeed."

"One does not require a great deal of knowledge

about royalty," she shot back at him. "They rule things. The end. Everything you need to know about your average, run-of-the-mill member of any royal family can be summed up like so. It's what makes them so presumptuous."

Zeus could not deny that. What astounded him was that…he wanted to.

But Nina was still speaking. "No, what I know too much about is the tabloids. The paparazzi. Just because I've enjoyed six months to myself doesn't mean my solitude will continue. Sooner or later, someone will remember me. Then they'll all find me. And worse, my baby."

She rubbed that belly of hers again, currently housed in a dress he suspected might possibly have been used as a circus tent. When he knew that her actual figure was so sweet and ripe that he found himself hungry even now. For he could see—what little of her he could truly see—that this pregnancy had ripened her further.

Zeus had the blistering notion that he actually *wanted* her to be carrying his child. He *wanted* this ripeness to be his. All his.

He shoved that aside.

Because he couldn't believe such a notion could cross his mind, much less bloom the way it seemed to be doing.

"Are you saying that the paparazzi have already found you?" he managed to ask past what amounted to a full-scale riot inside of him.

A riot her ripeness, so close to him, did not help.

"I don't think they have, but who can say where a

photographer with a nasty telephoto lens might lurk?" Again, that edgy smile. "The more my pregnancy shows, the more likely someone is to do the math. It will be worse once the baby comes."

"I see. You thought you'd come to me and try to get ahead of mathematics."

"No, it occurred to me that the math being what it is, I can expect that whether I wanted to involve you or not, you would end up involved." She sniffed. "Now or later. I decided to come ahead of the inevitable exposé to let you know what my demands are."

"See? I told you there would be demands." He smiled benevolently at her and found it delightful when she gritted her teeth in response. Far easier to deal with that sort of thing than any *ripening*. Much less his response to it. He was going to have to sort himself out. Later. "There are always demands. It's almost as if demands are the point of these little scenes."

"I've researched Theosian law," she said, without any indication she'd heard his comments. And Zeus was not used to being so soundly and repeatedly ignored. He couldn't tell if he hated it…or if his reaction was a bit more intense. And was something more like admiration. "Apparently, one of your ancestors so enjoyed spreading himself about that it was written into law that all royal bastards must be given a certain stipend from the crown. To keep them in an appropriate style, though not under the same roof, as that might offend any given queen."

Zeus laughed out loud. Of all the things he'd imagined she might say, it wasn't that.

"Ah, yes, the bastard clause." The clause that every

young royal Theosian man was lectured about extensively as he set to head out into the world and misbehave. He hadn't heard it mentioned by anyone outside the palace staff in ages—no doubt because he was considered such a lost cause. "It may surprise you to learn that the clause originated from the betrayed Queen in question, because she preferred to make public her husband's indiscretions. I think you'll find we haven't used it here in generations."

"Then I suppose I've come to ask for the usual amount of support," Nina replied easily enough, though her chin notched higher. "I'm not one for charity. I've already spent a lifetime being force-fed it while being told how grateful I should be for each and every sour bite. If it were up to me, you would never have seen me again. I would have made my own way in this world, and happily. That was my intention."

"So you have now stated twice." Zeus sighed. "I do hope you're not going to get boring on me. That would be a tragedy indeed."

She did not look like she agreed. And the Theosian sun made love to her as she stood there, facing off with him. It danced over the spun straw of her hair and the sensual bow of her lips. It was the sort of light that most women of his acquaintance avoided, and for good reason.

But it only made Nina that much more beautiful.

Inarguably lovely.

You need to remember who you are, a stern voice within him piped up then.

"I found a perfectly decent situation in England," she told him. "It would be hard, of course, but I'm not afraid of hard. I believed I could do it. I began to think I *would* do it, damn it…" Nina smiled a little ruefully. "Until it occurred to me that this baby is neither an orphan nor a prince. He or she should not have to pay for the sins of either."

Zeus heard a swift intake of breath. It took him a moment to realize it was his.

Nina straightened her shoulders. "Just as this baby doesn't deserve the lengths I'm willing to go to for freedom, it also doesn't deserve to be cut off from the kind of life it could have, just because its father is you."

An uncomfortable sensation worked its way through Zeus then, though it took him far too long to recognize it. Much less name it.

But he was fairly certain it was temper. When he had learned, so very long ago, that his own temper was useless and it was far better to poke and prod and play games, so that others could experience theirs and lose control.

He'd learned how to be very, very good at that.

And he had come to think of temper as weakness. Because what was it but emotion, twisted around and easily manipulated by men like him? He allowed himself none of that, either. Yet there was no mistaking it. The curl of a kind of smoke winding around inside him was very clearly temper.

How…astonishing.

"So, like every other woman who has ever pursued me," he said, drawling out the words and making sure no hint of temper leaked through, because he didn't know why it should. He refused to feel such things. Or any things. "You are after me for my money."

And he watched, too fascinated for his own good, as Nina's pretty brown eyes flashed. This orphan, this little brown hen, had never been what she seemed. He did not know how he had suffered through any number of interactions with Isabeau before he'd come to understand that.

But once he'd begun to see her, all too plainly, he couldn't unsee her.

He only saw *more* of her.

She had pride, this creature. And if he wasn't mistaken, a healthy dose of a burning need for retribution about her.

In other words, she was perfect.

"Yes," she said, as if she knew the direction his thoughts had gone. "I want your money. I see no reason this baby shouldn't be raised like the child of a prince it is."

"Then I have some deliciously good news for you," Zeus informed her with a little bow, because he couldn't resist a flourish. Not when his endgame had just altered completely. "Assuming this isn't all an elaborate ruse that will be uncovered shortly by the palace's medical staff, allow me to be the first to congratulate you."

"Why?" she asked, suspicion stamped all over her. "For what?"

Zeus only gazed down at her, that temper still curling around and around inside him, though he was happy to discover it did not inhibit his enjoyment. That would have been a tragedy.

"On your nuptials," he told her.

"My…what?"

"Oh, happy day," Zeus said, letting his voice carry and rebound back from the pristine walls like so much dizzy heat. "We are to be married, little hen. You lucky thing. Women have been jostling for that position since before I was born."

"Not me!" She looked almost insultingly horrified. "I don't want to marry *you*!"

Which, he could admit, was another reason she was perfect. Zeus could not have tolerated any of the women who did actually want to marry him, and quite desperately. They longed for either the man they thought he was or the throne he would take, and either way, it wasn't him.

Only this woman, only Nina, would do.

"I am afraid that what you want does not signify," he said, only the pulse he could feel hammering away in his neck indicating that he was perhaps not as calm as he was pretending. "You should have done more research. If you had, you might have found that here on Theosian soil, the heir to the kingdom belongs to the crown."

Her eyes widened. Almost comically. "That can't possibly mean what I think it does."

Zeus rocked back on his heels, all the strange emotions and memories of this encounter washing over him. But he concentrated on her dismay instead.

"I am the Crown Prince. If you are carrying my heir, I have every right to do with you what I will." He allowed himself a smile then, one that in no way hid the truth of him, and enjoyed it when her eyes widened farther still. “Welcome to Theosia. I hope you like our little island. You will one day reign as Queen.”

Nina cemented her place here by looking ill at the very idea. Not triumphant. Not thrilled. *Ill.* “That will never, ever happen. Never.”

“Oh, but it will, my little hen,” Zeus replied, something perilously close to happy, for once. He told himself it was because the pieces of this last part of his plan were coming together so beautifully. And for no other reason. Because there could not possibly be another reason. Zeus would not allow there to be. “You can depend on it.”

CHAPTER THREE

EVERYTHING HAPPENED A little too quickly then.

So quickly that Nina found herself perilously close to dizzy.

Zeus moved across the vast room, striding like a man with purpose instead of the monument to idleness he usually appeared to be in all things. He swung open the doors to his chamber, said two words, and half the palace staff seemed to flow in. He barked out orders, and for all that he lounged about Europe—acting as if he was too lazy to lift his finger when he could find any number of willing women to lift it for him—it was clear that his staff knew this version of him well. Peremptory in the extreme.

Princely, something in her whispered. *A man who is not only used to command, but infinitely comfortable in it.*

That made her head spin enough, because that wasn't Zeus. Not the Zeus the world knew entirely too well.

But the voice within her wasn't done.

Just like that night, it murmured, so that more of that wild heat charged through her, setting her aflame.

The way it had when she'd seen him again. And when he'd called her *little hen.*

Because the Zeus he'd become that night had been…intense. Demanding.

Different.

But she didn't have any time to take any of that in as she was marched from his rooms by a phalanx of aides. Who, at least, acted more polite and solicitous than the initial butler and the whole of the palace guard had. They swept her through the halls of the palace, climbing from one fairy-tale level to the next, one of them talking in a low voice into her mobile as they moved.

They arrived at their destination, another suite of graceful, expertly appointed rooms that looked, on the one hand, like every suite of rooms she had ever stayed in at places like this—though she'd never stayed in one quite as lovely. For this was the Palace of the Gods, so everything was that much brighter and inlaid with gold and silver. As if the light filling every room was not the weather, but a part of the planned decor. She was taken to a small salon, dappled with light that poured in from a shaded balcony outside.

"You will wait here," said the aide with the phone, who Nina suspected was the one in charge. Though the older woman managed to make the very clear command sound as if, maybe, it had been Nina's idea and she was only confirming it.

"I would love to wait," Nina replied as she lowered herself down to a settee that was so much more comfortable than the one she'd been sitting on before that she rather thought they shouldn't share the same name. She sat and smiled up at the woman. "But I'm afraid the baby won't. If I don't eat soon, neither one of us is going to be very happy."

The older woman looked at her moment, then snapped her fingers. Confirming that she was, indeed, in charge of this particular set of staff—and also setting one of her underlings running from the room.

"Then, of course, you shall eat," she said.

Nina was almost too grateful to bear it. "If you know where my personal belongings are, I can feed myself. I have snacks in my bag."

"Your personal belongings are being looked over by the palace guard," her aide said, sounding sorrowful. Though her eyes remained shrewd. "Security will do as they like, you know. But not to worry, we'll have something from the kitchens shortly."

And Nina could not have been more surprised when, not five minutes later, the underling reappeared. He was trailed by another staff member pushing a cart, who then began to lay out the makings of a hearty afternoon tea. But in Theosian style, with dishes of grilled fish to go along with finger sandwiches, mountains of vegetables and fresh fruits, hard cheeses, pots of herbed butter, and loaves of fragrant baked bread.

By the time another set of people appeared before her, she felt better than she had all day.

Which was maybe why, when one of the new people introduced herself as a doctor and announced that she was there to check on Nina's health—and the paternity of the baby she carried while they were at it—she was less outraged than she might otherwise have been. Because, as ever, she was a realist. She had known before she came here, no matter how grudgingly, that there was no possibility anyone would simply take her word for it. That was not how powerful men operated, whether they had their own palaces or not.

She followed the doctor and her cheerful, efficient team into the next room, a small study with stacks of books on whitewashed shelves and bright blue flowers in handcrafted vases. And there submitted to all necessary tests. Whatever it took to make her case in a place where her word wouldn't do.

The story of her life, really.

"You must be tired," said the aide from before, coming in to collect her once her exam was done. "After all the traveling, and then such a long day in the palace. Perhaps it would be best if you rested, no? Do feel free to ring should you require anything. Shall we say, a light supper later this evening? The kitchen will bring it up at the hour of your choice."

"I appreciate the concern for my feelings," Nina said dryly. "But I'm not the least bit tired."

"I feel certain you must be," replied the other woman, implacably.

"You could simply say that I'm to be locked in these quarters until such time as the paternity of my baby can be determined," Nina said. Then smiled. "I think we'd both respect each other more, don't you?"

The other woman inclined her head, but her shrewd gaze warmed. "Indeed, miss."

"You may call me Nina." And Nina had the strangest sense of vertigo, because she couldn't recall the last time she'd been the one to offer her first name. She had always been the one who had to mind her manners constantly around her betters.

"I am Daphne," the woman replied. Her mouth curved. "And I will let you know when you're free to move about the palace."

"See?" Nina asked. "Isn't that better?"

Daphne smiled wider, then clapped her hands and emptied the suite, leaving Nina alone.

For a while, she stayed where she was, staring at pretty blue flowers in small earthenware vases while inside of her everything was… Zeus.

That night six months ago was all tangled up in today, a temple of light and all his dark-honeyed glory, as if baklava had taken human form and called itself a prince.

Nina let out a long, shuddery breath.

She got up, then went out of the study into the atrium that took the place of any central hall. She could see into the first salon and was pleased to find they'd left her the remains of her tea, which made her smile despite herself. Because if she needed to, she would have thrown open these doors and stormed the palace kitchens if she was hungry.

Clearly, Daphne knew that and had removed the temptation to leave here.

She walked into the center of the atrium, where a fountain gurgled sedately, appreciating the glass ceiling and the greenery everywhere. Slowly, she turned in a circle. She could see the bedroom beyond two blue doors, a massive four-poster bed set against a wall done in mosaic. There were several other rooms, but their doors were shut, so she could only guess what was behind them. Some of these palatial guest quarters had screening rooms and bowling alleys, their own elevators and private pools. Boardrooms and full offices for government and business-minded guests. Palaces these days were equipped to cater to the needs of visiting royalty and all of their expectations on the high end, and questionable guests like Nina in more self-contained units like this.

And then she laughed at herself, because the atrium alone was larger than any place she'd lived in the last six months. Maybe she'd have been happier if she didn't know it was the sort of smallish suite Princess Isabeau would have sneered at—but deemed good enough for Nina.

She shook off memories of the wretched Isabeau and followed the light. Through the bedroom and out onto the wide balcony that she found waiting for her, wrapping around the side of the corner suite she occupied.

There was a shaded part of the balcony and then a far sunnier bit. Nina went out and stood in the sun for as long as she could, letting the heat sink into her bones and chase away the lingering cold after her last couple of months in England, then she made her way back into the shade. She found the chaise with the best view, straight out into the sea, and settled herself there.

And then, listening to the waves and staring at all that deep blue, she found herself getting drowsy. Despite her claims. She told herself it was all the food she'd just eaten. It had nothing to do with the day she'd had here.

Nina wasn't getting *soft*.

And as she drifted off into sleep, all she could see was that bright, impossible light growing even brighter, and then Zeus stepping out of it, shining far hotter than the lot.

So it wasn't as much of a shock as it might otherwise have been when she woke to find Zeus standing over her once again.

She was glad she'd worn her most hideous skirt, wide like a tent. Because it functioned like bedding, and she knew without having to look that she was properly covered. And then laughed at herself. The man had already seen her naked. That was why she was here in the first place.

Nina rubbed her hands over her eyes, then over the rest of her face, mostly to check to see if she had been caught drooling.

Then she tried to focus on Zeus, standing so still in the kind of dark bespoke suit that she associated with his inevitable presence across all the capitals of Europe. Cut to make him seem even taller, even broader, even more perfectly shaped. A love letter to his perfect body. The sky behind him was turning a deep blue, smudged with orange and pink, from a sun just set, as if it had prettied itself just for him.

And Nina felt breathless, as if the whole world was holding its breath when really, that was just her. She tried to force herself to breathe normally again. She assured herself it had nothing at all to do with the man standing at the foot of her chaise. She was pregnant. Surely she could blame any odd physical sensations on that.

Not on Zeus and the sunset all around him that made him look even more ancient and unworldly.

"I take it you've learned that you're the father of my baby," Nina said.

She blamed the rasp in her voice on her nap.

Zeus only looked at her a long while. The sky continued to put on a show behind him. "It seems we are to be parents, little hen."

And Nina had never minded that nickname from Isabeau. She hadn't liked it, but it hadn't *bothered* her. Isabeau had imagined it held more weight than it did.

But it was very different the way Zeus said it. And he *kept* saying it.

She had tried to ignore, earlier, the way his mouth moved over those words and, worse, the echo of them inside her. But his little hen was in danger of burning alive.

"At least we've established that I'm not a liar," she said before she immolated where she sat. She smoothed her hair back from her face, then remembered that she'd deliberately left it wild. So she dropped her hands again and folded them the only place they folded now, up above her belly. "But I have no intention of marrying you."

"I already told you that your intentions cannot matter in such a case." He waved a hand when she started to protest. "I have avoided matrimony the entirety of my life, Nina. I will require sustenance if I'm to discuss such a drastic change in my dissipated lifestyle any further."

Nina sat up straighter as lights appeared, and it took her a moment to work out it was from the lanterns hung on all the overhangs. And then she couldn't think about *lanterns*, because Zeus was beside her, leaning down—

And for a moment, she thought, *Yes, please, again—*

But all he did was lift her to her feet. With an economy of movement that reminded her, with a rush of sensation, of the way he'd tossed her this way and that six months ago.

She did not need the reminder.

Because it was easy to dismiss Prince Zeus. A playboy, a reprobate, a deeply unserious man who prided himself on being wicked to the core. It was easy to dismiss his beauty and make salty remarks about the fact he didn't have anything better to do with his time *but* work on that abdomen. She'd heard all of those things from snippy aristocrats in balls and palaces and had thought many of them herself.

But no matter why or how he came by his physicality, he certainly knew how to use it.

She knew that firsthand.

Nina didn't like that. Just as she didn't like the way everything inside her had leaned into that *yes*. And she *really* didn't like the fact it was only in Zeus's arms that she felt like her old self again. Graceful. Lithe.

She pushed away from him, hoping her feet would hold her. Then she felt a bit sad when they did—which was unacceptable. She shouldn't *want* him to hold her. "I'm not sure that stuffing yourself full of food is going to garner you the results that you want. I don't need to eat to know that I'm against marrying you. I don't even need a lifetime of dissipation to know it."

"My dear Nina," he said as he indicated she should

walk with him down the length of the balcony toward the corner. "The food is for me. I'm very hungry. I'm given to understand that my tea went astray."

Nina felt as if she'd betrayed herself, because she had the strangest urge to laugh at the look he swept her from beneath lashes that no man should be allowed to possess. She shouldn't find him *amusing.* What was the matter with her?

"How could the Crown Prince's tea go anywhere?" she asked. "I would have thought that, given your station, every chef in the kitchen would drop everything for the privilege of serving you any snack you desired."

"You're missing the point of the comment," he said, walking beside her with all the dignity of the prince he was. And yet still, she was certain she could detect something wilder beneath it. There was that sort of roll to the way he moved. As if the reality of him was caged somewhere deep within. *Stop telling yourself fairy tales,* she snapped at herself. "I'm attempting to make small talk. I understand that is the basis of any marriage."

"Funnily enough, I thought a good marriage was based on respect," Nina replied. She couldn't remember her parents or their marriage, but she was sure theirs had been a good one. Because it had to have been. She knew it did. "Friendship. Support of each other. Little things like that."

"Please tell me people don't sit around all day discussing their supportive impulses." Zeus shuddered. "That sounds markedly tedious."

"Best to avoid the institution, then," Nina said tartly.

And then wondered what she was playing at, because the way his mouth curved made her glad. When it shouldn't. Nothing about him should make her *glad.*

They turned the corner, and Nina's breath caught against her will. On this side of her rooms, the balcony was much wider. There was a small pool and a hot tub some distance farther down. But closer in, a dinner for two had been set up at a cozy round table. There were lights strewn on wires above, making everything seem magical. And with every step, the dark seemed to get thicker and the lights brighter.

Like a fairy tale, whispered a voice inside her with entirely too much wonder.

She ignored it. The way she always did.

Nina wanted to tell him that she wasn't hungry, and that even if she was, she didn't want to eat a private dinner with him. Anything to put the distance between them that should have been there automatically, given how their night together had ended. But as she drew close to the table, she could see the spread awaiting them. And she suddenly realized she was starving.

Again. Always.

And clearly the baby agreed, because it kicked her, hard.

Zeus helped her sit with an exaggerated courtesy that Nina had last seen him display toward the elderly Queen of a tiny northern country. She wanted to snap at that gesture, too, but she didn't dare.

Because she was afraid that if she opened her mouth, things she shouldn't say might come out.

Instead of sitting across the little table, Zeus pulled the chair around to settle himself next to her, only smiling blandly as the staff appeared and rearranged the table until it looked as if there had never been any choice at all for him to sit anywhere but there.

What must that be like, Nina wondered. That certainty. That knowledge that no matter what, his choices would always be supported and celebrated. And it was more than that. *His* every choice was a command.

"I hope you do not find dinner with me too much of a trial," he said as the staff retreated and left them to their own devices. "Many do, I fear."

He did not look as if he feared anything. Nina tried not to look at him and took in the feast before them instead. There were serving dishes taking up all the available space on the table, filled with all manner of savory delights. And to her astonishment, Zeus served himself, and her, with the same innate grace he did everything.

She did mean everything.

Stop that, she ordered herself, frowning at her own…idiocy.

"When is a trial too much?" she managed to ask. "I don't know how I would begin to measure."

"Did you learn this kind of wit in the orphanage?" Zeus's voice was mild, and yet still a caress. "I know you didn't learn it while at the mercy of Isabeau the humorless."

"It's a natural talent," Nina found herself saying. "Not everyone can be born into a royal family. Some of us really do have to rely on our wits."

He was toying with his food almost absently, but his gaze was intent. And on her. "What warms my heart is the notion that we will be having this conversation for the rest of our lives."

She felt that same surge of instant denial rush through her, but she caught herself.

This was Zeus of Theosia. He lived to be provoking. Letting him succeed in provoking her was letting him win. And she might have been carrying his child, but she had no intention of letting him win anything. Not if she could help it.

She was determined that she could.

"You're going to have to explain your reasoning to me." She lowered her gaze to her plate and took up a forkful of rice laden with spices. "Six months ago you engineered a ridiculous French farce of a setup to get out of one marriage. Why would you want to jump into another?"

"I consider myself several steps above a French farce, thank you," he said reproachfully. But his green eyes were gleaming, brighter than any lantern or string of lights. "Perhaps I have finally seen the error of my ways."

"I doubt that very much."

"I do rather like the error of my ways, now that you mention it," he said. "It could be that as my father grows ever more frail, I am filled with a sudden burst of filial devotion and wish to give him what he's always wanted—a wife and a child. One-stop shopping."

"That's almost sweet." Nina smiled at him. Sharply. "Which is how I know that's not your motivation."

"I shall have the palace's legal team deliver the relevant proclamations to your bedchamber," he told her. "I think you should find them interesting reading. The crux of the matter, I'm afraid, is that I don't have to offer you any explanation at all."

"Very well," Nina said and shrugged. She returned her attention to her food.

And, because she'd been raised in a harder school than this, she proceeded to ignore him as she tasted all the various dishes he'd arranged on her plate. The flavors were as bright as the lights above her, but she could hardly take them in.

Because Zeus lounged there beside her, simmering with intensity and entirely too male. She couldn't pretend she wasn't aware of him. At least not to herself. She was hardly aware of anything else. Still, she ate her dinner as if she was entirely on her own, gazing out over the sea as a tender moon began to rise.

And she would have carried on in the same vein, because he was apparently prepared to sit there in brooding silence for as long as she could maintain hers, but the baby began kicking again. Extra hard, so that she had to stop and press her hand against the point of impact.

She didn't even mean to look at Zeus while she did it, but she couldn't seem to help herself. And she found an arrested sort of expression in those deep green eyes.

"The baby's kicking," she told him, though she immediately questioned why she was telling him anything. It would have been far easier to say nothing and keep on doing what she was doing. Far less intimate, anyway. Because though she would have told a stranger on the bus that the baby was kicking, it was something else again to tell the man who'd helped make that baby.

Or maybe it was just that the man was him.

It was something about how green his eyes were, perhaps. Or how, just for a moment, she got a glimpse of the man she thought she'd seen that long-ago night.

Nina didn't like to think about that night in such detail. She'd been confused, that was all. That was the sort of thing that happened when a person accidentally fell into the arms of a notoriously wicked prince, proceeded to give him her virginity, and then stayed up the rest of the night—very nearly every moment of it—compounding the error.

Repeatedly.

And in between those rounds of experiencing so much pleasure that she couldn't believe she'd lived this long without it, they'd talked, too. The way people talked when they never expected to see each other again, she understood now.

She hadn't understood it then. *Then* she'd been wonderstruck at finally—*finally*—being seen. For herself. Her real, true self.

Nina definitely didn't like to remember that.

Now she was carrying the baby they'd made that night. And she was sitting high up on a magical balcony in a palace dedicated to gods, looking at the closest example to one she had ever seen on earth.

For a moment she thought he'd smirk, make a droll remark, do his *Zeus* thing.

Maybe that would be better.

Instead, the ancient mask seemed to crumble as she watched. Zeus leaned forward, suddenly looking nothing like that lounging, lazy creature who all the world thought they knew so well because he was always performing for them.

He wasn't performing now. She was sure of it.

"Here?" His voice was gruff and low, his hand hovering over her belly.

Nina told herself she was being efficient, that was all, as she took his hand in hers and guided it to the spot where the baby he'd helped make was using her ribs as a drum.

She'd felt the baby kick for some time now, and still, it felt miraculous. Every time. She could still remember the very first time, the sudden quickening that had changed everything. Because the baby had kicked and she'd known, beyond any of the doubts that might have chased her through those first few months when she'd worried about how her life would change, that they were in it together. Her child and her. Forever. She'd started preparing to come to Theosia the very next day.

But Nina had done all that alone.

This was something else again. Taking the hand of the man who'd fathered her baby and placing it on her body, and then watching as that hard, starkly sensual face of his lit up with wonder.

Something inside of her seemed to shatter, though it wasn't a breaking. It was a kind of shattering that went on and on, too thick and too hot.

And it seemed to take a very long while for Zeus to pull his hand away again.

Nina felt…changed. There was that shattering inside her, and now there was the imprint where his hand had been. She could feel the heat of it, charging through her. It kicked up feelings she thought had only ever been fleeting, only that one night, and never to be repeated.

It made her feel…fragile, somehow, that she'd been wrong.

Zeus sat back in his chair, and his gaze was inscrutable. "Why don't you want to marry me? It's very disconcerting, given women usually fling wedding rings at my feet and beg for the privilege. Are you only saying it to distinguish yourself from the masses?"

That didn't entirely break the spell, but it went a long way toward it. Nina laughed. "I have absolutely no wish to distinguish myself in your eyes."

She thought he might take offense to that—really, she'd *meant* him to take offense to it—but instead, he only smiled lazily.

"One of the things I like most about you," he told her, gaze and voice as dark as the night around them, "is what a liar you are."

"Strange. That sounds like a compliment. And yet."

"Oh, it is."

He moved forward and took her hand in his, and every single instinct she had screamed at her to snatch it back. *Now.* Or he'd know. Or he'd see it, that shattering in place of who she'd been only moments ago. Or the way that all that glimmering within her turned quickly into a molten fire when he touched her.

But then, when his gaze found hers and glinted with wickedness again, she suspected he already knew.

Nina didn't snatch her hand away the way she wanted to, and badly. She left it in his, painstakingly aware of the way his fingers moved over hers, kicking up storms of sensation everywhere he touched. And she had never considered a palm particularly sensitive before. It was functional. Useful. She'd scrubbed too many floors for her to believe anything else.

But with her hand in his, she found she could feel... everything. As if her palm was the center of all possible pleasure, and only he knew how to make it all ignite. And more—every place he touched seemed connected to the strings of fire already lighting her up inside.

And the more he moved his fingers this way and that, almost as if he didn't know what he was doing when she knew he did, the more she burned.

Oh, how she burned, and she couldn't seem to make herself stop.

"What I'd like to know," Zeus said, after a very long while—or possibly only a very few moments, she couldn't tell past the need and longing clashing about inside her—"is what exactly you are hiding."

She made herself sit up straighter.

"I have nothing to hide," she replied. As placidly as she used to respond to the vile insults and occasional shoes Isabeau had lobbed at her head. "I never had much of a personal life to begin with, and what little I did have was sold out to the paparazzi so you could avoid your existing commitments. There's nothing to find except this baby. And nothing to hide—the world is already well aware of how it was made."

She didn't say, *You saw to that, Zeus.* Why bother? He knew what he'd done.

"And yet you go to such lengths to hide yourself," he murmured, still playing with her hand. "Why would anyone do such a thing? Unless there was something hidden away in there they didn't want the rest of the world to see."

"Maybe I resented forever being on display," Nina retorted before she thought better of it.

And if he'd smirked at her the way he did so often, she would have collected herself. It would have served as a dose of much-needed cold water over the head and restored her to herself. She would have gone off on a different tangent, hopefully chastened. Or she would simply have pulled her hand from his and returned to the exquisitely prepared food waiting for her. As serenely as possible.

But he didn't smirk at her. He only waited, the force of his bronze tension moving in her like the beat of her own heart.

And that beat was hard. Deep. It almost knocked her out of her seat.

"I went into the orphanage when I was five." Nina asked herself what on earth she was doing even as she spoke. But then again, none of this was a secret. It was only that no one had ever asked. "My parents were killed in an accident. A slick road in winter. No one's fault, these things happen, and so on. All the same, they died and I went into care. And then, every Sunday for the next ten years, I was trotted out to sell myself to potential buyers." She laughed, but only a little. "Excuse me. I mean, to *charm* potential adoptive *parents*."

He looked at her, frowning slightly. "Surely a cute five-year-old girl should have gone in a snap."

"You would think so. And I did. But they always brought me back."

"You can return a child?" Zeus asked in what looked like astonishment.

Laced with disbelief.

She had never liked him more than she did at the sight of that untutored reaction, but she couldn't dwell on it. Not now.

"It turns out that you can return a defective one," she said quietly. "I had night terrors and no one could deal with it. So after I got to be about ten, they started telling the prospective parents I had emotional problems. That way they didn't bother to take me for a test run only to come back the next morning, complaining of how difficult it had been and how spooky I was. And how that wasn't what they were looking for in a child."

His grip on her hand tightened. "I'm sorry," he said.

And that, too, struck her as alarmingly real.

She didn't want to deal with how the notion of Prince Zeus *being serious* tumbled through her. The things she wanted it to mean that she knew it didn't.

Because he'd showed her who he was. She needed to believe him.

"No need to be sorry. I much preferred not going off into strangers' homes, knowing perfectly well that it wasn't going to work and then being returned like faulty merchandise."

He looked as if he was going to say something, and it was suddenly clear to Nina that if he offered her any pity—if he even looked like he might—she would break into pieces.

She hurried on before he could put that to the test. "But I still had to stand there every Sunday, on display. I was counting the days until I turned sixteen and would be set free. Instead, on the day before that happened, Isabeau's publicity team felt that in light of her recent spate of scandals that year, she ought to make a grand gesture. And I was it."

"I remember," Zeus said.

And it was amazing, truly, how much Nina wanted to ask *what* he remembered… Was it the stories that had been plastered everywhere on her sixteenth birthday? Her personal pain exploited so a spoiled princess could play at looking merciful and good? Or was it the times he'd seen her over the years after that, trailing around after the same spoiled princess who loathed her forced benevolence, hated that she couldn't rid herself of Nina without a good reason to feed to her public, and had gone out of her way to be cruel?

Or was it possible that he remembered that night and the things they'd talked about when they weren't turning each other inside out? The same as she did?

But she kept her questions to herself.

"Living with Isabeau was like living in a glass bowl," she said, though she still wasn't sure why she was telling him this. Because he was the father of her child and he was *here.* Because he was beautiful. Because his hand was wrapped tight around hers, and she couldn't seem to stop herself. "There's the world forever looking at her and everyone around her, but that's not the worst of it. Even in private, every moment is watched. All the people who lurk about the palace, everywhere, like little spies. Reporting back anything and everything they can to gain favor. Currying goodwill and leverage with their reports. Isabeau herself, always there to criticize, cackle, and cut everyone down to size. But especially me, because she didn't actually choose me. Her people did. Something she wanted to make sure I knew. She wanted to be *very* sure I was never under the impression she'd wanted me anywhere near her."

It didn't hurt her to think of these things. Nina was only ashamed that there had ever been a part of her that had wished she and Isabeau could have been closer.

"You decided you would hide your real self away where no one would find you, no matter how hard they looked," Zeus said in his dark, rich voice. "Is that it?"

It was so tempting to lean closer. To thread her fingers with his, then see if he would do what he did last time and lean across what separated them to fit his lips to hers as if that had been their destiny all along—

Nina tugged her hand from his. "This isn't going to work."

Zeus stayed where he was, his elbows on the table, all of his attention focused on her. She saw the way his gaze darkened. "I don't know what you mean."

"You do."

His mouth curved into what she would have said, on someone else, was a self-deprecating sort of smile. But this was Zeus of Theosia.

Still, she couldn't seem to breathe properly when he reached out a hand and toyed with a bit of her dress between his finger and thumb. Then he moved that finger and thumb to trace his way over the swell of her belly.

Where their baby was curled up between them. And would be a person, in the world, in a few short months.

Linking them together no matter what. Like it or not.

No matter what either one of them might be hiding.

"The trouble is," Zeus said when he looked up again, his gaze pinning her to her seat, "I've seen the real you, Nina. I know the difference."

CHAPTER FOUR

ZEUS EXPECTED HER to pull away, and she did. Nina sat back so quickly that the chair scraped loudly against the stone, and he knew that if she hadn't been hampered by her newly rounded body, she would likely have stood up and stormed away.

He could see that she was considering it, even now, no matter that it might take her a moment to rise.

But then, as he watched, her face took on that studied blankness he recognized too well. It was the particular expression she had always worn in court. The very expression that—coupled with her pointed inability to dress in any kind of fashionable manner, no matter how objectively chic the garments she was butchering—had first caught his attention.

Because it was so odd. And the longer he looked, the less sense it made.

"I don't think you should read quite so much into that night," she told him now.

In a tone it took him a moment to place. She sounded as if she felt sorry for him. As if *she* pitied *him*.

He nearly laughed out loud but contained himself. "I'm not sure any reading is required, little hen. You appear to be blooming with the consequences of our choices that night. I believe the book is written."

One expression after the next moved through her brown eyes, though none appeared on her face. He had spent a long time perfecting his own public face, and he knew precisely how difficult it was. And more, what kind of dedication it took.

She was a puzzle, this commoner who would become his Queen, and he was going to enjoy solving her. Piece by delectable piece.

"I will admit that I took a certain satisfaction in making myself…unpalatable. It was my own private rebellion against Isabeau." Her chin lifted then, and Zeus didn't know what it was about her that made his chest so tight. Maybe it was this. This hurling herself at windmills when even Don Quixote would have called it hopeless. But not Nina. "You know you're a good-looking man, Zeus. Usually you're the first to say so. I merely took the opportunity to taste what the many crowds before me have tasted."

"Another lie. How intriguing."

"I'm sorry that you no longer rate your charms as highly as you used to do."

He smiled. "You were an innocent, Nina. Beneath all that bravado. Believe me, I remember it."

What he didn't want to say to her was that whether she'd been hiding or not, it was as if the alchemy of that sudden blast of fire between them—mixed with her unexpected untouched state—had changed him, too.

Because he still didn't care to accept that change.

But he'd never had a night like that.

Not ever.

Zeus had never planned to admit that. To anyone, least of all himself. And he wouldn't have. He would have taken his strange reaction to her—and to what they'd shared, and to what he'd done—to his grave.

That had been his intent.

Had she not shown up today, even more beautiful than he remembered.

He remembered too well. That was the trouble. It was those curves, certainly. But it was also the slow laughter in her gaze that always seemed to be there, at the ready. It was the way she'd matched wits with him and had actually succeeded. It was her sheer delight in each and every new thing he'd taught her. The things her body could do. The things he could make her feel.

The things she had made *him* feel. It was that part that haunted him.

And now there was a child.

His child.

And Zeus might not have wanted the things his father was so determined he should. He might, in fact, have made it his life's work to make sure that where he was concerned, his father never got the slightest bit of satisfaction.

Because he'd made a promise. And he couldn't go back on it now. His mother had never had anyone but him, he had adored her, and even he hadn't been able to save her.

This was all he could do. Accordingly, he'd been doing it for years, letting the world think what they would about him—just so long as his father thought the same, and despaired.

He would keep playing this game as long as necessary.

One thing that was true about Zeus was that he was committed.

But he had known the moment he saw her that his plans could use some changing up, here at the end, and she was the perfect pièce de résistance.

"I'm not innocent anymore," she was saying in that same way, as if she thought this was a fair fight. When she had no idea what games he was playing here. But that didn't make her any less appealing. He wondered idly if anything could. "You've seen to that, and thoroughly."

He was delighted by that, and the hint of pink that rose in her cheeks. *"Thoroughly,"* he echoed. "That is one way to put it."

The pink in her cheeks got brighter. "Right. So. No need to talk about it, I think."

"What I wonder is what would happen if you no longer hid yourself away," he said. "Even now you dress to hide. You put your hair in this mess. Did you do this in your orphanage? Is this the real reason no one chose you?" He could see from the mutinous look on her face that she had done exactly this. He smiled. "What if, for once, you stopped concealing yourself in plain sight?"

And for a moment, he thought she might let her defenses down. Her pretty face softened, and he almost forgot that he was asking her to marry him because it fit so nicely into his endgame where his father was concerned. He almost forgot about the vow he'd made to punish the man who had ruined his mother's life. He almost thought—

But that was madness.

"There is no hidden part of me that wants to marry you, Zeus." And then she seemed to hear herself, out here where there was only the moon and the sea as witness. She shifted in her chair. "I have no intention of marrying anyone. I will have this child and we will be a family. That is more than enough for me."

Zeus didn't think Nina had the slightest idea what *enough* was. And what he wanted to do was pick her up, carry her inside, and prove it. Over and over, the way he had six months ago, ruining them both.

But he didn't.

Because he only played the part of a man unable to control himself.

"You understand that this is Theosia, do you not?" he asked.

"I could hardly forget it while staring at its most overexposed advertisement, could I?" she retorted.

And Zeus's trouble was that he liked that this woman, who should have been the most in awe of him—the most tongue-tied, the most intimidated to find herself once again in his presence—was none of those things. Not then, not now.

She was as unafraid of him as she was unimpressed with him. And what did it say about him that he liked it? That he liked *her*?

"Then you must know that your options are limited here," he told her. Instead of all the other things he could have told her. "I do not require your consent to wed you, Nina. Know this now and spare yourself a fight you will not win."

Nina vibrated in her chair. "Is that a threat?"

He laughed. "Of course it is a threat. What else would it be?"

"But why?" She sounded more desperate than before. "Why do you want this? Because I know you don't want me. And I've already indicated that I intended the baby should know its father, or I wouldn't have come here at all. Why isn't that enough?"

And Zeus had the strangest urge to tell her. Even though he knew better. For what woman would wish to hear that she could be yet another game piece in this endless war with his father? What man would confess it?

He wanted to tell her all the same. And not because he thought she might understand. Since when had he required understanding? But because she was different. She always had been. And he was the only one who had always known that she was beautiful, there beneath the clown show she'd put on. He had seen things in her she'd never shown anyone else.

Maybe Zeus wanted to see if it was at all possible that someone could see such things in him—

But that was his weakness talking.

And he'd chosen his path a long time ago.

He would not lose his way now, no matter the temptation.

"The child, Nina," he told her, with enough severity that he almost believed it was the whole of his reason to marry her. And then, as the words sat there, he understood they were not a lie. Not quite. "That is why.

Whatever else I might be, I am also a Prince of Theosia. No child of mine will be born out of wedlock."

Her mouth moved, but no sound came forth.

And Zeus shook his head as he gazed at her. "I might not care much for my father, but I believe that every child should have one. If at all possible."

She held his gaze for what seemed like an age, then dropped it.

"What did your father do to you?" she asked softly.

"It is what he didn't do." But he would not speak of this. He refused.

Zeus rose then, gazing down at this woman who had already upended his world. He thought that perhaps he should have taken against that, but the truth was, he liked it.

She was not boring, this hen of his, and he would have liked her for that alone.

But there was a child to consider. And to his great astonishment, he hadn't been lying when he'd said those things to her about wedlock and fatherhood. Even if, were he to be scrupulously honest, he hadn't actually known he had such traditional notions knocking around inside him.

Until now.

"We will be married," he said, and though he knew he sounded severe instead of his usual lackadaisical self, he did nothing to temper his voice. "Soon. I suggest you come to terms with it. If you do not, nothing will change, I should not like to see you so needlessly unhappy, Nina."

Her eyes narrowed. "You are all heart," she murmured.

Zeus left her there, out on the balcony with the sea all around, to think over her choices. And because if he didn't walk away from her, he wouldn't, and he couldn't indulge that kind of need. Not when it was nothing so simple as a forgettable pleasure.

It was harder to leave her rooms than it should have been.

Zeus tried to distract himself from the greedy longing storming around in him by imagining what form of rebellion she would take on now. Would she still try to look a mess, as it seemed she had in both previous parts of her life? Would she fashion herself Princess Pigsty?

He thought that sounded entertaining.

But it wasn't her little rebellions that kept him up that night. It was the touch of her hand to his. The press of her belly beneath his palm. The way she'd tried to hide the way she was breathing when he'd toyed with her fingers.

That flame. That need.

The night he told himself he could barely remember, yet had never forgotten.

He was thin-tempered the next morning when his butler let her in again, leading her out to the morning room.

And yet, one look at her and he felt fully restored.

Because Nina had clearly chosen her next rebellion. Sheer perfection.

She stood before him looking nothing short of edible, no sign of the clownish buffoon she'd played in Haught Montagne to be seen.

Her blond hair was woven into a crown of braids

atop her head, showing off her slender neck and wide mouth. And instead of yesterday's tent, she wore something clingy enough that he could see her generous breasts and that marvelous bump, but all the rest of her, too. Her delicate shoulders, her lovely legs.

She was beautiful. She always had been, but today it was on display.

"Did you find a hairbrush in your bathroom suite?" he asked mildly.

Nina glared at him but straightened her shoulders. "I might as well marry you as not, I suppose."

"I'm touched," he said. "Deeply."

He did not rise from the small table where he took his breakfast. The expansive windows let the sun in, and he liked to bask in it while he sipped at an espresso and tracked various items of interest in the financial pages. Only after this ritual did he venture into his actual office, where he spent more and more of his time since his father's decline these last months had forced the reluctant Cronos to shift the bulk of his duties to his son. Zeus had gone to great lengths to make himself seem ineffectual—as if the kingdom ran itself. If anyone outside the palace even knew he had an office, they assumed it was a PR affair kept on hand for no other purpose than to clean up the messes he made.

He had one of those, too. But that wasn't what he did all day.

Another thing he did not intend to share.

Zeus waved Nina into the seat opposite him and then leaned back to give off his usual impression of an indolent little princeling. The one she already thought he was. So she could truly contemplate the step she was taking.

Nina took her time sitting down, and he couldn't tell if her discomfort came from him—or the fact that she'd proven his point by effectively unveiling herself. And he liked his games, it was true. But it was untenable that she should sit with him in *discomfort*.

"The first time I noticed you was at an opera some years ago," he said, though he would have sworn he had no such memory. That she had been there, like wallpaper, until he'd decided to use her as a weapon to effect his escape. Yet it seemed he could remember that night in Vienna with perfect clarity. "You sat just behind me, and I did not hear a note. All I could think was that you smelled of strawberries."

"That's because I was eating them," Nina replied in that bland way of hers. Her lips twitched. "Dipped in chocolate, naturally, or what's the point? Perhaps you were hungry."

He lifted his espresso to his lips and took a sip. "It fascinates me that you will not take a compliment."

"While it fascinates me that you're so determined to give them." She lifted a shoulder. "I don't need to be complimented by you, Zeus. The fact of the matter is that if I were choosing husbands, I would not choose you, either."

"I'm devastated. And you are still trapped. My condolences on the life of hardship that awaits you here."

But she'd settled into her chair, despite his sardonic tone. And was clearly leaning into this topic. "You're selfish. Your behavior is atrocious. That's on a good day. As far as anyone can tell, the main purpose of your existence appears to be racking up as many sexual encounters as you can and flaunting them in the tabloids."

"You say that like it's a bad thing."

Nina sighed. "As far as I'm aware, marriages like these survive because certain understandings are put in place from the start."

She was more correct than she knew, but Zeus did not let himself react. He bit back the automatic response that leaped in him. And waited until he was calm enough to shrug.

With all expected indolence.

"I cannot say I have concerned myself overmuch with the state of marriages, royal or otherwise," he said.

Across from him, Nina shifted in her chair. "I know that Isabeau had every intention of continuing her usual exploits while married to you. She talked about it all the time. All she needed to do was pop out an heir and then, duty done, she could return to doing what she truly enjoyed. The expectation was that you would do the same. And that neither of you would care."

"And am I to expect the same understanding with you?" he asked. "Or are you worried that's what I want?"

He forced himself to sound bored when he was… not. He unclenched his jaw. And his fist. And did not allow himself to contemplate this woman with other lovers. The very idea made everything in him…burn.

Not that Nina noticed.

"Oh, no, you misunderstand," she said airily. "I already know my part."

Everything in Zeus went still. Dangerously still.

Alarmingly still, even. Had he been paying attention to anything but her, he might have heeded those alarms.

"I beg your pardon. Do you have some lover you feel you cannot give up?"

Because if she did, he would rip the man apart. And then the world.

He opted not to ask himself why he, who had always professed he could not begin to understand the notion of jealousy or possession, felt both here. To a disturbing degree.

"It's not about *me*," Nina said, frowning at him. "It's for you. I want you to go out there and do whatever it is you do so that I don't have to worry about it."

There was no answer she could have given that would have stunned him more.

"So you don't…have to *worry* about it?" He could do little more than blink in astonishment.

She nodded enthusiastically. "It's a perfect solution. I'm sure your sexual demands are very… Well. *Demanding.* And I certainly couldn't keep up with all that." Nina waved a hand. "You should go out there and keep spreading it around, the way you always have. You have my blessing."

And that strange temper kicked through him all over again. Laced through with what he could only assume was outrage that this woman who would be his wife was offering him carte blanche to carry on as if he were to remain single.

It felt blistering. Life-altering.

Yet the strangest part was, he knew that what she

was suggesting should have thrilled him. Zeus had never been any particular fan of monogamy. He had often advanced the theory that it didn't truly exist. That it was only fear masquerading as all the pledging of troths and other such horrors.

He should have been delighted with this, and yet he was not.

Not at all.

"This way, everyone's happy," she was saying brightly. *Happily.* "You can do what you do best. And I—"

"What is it, pray, that you do best?" Zeus growled. "I shudder to think."

Nina cast a look his way that suggested he was being strange. "I don't know what I do best. I've never had the opportunity to find out." But she studied him for moment, tilting her head to one side. "I thought you'd be thrilled. You do not look thrilled."

"You're awfully quick to forgo the pleasures of the flesh, Nina."

She laughed, which was somehow the most insulting thing yet. "I think I'll survive."

"Will you?"

And he didn't mean to move. Zeus would have sworn that he'd had no intention of doing anything of the sort.

But then, as if he had no part in it, his hand was reaching out. And then he was leaning across the small table until he could hook his palm around her neck.

And then pull her face to his.

He could taste her startled exhalation. He could see the shock in those warm, pretty brown eyes.

And everything about her was sweet. Soft.

But he kissed her like a drowning man, all the same.

Hot and hard, like he was setting a fire, then throwing gasoline on the blaze.

And it was like the six months that he knew had existed between that night with her and now simply… disappeared. As if they'd been shadows that he'd traveled through and nothing more.

Because this, finally, was vivid.

It was *right*.

It was the opposite of boring.

Without lifting his mouth from hers, Zeus moved from his seat, rounding the small table so he could lift her up and pull her into his arms. And she fit differently, with that beautiful belly between them, but somehow that only made it hotter.

They had made a child, and he could feel the solid weight of the baby between them, and still she kissed him with all of that passion, all of that need, that had haunted him for half a year.

Maybe it had haunted her, too.

He kissed her and he kissed her, deeper and wilder with every stroke, until he got his answer.

Then he kept on kissing her, until he'd almost forgotten that he was marrying her for any reason but this.

This slick perfection. This unnerving sense that he was home at last.

That thought sobered him too quickly. This was about a narrative, that was all, and he needed to be in control of it. He needed to make sure she was seen the way he wanted her seen. The same way he made sure he was seen in only one way outside his office. *Home* had nothing to do with this. Zeus didn't know what the word meant.

He pulled back so he could rest his forehead on hers, letting one hand move down to stroke the belly between them at last.

Because he knew every other part of her. He remembered it all. In extraordinary detail.

Her eyes were closed, and she was breathing heavily. It took her a long time to look at him again, and when she did, she looked dazed.

"That can't happen again," she told him, very distinctly.

But all he could do was stand there, sharing breath with her while his sex shouted at him and every part of him urged him to get closer. To keep going. To do whatever was necessary to have her naked and beneath him, sobbing out her joy as they found each other again—

"Zeus." Her voice cracked a little on his name. "This *can't* happen again. Ever."

"Somehow, little hen," he murmured, reaching up to slide his hand along her pink-tinged cheek and brush his thumb over her lips, "I think that it will."

When she pulled away, he let her. Just as he let her rush from out of the room. But he could taste her on his mouth again. At last. He could feel the press of her body against his, like she'd marked him.

And he found himself smiling long after she'd gone.

CHAPTER FIVE

THAT KISS COMPLICATED EVERYTHING.

It was bad enough that Nina had agreed to marry him. She'd lain awake that first night, staring at the ornate ceiling that arched high above her. She'd listened to the sound of the sea outside. And she'd asked herself what on earth she thought she was doing here.

But came back, always, to her baby.

How could she reasonably refuse to marry her baby's father? She'd argued with herself all night. Because certainly, she had her issues with royals in general. This child would be a crown prince or princess. Nina had never met one of those she didn't have deep suspicions about in one way or another, but that didn't mean there couldn't be a perfectly lovely version.

Was that good enough reason to deny her child its birthright?

The fact of the matter was, she wasn't romantic, despite the odd daydream. Not really. She had congratulated herself on that, lying in that vast bed in her guest bedchamber, running her fingers up and down her sides and over her belly as she tried to get used to sleeping on one side or the other.

I can make decisions based on what's good for you, she told her baby. *Not silly little fairy tales of true love.*

She might have dreamed of romance and other such things when she was with Isabeau, but that was only because the Haught Montagne court had been devoid of any such tender notions. And because she'd been sixteen when she'd first gotten there and might have been foolish enough to think *what if* in those first few months. Before Isabeau had stopped pretending and had showed her true colors. When Nina had let herself imagine that there might be a place she belonged.

Her years at Isabeau's side had cured her of such foolishness. And watching Isabeau's many passionate entanglements—all while she was so determined to marry Zeus—had soured Nina on romance completely. Zeus's own exploits, extensively covered in the press, had suggested to her that love was nothing more than a cynical bid to sell more column space in greedy magazines.

Nina had always told herself that when she was finally set free, she would go out into the world and follow her heart wherever it led without involving the tabloids at all.

But what she'd discovered was that she liked following her heart well enough—but only in terms of the many destinations she could finally explore on her own terms. She'd never had any interest in following her heart to *people*. Not once in her first two months of travel, before she'd started to feel so wretched, had it even occurred to her to try out a *passionate entanglement* of her own. Maybe she should have.

She'd loved what little part she'd taken in the happy

nights in the various hostels where she'd stayed. It had seemed like such a different world, all these heedless young people, dancing and drinking without a care—night after night, as if no one was watching them. Because no one *was* watching them.

But she'd never followed through on any of the invitations, spoken or unspoken, that had come her way.

A romantic would have, surely. A romantic would have wondered *what if.*

That had been what decided her. If she was the kind of woman who intended to hold out for love, that would have been one thing. But she wasn't. She was practical. A realist. Love was for silly girls in skimpy dresses, filled with wonder and maybes. Not grown, weathered women who knew better, who'd already been called a horrid disgrace in at least ten languages. And if she wasn't the sort who was going to hold out for romantic love, she might as well marry the Prince, who had his own, likely nefarious, reasons for marrying her—but what did that matter?

It was about her child in the end.

That was the only love that mattered.

She'd marched off to find him that morning, filled with a sense of purpose and even pleasure that she could secure her child's future like this. Almost as if, finally, she'd relegated her memories of her own cold, hard childhood to the dustbin.

Then Zeus had kissed her and ruined everything.

Because now she was forced to lie in her bed, night after night, and wonder if the reason she hadn't used her travel time to experiment in all the ways everyone else did was not because she was so practical and *above it all.*

She was terribly afraid it had been because of him.

After all, she'd only started on that adventure in the first place because of her night in Prince Zeus's arms. And once the scandal had broken, she had happily left Haught Montagne. Then marched out into the world, telling herself with every step that she barely remembered a thing, because all that really mattered was that she was free of Isabeau at last.

But even if that were true—and it wasn't—his kiss brought it all back.

Because the man tasted like sunshine and the darkest nights, sin and sweet surrender, and she remembered every single thing she'd ever done with him. Every last detail of that long, languorous night. Almost as if his betrayal of her come morning didn't matter.

Now she was more than six months pregnant, trapped in the Palace of the Gods with the only man she'd ever met who could reasonably suggest he might earn that title in the modern world. And Prince Zeus, the wickedest man alive, was insisting she marry him.

Nina couldn't come up with a good enough reason why she shouldn't.

But she'd regretted it the moment she said she would.

Not just because he'd kissed her—and she'd betrayed herself entirely by kissing him back like a desperate woman, a shocking truth she was still struggling to come to terms with—but because the palace staff descended upon her soon after, the inevitable Theosian courtiers in their wake.

And as they began to play their little games around her, it occurred to Nina that she hadn't even thought to have *this* nightmare.

"I can't have a staff and all those horrible aristocratic groupies," she told Zeus one night at another one of the dinners he insisted upon. Tonight he wore a crisp linen affair that would have melted into a tragedy of wrinkles on anyone else in this climate. On Zeus, it did not dare.

It seemed at odds with the man she'd glimpsed in his offices earlier that same day, when she'd been wandering about on one of her art walks, looking… focused and somber as he spoke in low tones with his ministers, none of them the least bit groupie-ish. Almost as if he took his job seriously when no one was watching him.

She didn't know where to put that. Particularly when he showed up looking every inch his rakish, playboy self.

"Some of the aristocratic groupies you disdain are my cousins, Nina," he replied, genially enough. But she was sure she could see behind that mask of his. Maybe more than she should.

"They are a pit of snakes, waiting to strike."

Zeus laughed. "Fair enough. But you cannot hate a snake for merely following its nature."

"I can choose not to put myself in striking distance." He only gazed at her, and she blew out a breath. "The last thing in the world I want is a set of my own courtiers. They're already circling around me, looking for a head to bite off."

"They are no match for you, little hen."

Another ecstatic sunset was stretched out behind him, framing him in deep pinks and oranges. And Nina's pulse was too quick, another betrayal, suggesting as it did that she was *afraid* when she was not. Why should she be afraid? What were a pack of status-hungry aristocrats to her?

But her pulse carried on making her a liar.

"Perhaps it is not the sad reality of palace courtiers that you dislike," Zeus said, almost as if he was addressing the sunset instead of her. "Here they do not creep about the palace at all hours, as in Haught Montagne. They are only allowed in at my discretion. Perhaps what you cannot fathom is facing them without your usual armor."

"I don't know what you mean," Nina threw back at him.

Even as her stomach dropped and her pulse picked up again. Because she did know. One of the reasons she hadn't minded all those terrible articles about her was because…they weren't about her, really. They were about the character she'd played to annoy Isabeau. Or even, in some cases, about the ungainly orphan girl no one had ever wanted. That was also not her, because she'd wanted her own parents, not new ones. After a certain point, she'd taken pleasure in being overlooked.

She'd hidden herself her whole life, but not here.

Here, she dressed as if she considered herself just as pretty as any idle aristocratic courtier whose job it was to look lovely at all times. She did her hair and took care with her appearance for the first time in her life. And yes, she was doing it because Zeus had challenged her. Because he'd suggested she couldn't handle showing herself.

But she hadn't expected how much she would hate the fact that the sort of people she disliked most could see her, too.

"Nina."

She only kept herself from jolting by the barest thread. And that was before he reached over and took her hand, sending that rush of heat and longing shooting through her, lighting her up. Everywhere.

His gaze was intent. "Hiding in the way you have may have amused you, but it also gave them ammunition. Imagine if you denied them even that. It is possible to keep a boundary around what is private, what is yours, without playing at dress-up."

"Is that what you do?" she managed to ask.

And she knew she'd scored a point when that gaze of his shuttered. Behind him, the winter sun dipped below the horizon. Zeus let go of her hand.

Nina had the distinct thought that, perhaps, she was tired of point scoring.

But that felt far too much like an admission of something she refused to accept, so she swept it aside and attended to yet another spectacular feast laid out before her.

"Whatever you think of courtiers, you must choose a staff," Zeus said after a moment or two. In his usual manner, all ease and male grace and that wickedness beneath. "Not for your personal needs, as I am sure you will tell me you can take care of yourself, but because you will be Queen one day. And there will be a great many considerations it is better a staff handles. I think you know this."

Her hand was still branded by his touch. Her body was still reacting to that jolt of its favorite source of heat. And Nina wanted to argue, or maybe succumb to the pressure inside her that felt too much like a sob—but Zeus had that look in those gleaming green eyes of his again. That wicked, knowing light when she was determined that no more kissing would occur.

Because when he kissed her, she couldn't think straight.

Nina couldn't have that. She was a practical, rational, capable woman. She would not allow *kisses* to sidetrack her.

Even if kissing Zeus again was all she thought about some days.

To her eternal shame.

Zeus made himself scarce at certain hours of the day. And now and again she saw him as he apparently tended to the actual business of running his country, which was clearly a secret. Maybe the biggest secret, certainly outside the palace walls, and one she clearly didn't know how to process. Nina decided that instead of processing any of these things about him that didn't fit—or picking courtiers she didn't want or staff she didn't trust—she would dedicate herself to what she did best, instead.

That meant she hid in the palace library and reveled not only in the books but in the fact that no one questioned her right to sit around and read as much as she liked about whatever she liked. Or to sit in a window seat and daydream. No one came to lecture her.

No one demanded she attend them. No one punished her if she wandered off by herself for hours.

Daphne learned quickly to track her down in the stacks, where Nina could always be found sitting with her feet up, a book open in her lap.

If she didn't look too closely at her situation, she almost felt free.

Or at least off on the sort of holiday she'd always longed to take after she finished seeing the world.

But on the first morning of her second week in Theosia, Daphne hurried her through her breakfast, then told her there would be no library time today.

"Library time is the only thing keeping me sane," Nina told her aide—who she had made the head of her staff. They had both stared at each other, then nodded, and that had been that. Painless, really.

"I have faith in your sanity," Daphne replied. "In or out of the palace library."

And then delivered her to the airfield, where liveried servants waited to escort her onto a waiting plane. Zeus was already there, reclining in a leather seat as if it was a throne. Or as if he wanted her to think it was.

"Where are we going?" she asked as she sat down in one of the bucket seats, aiming a smile at the hovering air steward. She declined refreshment, her gaze on the man across from her. And the way he looked at her, all that dark green heat.

"I've spent the week planning how we will reveal ourselves to the world," he said when the steward was gone.

"Reveal ourselves?" Nina didn't like the sound of that at all. "I don't know what you mean. You are over-revealed as it is, surely. There was a swimsuit edition of you only last month."

"I do look fantastic in a swimsuit," he said, as if she'd been lavishing him with praise.

Nina could only roll her eyes. Because he was right. He did.

"Come now," Zeus chided her, his mouth curving. He propped up his head and all that dark blond hair with one hand. "You cannot possibly imagine that you can turn up out of the blue, hugely pregnant with the child of a prince, and reveal nothing about how you came to find yourself in this state. Especially when that prince is me. And then, of course, we have decided to marry. It will need announcing."

"I don't see why."

He only smiled. "You do. You don't want to see why, but you do. It will be reported on either way. Better to attempt to control the narrative."

"Alternatively, we could try just going about our lives," Nina said dryly. "I think the world would catch on, narrative or no narrative."

"You worked for Isabeau for far too long not to know how this works," Zeus said, too much laughter in his gaze. Mocking laughter, she thought. "You know this game as well as I do. Why are you pretending you don't know how to play?"

She tried to ignore the way her pulse rocketed around, because it had nothing to do with anything. It was proximity, that was all. Maybe it was biology. Maybe a pregnant woman couldn't help herself from feeling this way in the presence of her child's father. Maybe the need to want him was in her bones.

But that didn't mean she planned to surrender to it, either.

She tried to think strategically, the way she would if she had a little more distance from the scenario. The scenario being a wicked prince who looked at her as if he wanted nothing more than to taste her. If she were Zeus, what would she do? And why would it require a trip?

And he was right. She did know.

"You're staging some kind of engagement scene," she said after a moment or two. "You want to start them all talking about us again."

She almost said *on your terms*, but she remembered herself. The last time they'd been talked about had been on his terms, too. The only difference this time was that he was telling her what he was doing in advance.

Nina was tempted to feel a bit of outrage about that but couldn't. Because the way his smile broke across his face felt like a reward, and it made everything in her…shift. Then roll.

Then keep right on rolling until it became a molten, hot brand between her legs.

"Very good, little hen," he said.

And God, the way he said that. *Little hen.* It shouldn't be allowed.

Her breasts seemed to press against the fabric of her dress. She had to tell herself, sternly, not to squirm in her seat. It would only make things worse.

"I don't know what makes you think you can call me that," she said, because she was reeling. And because she was desperate for some hint of equilibrium.

"You do know that Isabeau called me that as an insult, don't you?"

"It's different when I say it."

It wasn't as if there was ever a moment in Zeus's presence when his arrogance didn't seem to take over the room. Or the taxiing plane, in this case. But every now and again, it seemed to boil inside of her. "How is it different?"

"Because you like it when I say it, Nina."

And suddenly, it was as if he had gripped her between his hands and was squeezing tight, forcing all the breath from her body.

All she could think about was kissing him. Hurling herself from her seat and finding his mouth with hers. The wild longing seemed to expand within her, crowding out any possibility of anything else, even breath—

You need to stop, she ordered herself. *Now.*

Nina made a little show of rubbing her belly and murmuring to the baby, who was fast asleep inside her. And then wondered if that was the kind of mother she was going to be. The kind who shamelessly used her own child to get out of awkward moments of her own creation.

"Why do you look sad?" Zeus demanded, still lounging there as the plane began to gather steam along the runway. "Surely you cannot be so distraught over the use of a nickname."

"First, I can be distraught about anything I wish," Nina retorted. "Whether you like it or not. But I was thinking about motherhood."

Their gazes seemed to tangle then, and suddenly everything seemed…stark. Stripped down in ways she wasn't sure they had ever been before—not since that night. Not since they stayed awake as the hours grew narrower and told each other things that could only belong in moments like that.

Stolen. Illicit. Never to be repeated.

She had no doubt, as the plane leaped from the earth, that Zeus was remembering the very same thing.

Are you lonely? she had dared to whisper, there in his vast guest rooms in the old Haught Montagne castle. A far cry from where she lived, down in the servants' quarters.

He had held her beside him, pulled fast to his side because they had not let each other go all night, but he did not laugh. The look he gave her was...quizzical.

What would make you ask such a thing of me? I'm forever surrounded by people. I could not be lonely if I tried.

An orphanage is filled with people, she'd replied. *And yet it is the loneliest place on earth.*

He had looked at her for a long time, still not smiling, so she had no choice but to notice how truly beautiful he really was. All those sculpted lines. That heartbreakingly sensual mouth. *Princes do not believe in loneliness*, he had said.

She had traced his cheek, his jaw, with her fingers. She had wanted to remember this, remember him, with everything she was. *I don't think it works that way.*

He had rolled her over to her back, setting himself over her again, and already she had been soft and ready for him. It was as if, after that first impossible kiss, he had made her body his.

And she had loved it.

Yes, he had whispered harshly. His green eyes glittered. *I am always lonely.*

And then he had thrust deep inside her, and she had stopped doing anything so difficult as forming words.

Now, Nina was glad they were on a plane. And that takeoff was a distraction. And that she could fuss around with the new maternity outfit she wore, one of the many items of clothing that had appeared in her bedchamber over the last week. She'd gone and looked for the clothes she'd come with, only to find them missing.

I will be certain to take it up with the palace laundry, my lady, Daphne had said mildly enough. *But who can say when I'll be able to speak to them? You had better wear these things in the meantime.*

Nina hadn't had any doubt whose order it was to dress her differently, but still. She thought she ought to protest. She ought to put up *some* resistance, surely. But the look of pleasure and heat in Zeus's gaze the next time he saw her in something that accentuated her new curves…did something to her.

A bit of acid stomach, perhaps, she told herself tartly as the plane hit cruising altitude and the man across from her was still lounging there as if propped up by indolence instead of his own arm.

And she thought, with great clarity, that discussing the moment they'd had at takeoff might actually kill her.

"What is it you do when you disappear all day?" she asked instead, though she suspected she knew. As impossible as it was to imagine this man doing anything virtuous—or even vaguely responsible. "I would have thought debauching virgins was something you had down to a science, requiring very little time. And more to the point, I did think most of your trysts occurred at night."

He treated her to one of those smiles of his, wolfish and edgy, a perfect match for the heat in his green gaze and the echoing blast of fire deep inside her.

"I don't think you really want to know."

"You don't have to tell me, of course," Nina said with a shrug. "After all, ours will be two very separate lives."

She didn't think she was imagining the way his jaw tightened at that. "I don't know that either one of us has the faintest idea what our lives will be like. But we were speaking of motherhood, were we not?"

"Indeed we were." She felt as if she'd dodged a hard punch there, or maybe caught it, because her breath seemed to come a little quicker. "I don't remember my mother, you see. Not really. I have vague impressions of a kind voice, a hand on my cheek. Though I can't say that those are actual memories. They might just as easily be things I thought I ought to imagine. Some of the kids at the orphanage could remember everything, back to when they were in a cot, staring up at their parents. But not me. You lost your mother, too, did you not?"

He was still lounging, but somehow, he looked more like a predator set to pounce than he did relaxed in any way. "I did. I was eleven."

Nina nodded. "Then you remember more."

Still, he didn't move. "I do."

The prickle of some kind of warning moved over her then, though she couldn't have said what it was. She looked down at her bump instead, smoothing her hands over the soft, stretchy material that somehow managed to both emphasize her pregnancy and make her look more delicate at the same time. It shocked her how much she liked it, when she'd spent so many years concealing anything real about herself—loath as she was to admit it. Not only choosing the most unflattering clothes, but wearing them two sizes too big, or too small, so she always looked misshapen. All for the reward of hearing Isabeau's shriek of fury every time she walked in the room.

I cannot bear the sight of you! the Princess would scream. Which meant Nina could retreat and have an afternoon to herself.

But she hadn't simply gotten used to the subterfuge—she'd liked it. And yes, maybe hid there, too. Because she hadn't changed the way she'd dressed when she'd gone traveling. She'd continued to do nothing with her appearance except make herself look worse.

This was the first time she'd tried to look pretty. And somehow, it felt important that it was with Zeus.

"I hope that I do all right," she said after a moment. "With mothering. I have no examples to look up to."

"You will be an excellent mother," he said, his voice something like rough.

And Nina didn't realize how badly she'd needed to hear those words until he said them. How she'd longed to hear someone say that to her. "I hope so," she whispered. "But it seems such a complicated thing, to raise a child. I was raised by a committee of disinterested matrons. Who knows what harm a single person might do?"

Zeus got an odd look on his beautiful face. As if she had somehow disarmed him.

"My mother was lovely," he said, his voice gruffer than she'd ever heard it before. "Being a small child in a palace is not, perhaps, the laugh riot you might imagine. But she made it fun. Everything was an adventure. We were always playing games, and looking back, that's probably because she was closer in age to me than to my father. The courtiers you hate so much were not kind to her. But that was just as well, as it meant we spent more time together. I would say that in terms of mothering, she taught me that it doesn't matter what you do as long as you make sure to do it with intention. I have lived by that ever since."

And she could tell by the look on his face that he had never said such things to another. She would be surprised if he'd ever said such a thing out loud before. Maybe because she knew he hadn't, she had the strangest urge to go to him. To move across the little space between their seats and put her hands on him. Hold him, somehow. This hard, bronze statue of a man.

But she did not dare.

He might not let her. Or worse, he would—and she would not know how to stop.

"I will do my best," she told him instead, feeling that starkness between them again. As if there was no artifice, no masks. Just the two of them.

She pressed her palms against her belly, as if already

holding their child. The way she hoped she would, with love and wisdom, as long as she lived. And was surprised to discover that she was blinking back tears.

"Before we confront our deficiencies as parents," Zeus said in a low voice, "which in my case will be epic indeed, I am certain, there is the little matter of our wedding."

She didn't want to look at him. It felt too fraught with peril. She blinked a few more times. "I already agreed."

"Your agreement was unnecessary, yet still appreciated." He only smiled, faintly, when she glared at him. "Before our wedding, we must turn our attention to presenting our relationship to the world. Our adoring public, if you will."

Nina sighed. "They will all find out soon enough. I'm sure you'll see to that personally."

Zeus made a tsking sound. "I think you know that's not quite how it works. Scandals are much easier to sort out than brand-new story lines, drip fed into the world to create a new impression of existing characters."

Nina made a low noise and directed her attention out the window, where everything was bright blue and sunny. This high above the clouds, surely no one should have to concern themselves with these concocted displays—the lives the public thought people in Zeus's position ought to be living, not the lives men like him actually lived.

"I hate all this," she said, more to the window than to him. "Constantly having to come up with these stories. Pretending to be whatever *character* it is the papers have decided I ought to play. I can see it now. *Queen Hen, clucking her way across Theosia.*"

And with her not hidden at all, but out here looking like *her.*

She shuddered.

"Nina. Please. No one will call you *hen* but me."

She looked back at him, and as ever, Zeus looked at his ease. She told herself that it was annoying, but somehow, she felt a little bit less…fluttery.

He waved a languid hand. "I only spend time with beautiful women, as you know. Therefore, it follows that the woman I marry must be the most beautiful of all."

"I think you're forgetting something," Nina said. He lifted his magnificent brows. "We already created one scandal. They already think I'm a mercenary gold digger. That was when I simply slept with my mistress's fiancé. What do you suppose they'll call me now?"

"Whatever I ask them to," he said, as if the matter was already settled, the articles already written.

She could feel the dubious look on her face. "Is that how it works? You think you're in control of the tabloid cesspool?"

But Zeus only laughed. "Nina. We're going to tell them a love story. Don't you know? All is always forgiven with love."

CHAPTER SIX

ZEUS DIDN'T KNOW what was worse. Nina's look of outright horror at his use of the word *love*. Or the fact that he'd actually spoken of his mother.

Of his own accord.

He spent the rest of the flight to Paris being outrageous and needlessly provoking to make up for it.

Because he would rather have her looking at him the way she normally did. As if he required extreme forbearance.

It wouldn't change the fact that he wanted his father—and the rest of the world—to think that the most notorious prince in the world was head over heels in love with what was considered his worst scandal yet.

Once in the City of Light, a waiting car swept them off to his favorite hotel, a discreet affair on the Left Bank that suited both his sense of luxury and his need for discretion—but only sometimes.

"I'm surprised that the Theosian crown doesn't have property in Paris," Nina said once he told her where they were staying. When any other woman he knew would simply have sat there quietly, possibly murmured a few superlatives about both him and his choice of lodging, and tried to look appealing. Then again, Nina didn't have to *try*. "Haught Montagne maintains residences in most major cities. I thought everyone did."

"The kingdom has several residences here, in fact." He thrust his legs out before him in the back of the spacious car, slumping down a bit in his seat so he'd look as rumpled as possible. "I do not always wish to have my every move dissected by the palace."

She nodded briskly. "Because they're evil."

Zeus only sighed. "I like an enemy as much as the next person, but there's something you must remember about palace staff." He turned toward her so he could hold her gaze with his. "We are the product, and they are responsible for keeping that product in as pristine condition as they can manage. Yet the product also has all the power. So what are they meant to do?"

Her gaze was steady on his. "You think of yourself as a product?"

And he kept finding himself in moments like these with her. Perilously close to being his real self around this woman when he liked to pretend he couldn't even recall that he'd ever had a real self to begin with.

"I know exactly who I am," he replied.

Possibly with a touch too much heat.

"But—" Nina began, frowning.

"I cannot speak for other palaces, but I know that I give my own nothing but trouble. And yet they manage it all magnificently." He lifted a brow. "I'm surprised that a woman elevated from the orphanage, and with such a chip on her shoulder to match, would not care for the plight of honest, hardworking servants."

She let out a small sound and looked down at her belly. Then rubbed it the way she did when she was avoiding him. He found it more fascinating every time he saw her do it. And adorable.

Because he was impossible to ignore.

"I don't really think it fair that you are utterly shameless yet think you can go about shaming others," Nina said after a moment.

He bit back a smile. "Courtiers, on the other hand. Truly the dregs of humanity. I fully agree."

"You have more courtiers than a picnic has ants."

"They like to froth about me, it's true," he said. He had always liked it that way. He had always liked to go about in a jostling, happy crowd, the more loud and obnoxious the better. Back in his university days, he'd had the company of his best friends, Vincenzo, Rafael, and Jag. He sometimes thought those days in Oxford were a dream, because they had been the easiest of his life. Good friends. The time to hang about in pubs, heedless and young and magnificently rich.

But that was the trouble with a load of princes as best friends. They did, sooner or later, have to head back to their kingdoms to handle the responsibilities.

Even him.

And now he had a great many more people who liked to call him a friend, yet only the same three real ones. He'd replaced quality with quantity, and he could not say his life was richer for it. But it helped him play his part.

For the first time, he found himself wondering if it was worth it.

The question shook him.

"You're an interesting case," Nina said, looking at him as if to study him as they slid down Parisian streets and past iconic cafés. And Zeus shoved aside that odd feeling inside—because he'd made a vow. That made all this worth it, full stop. "You've never met a crowd you didn't like. And yet you wander around your own palace quite alone."

"The palace calls for gods, not courtiers, Nina. It's in the name. I can only obey."

"I'm almost tempted to suggest that everyone's favorite wicked prince has a public *and* private side. Yet you go to great lengths to pretend otherwise." He could feel her gaze on him. "Why?"

He sent a lazy look her way and tried not to think about the picture she presented. Sitting next to him in the back of a car, her long legs visible now and crossed at the ankles. The rest of her was almost dainty, small and narrow-shouldered, with a belly so big it shouldn't have been possible for such a small woman to walk around with it.

And yet she did. Seemingly without complaint.

Already the perfect mother, he thought.

And when the usual surge of something too much like emotion crested in him, he shoved it away again. The way he always did.

It was already bad enough that he'd mentioned his mother and started questioning the vow he had made over her grave. He could not start thinking of himself as a father. Or of his own father. Because everything he'd said about his mother was true. She had been a bright light in every respect. But she had been very young and too silly for Cronos, who had dimmed a little more of her light each day until it was extinguished.

And so, with his endless criticism and neglect, King Cronos had taken the only thing that mattered to his son.

Leaving Zeus to return the favor.

By making sure that the only things that mattered to Cronos—his throne, his pure Theosian blood, and the line of succession that would carry forth his bloodline into the future—would be publicly, repeatedly, comprehensively bruised. If not stained beyond redemption.

The truth was, Zeus had never planned to have an heir. He had gone to great lengths to ensure he could not possibly father one. But now, in his bitter old father's waning days, he would present the dying King with something even better than no heir.

An heir from a bloodline his father would despise, when there was nothing he could do about it.

He could not have planned it better if he'd tried.

When Zeus was out of Nina's presence, he thought the plan was divine. He had not intended to impregnate her, but he was delighted he had. Everything fell into place with this particular woman carrying the heir to the throne of Theosia.

It was only when he was with her and she aimed that secret, tender smile down at her belly, or when she spoke of things like her fears of motherhood, that he wondered what, exactly, he was doing.

But only for a moment.

Because Zeus had lost his soul long ago. When he

was eleven, in fact, and his heart along with it. There was no getting them back now.

He told himself he hardly noticed the void.

His Parisian getaway was the two top stories of the quietly opulent hotel, far away from any other guests or nosy photographers. As soon as they arrived in the expansive suite, he had food brought in, because he knew by now that Nina was always hungry.

And as she sat in the living room and helped herself to the small yet epic tea provided, he welcomed in a smiling, diffident man with a briefcase connected to his body with a chain. Behind him came several more men, similarly attired.

They proceeded to set out their wares on one of the tables, and when they were done, they had set out the finest jewels that Europe had to offer.

"I don't understand what's happening," Nina muttered, but she was looking around with a sort of hunted look on her face.

"I suspect you do." Zeus went to take a seat next to her on the sofa she had chosen. He only smiled when she shot a fairly outraged look his way as his weight tipped her closer to him. He waved his hand at all the open briefcases, sparkling with rows upon rows of priceless, impossibly stunning rings. "Choose one."

Beside him, Nina simply…shut down.

"I wouldn't know where to begin," she said, and she sounded…different, somehow.

As if, unbowed by the entire house of Haught Montagne, and not too impressed with Zeus while she was at it, what had finally brought her to her knees was a private shopping expedition.

The woman was a revelation.

"If I may," said one of the men, looking closely at Nina. "I think I have just the thing."

He turned all the briefcases around and then did the choosing, presenting Nina with a selection of five rings instead of ten times the number. And every time she reacted, he switched the presentation until, at the end, only one remained.

And it was clear that no other ring could possibly have done.

It was lovely. Delicate, though it boasted a large, marquise-cut diamond set horizontally. It looked as if it had been designed for Nina's hand, so it nearly sang. Zeus watched as she looked down at it, an expression he couldn't read on her face.

Yet when the men had left, Nina pulled that beautiful ring off her finger and set it on the table before her with a decisive click.

"I can't wear that," she announced.

"Of course not," Zeus agreed, lazily. "I have yet to present it to you. On bended knee, very likely. It's a classic romantic gesture for a reason."

"No."

It registered on him that she actually seemed distressed, but before he could reach for her, she pushed herself off the couch and onto her feet.

"I can't wear that, Zeus. Look at my hands." And then, disconcertingly, she lifted her hands toward him, as if warding him off. "I spent ten years of my life scrubbing floors."

"No one will ask you to scrub floors while wearing a ten-carat ring, Nina."

"This whole thing is ridiculous," she threw at him. "No one will believe for one second that you're marrying a *servant.* A scandalous former servant. Because why would you?"

"I told you. This is a love story."

Because he needed it to be to really pour salt in his father's wounds.

That was what he kept telling himself.

She looked down at her bump. Then she lifted that same grave gaze to him. "No one will believe that, either," she said quietly. Yet with conviction—and he found he disliked it. Intensely. "I'm sure no one will have any trouble believing that I somehow fell in love with you, in my mercenary way, as gold diggers are wont to do. But anyone who has ever met you knows how impossible it is that you would ever fall in love with anyone."

Everything she said was true. And yet he wanted to argue—against the premise, against the names she called herself, against her description of him. Even though all of that was precisely why she was so perfect.

He opted to shrug instead. "And yet, why else would I marry if not for love?"

Nina only fixed him with that same look, much too grave for his liking. She stroked her belly. "I can't think of a single reason. Can you?"

She looked as if she was about to say something else, but then she squeaked a little. Her hands moved on her belly to press down, and because she was no longer wearing a tent, he could see the way her belly rippled.

When Nina looked at him again, her whole face was changed. Light. Shining.

And it hit him, suddenly, that when she wasn't wearing masks and pretending the way she'd had to do for so many years, this was what she looked like. Those brown eyes so bright they seemed shot through with sunshine. Her lovely face, open and happy. And that smile of hers, so charming that it lit up the whole of their hotel suite and likely outside as well, rendering Paris something other than gloomy this February day.

Rendering him…undone.

"Ouch," she said, but she was laughing. "Apparently our child would like to weigh in on this discussion. I'm almost certain it voted for no ring, no marriage, and no more of this silly game."

Zeus moved without thinking. He rose, moved to her, and then slid his own hands onto her warm belly. And he didn't so much hear the way she caught her breath. He felt it, as if she was inside him.

And he felt his child again.

He *felt*, and instead of shoving the feelings away, he stood in them a moment. He kept his palms against her belly and felt her breath come faster. He let all of that wash around in him until he hardly knew who he was, and then he kept on.

"I don't think you're translating correctly," he said as he felt the little drumbeat kick beneath his hands. "The child clearly wishes his parents to marry. He's adamant."

"*She* thinks that she would be just fine as an independent entity," Nina replied.

She pushed his hands away, but then their hands were tangled up together. That wasn't any better.

Zeus wanted to laugh at himself, because if anyone had ever dared try to tell him that there would come a day that simply *touching hands* with a woman would so nearly destroy him, he would have laughed.

But everything with Nina seemed charged like this. One slip away from total detonation.

Little as he liked to recall it, it had always been like this. From that night in Haught Montagne when he'd pressed into a moment that had bloomed between them, thinking she would frown and dismiss him, but she'd laughed. It had seemed preordained.

This had always been impossible to resist.

If she hadn't disappeared so completely after that night, walking away from a castle with little more than a backpack, by all accounts, Zeus would have found her. He had tried.

He didn't like to admit how hard he'd tried. He didn't like to think of that strange autumn at all, when he'd been…not himself.

But he needed to remember his endgame. That was what he'd told himself then. That was what had to matter now.

He needed to keep his promise. He would.

For a moment he could see his mother's face, tipped back in that marvelous laughter of hers that had become so rare near the end. He had been so small, and she had danced with him, around and around to the music of the sun and the sea. He remembered how she'd swung him up into her arms and kept going, twirling until they were both dizzy.

Then they'd done it again.

And by the time Zeus had grown to a tall eleven, she didn't laugh any longer, and she certainly didn't dance, so it had taken coaxing for her to let him pick her up and spin her around in his arms, trying not to notice how frail she was. How tiny.

How destroyed.

Zeus let go of Nina's hands and stepped back. For a beat, he didn't know what he would do. Maybe run? Shout? He did neither. Though it hurt.

He smiled at the woman he would marry, and soon. To fulfill the destiny he'd made for himself not long after that day in his mother's chamber. Then he went and assumed his typical position on the couch, as if it had taxed him sorely to stand.

And he opted not to notice that Nina looked at him for much too long, her expression gone grave again, as if she could see straight through him.

When he knew no one could.

He'd made certain of that.

"Now," he said, with his usual dark humor, though it stung more today than it should have. It made his ribs feel dented. "Let me tell you how this will go."

CHAPTER SEVEN

NINA LEARNED A lot about Zeus over the following weeks.

When he mounted a campaign, he did not play around. He had made their hotel in Paris their home base, and she quickly realized why. Its little-used front entrance was on a busy street, but its back entrance was gated and equipped with a security officer. That meant that Zeus could decide when and if to play paparazzi games.

First he started telling his stories.

He did not get down on one knee. Instead, he slid the ring on her hand over breakfast their first morning there and told her to get used to wearing it. Then he called in what appeared to be the entire Parisian fashion world, paying Nina absolutely no mind when she protested, and insisted they use the front entrance.

"You must mean the back," she said when he ended the call. The ring was heavy on her hand. It dazzled her, catching her eye with its sparkle every time she breathed. The more she gazed at it, the more impossibly magical it seemed.

Even on a hand like hers.

"The more of a commotion out in front, the better," Zeus said. He offered her that wicked curve of his mouth. "Trust me, little hen."

"Well," Nina said, blinking at the blinding jewel on her finger. "That's very unlikely."

Zeus only laughed, low and hot, so that it rolled around inside her and made her feel shivery. Everywhere.

By the time they came, in a horde, Nina certainly wasn't *ready*. But at least she'd eaten and tried her best to get used to the idea.

Ten slender and severe-looking men and women, almost all in black, took over the suite's small ballroom. They wheeled in racks stuffed with fabrics and garments. They conferred with Zeus, pursing their lips and frowning at her, but then murmured appreciatively when they draped certain fabrics over her.

They did not appear to need *her* input at all.

"I don't need all of this," she complained, in the middle of the melee.

But Zeus only eyed her as if she was something adorable. Yet edible.

"I do," he said.

It wasn't as if Nina hadn't witnessed a fitting like this before. She'd sat through far too many of them, in fact. What she hadn't experienced, however, was a fitting like this in which she was the center of attention.

Gown after gown, fabric after fabric. Her measurements were taken, then retaken, while theatrical arguments in French swirled on all around her.

At one point, standing on a raised platform while

a crowd of fashionistas revolved around her, she thought, *This is how a queen must feel.*

The ring on her hand seemed to buzz a little, as if it knew she'd actually dared to imagine herself in the role.

She sneaked a look at Zeus and found him watching her. He was leaning back against the far wall, another one of his dark suits looking as rumpled on him as ever. His ankles and arms were crossed, giving him the look of a sort of fallen angel.

But his green gaze was as hot as it was dark. And it was focused on her.

Nina flushed. And burned.

And yet she couldn't look away.

Almost as if she wanted him to see what he did to her.

When the fitting was finished, they left her with what seemed like an entire wardrobe that very same day. Yet promised to come back with what one stylish gentleman told her were *the important pieces.*

Nina both wanted and didn't want to know what those might be. Because she still couldn't quite accept that this was happening, maybe. Or because she and Zeus were left alone in a ballroom filled with racks of clothes. With no one else in this suite apart from his unobtrusive security detail.

He was still leaning against that wall. Like a taunt.

And all the things she felt, all the ways she burned, bubbled up inside her like a sob. She wanted to explode. She wanted to launch herself at him. She wanted—

"You must change into one of these new options,"

Zeus told her idly, though his gaze was still hot. Too hot. "You like art, do you not?"

She couldn't tell if she welcomed the shift in conversation or did not. And her cheeks were too pink either way.

"I question anyone who does not like art," she managed to reply.

"Then your task is to change into something appropriate for looking at art in Paris."

Nina lifted her chin. "Define *appropriate*."

He didn't smile, but his green eyes grew warm. He waved his usual languid hand, but this time at the racks of clothing.

But when she took too long, only staring at him like she couldn't quite comprehend anything that was happening—because she couldn't—he went and chose a few pieces himself.

Nina went up to the room he'd given her the night before, but she hardly saw it. She put on the simple dress he'd chosen, then sighed. Because it looked like nothing on the rack, but it fit her like a dream. The fabric was soft yet held enough of a shape that, once again, she could see the difference between her belly and her body.

And she blamed her hormonal state when she got a little teary at that.

She wrapped a bright scarf around her neck, knotting it carelessly, then pulled on the trench that slid over her shoulders like a hug. She looked in the mirror and thought it was all so beautiful that maybe, if she squinted, she was beautiful, too.

Just in case, she went and fixed her hair, too. And swept some mascara over her lashes.

When she came down the suite's winding stair, Zeus was waiting at the bottom. He took her hand and kissed the ring she wore, and she thought she wasn't the only one who felt shivery inside.

Then he led her to the nearest chair and helped her sit.

And she felt her mouth go dry when he knelt before her.

"I'm already wearing the ring," Nina managed to say. And she waved it at him, in case he'd forgotten in the twelve seconds since he'd kissed it.

"And it suits you," Zeus rumbled in reply. "But you will need shoes, I think, to brave the city."

Nina watched, then, as Prince Zeus of Theosia slid a delicate shoe, itself a near-operatic work of art, onto one of her feet. Then did the same with the other.

Like another prince she used to dream about. When she'd still believed in fairy tales.

She cleared her throat and reminded herself that these shoes, however stunning, were not made of glass. "I don't know if I can walk in these."

He pulled her up to stand in them, and she swayed, gripping him tighter.

"See?" she demanded. "It's a tragedy waiting to happen."

"Then lean on me, little hen," Zeus murmured, as she clung to him. "I promise, I will not let you or my child fall."

My child, she marveled. He'd actually said *my child*.

And the moment between them seemed dipped in

gold. He stared at her for what felt like a millennium or two, then lifted her hand and the ring to his lips once more.

"You do understand that no one will believe this is real," Nina whispered, though she felt...fragile and beautiful, both not herself and more fully herself than before. "Since when have you wanted to do anything in private? Yet you supposedly proposed to the servant you knocked up where no one can see?"

"But of course." He lowered her hand and guided it to his arm. "This will only add to your mystery."

And that night, he took her on a private tour of several of Paris's most famous museums. She found that once she decided she could walk in her shoes, she did. And they were more comfortable than the heels she'd had to trot in while chasing Isabeau around. So comfortable she kept forgetting where she was, or who she was with, the better to tumble heedlessly into one masterpiece after another.

"What made you think to do this?" she asked at one point, her eyes almost overflowing with the marvels she'd seen tonight.

"The time you don't spend in the library you spend walking the halls, looking at the art on the walls and in the gallery," Zeus replied. Then smiled when her mouth dropped open. "I know. It is so difficult to imagine I could pay attention to such things, but I assure you, I do."

"Thank you," she managed to say. Awkwardly. But heartfelt all the same.

And he didn't look like himself then. No lazy smile, no laughing gaze. He only looked down at her as if they could have been anyone. Just a man and a woman in front of a painting so famous it had its own merchandise.

Just a man and a woman, a pretty ring, and the baby they'd made.

Deep inside Nina, a voice whispered…*what if?*

But his security detail entered the room, and the breathless moment was gone. And afterward, Zeus took her to a restaurant so exquisite that there was no name on its door, and when he ushered her inside, the maître d' nodded as if they were regulars, then greeted them both by name.

And it was later, much later, when Nina felt drunk on good food and great art. And, if she was being honest, the man beside her.

"I'd like to walk back," she said when the car pulled up before them on the narrow side street. "Either my feet don't hurt or they've gone completely numb."

"Very well," Zeus said and then looked behind her, doing something with his chin to alert his team.

Her hand still felt strange with the ring on it, so she kept curling it into a fist and holding it up. As if, were she not careful, the ring would tip her sideways and take her tumbling down to the ground.

But then he solved the problem by taking that hand in his, and that was…

Nina told herself that she was drunk, even though she hadn't touched a sip of alcohol. She felt that giddy. As if she was graceful enough to turn cartwheels, walking down the street in the dark with a man so beautiful that every passerby who saw him stopped and looked twice.

And there were so many things she wanted to say to him, out here in these old streets. Points she needed to make, and then, while they were out here in the dark and the cold, perhaps a confession or two.

She was saved from all that, in the end.

Because by the time they arrived back at their hotel, a crowd had formed. Almost before she registered that all the people were waiting—and for them—the flash-bulbs began popping.

It was as violent as it always was, and that was before they started shouting.

Her heart slammed against her ribs. She almost tripped over her own feet and was grateful she was holding on to Zeus for dear life as he pushed on through the wall of noise and disorienting bright lights.

It was a fight to make it into the hotel lobby, where it was mercifully hushed—but Nina could still hear all the shouting from outside. Zeus's security detail led them across the lobby until they reached the private elevator that brought them directly up to their rooms at last.

Nina was shaking. She didn't realize until they were inside their rooms with all the doors locked that Zeus was laughing.

Honest to God *laughing.*

"Why do you think it was funny?" she asked him, letting go of him to hold on tight to the nearest wall. She tried to reach down to take off her shoes, but she'd forgotten that her belly was in the way.

And she had to hold herself back from kicking him when he came over and knelt down to remove them.

Just as she had to *not* punch him, hard, on his shoulder when she had the opportunity.

"You are shaking," Zeus said as he rose, his gaze narrow as it scanned her face.

"That was…" She shook her head. "I've been near scrums like that before, obviously. The last time they were shouting my name, I was half-asleep. This time I actually heard all the vile things they were saying about me. Or to me. I don't know how you can find it the least bit entertaining."

And somehow it felt right when he moved his hands to grip her shoulders. Gently enough, but they were still his hands. Holding her.

"Because that was all it took," he said, gazing down at her. "One evening out and here they are."

She could still hear the shouting in her ears. Her eyes were still dazzled by all the cameras. "Why do you want that?"

He looked confused—or whatever *confused* was on a man so convinced that if there was an answer worth giving, he already knew it. "We discussed this."

"We did not discuss it. You ranted on about telling stories and twisting narratives, but I didn't think…" But her voice trailed off.

"What, then, did you think it would entail?" he asked, his voice a gruff thread of sound. She didn't know why it sounded so loud when she'd heard real volume outside. And when she knew he wasn't shouting himself.

But all Nina could do was shake her head. "I don't know."

"Trust me." His hands gripped her a little tighter,

then he let her go. And she remembered, suddenly, that bronze mask in the halls of his palace. He had never resembled it so much as he did now—and there was no trace of laughter on his face. "This is exactly what I wanted."

But that was the thing, she thought later, shut away in her room with the lights of Paris pouring in through the raindrops that coated her window, like the tears she refused to let herself cry. She did trust that all of this was what Zeus wanted. But how was she meant to trust that what he wanted was any good for her or the baby?

I don't believe he asked you to trust that, came a voice from inside her. *He only asked you to trust* him.

Nina curled herself up in a ball and tried to sleep, but when she did, her head was filled with images of Zeus on his knees, playing Cinderella games.

The headlines started pouring in the next morning.

And Nina quickly realized that Zeus did not intend to give any supposedly soul-baring interviews to carefully vetted, sympathetic journalists. That was one way of rehabilitating a reputation, though one rarely used to good effect by royalty. Instead, he made certain that he and Nina were seen out every night, taking in Paris like lovers.

To drive the point home, he doted on her. He held her hand as they walked. He was always leaning close when she spoke. He helped her into cars. He gazed into her eyes over dinner tables, smiled fondly when she spoke, and looked—in every photograph Nina saw of them—like a man besotted.

This strategy, he informed her with glee, allowed

the tabloids and their readership to compare and contrast for themselves the difference between the arranged engagement to his Princess that he had clearly never wanted anything to do with, and the pregnant woman everyone now suggested he'd left Isabeau for. And would convince anyone who looked that the two of them were mad for each other.

He didn't need to announce any engagement, because the papers took care of that with their zoom lenses. The speculation about the ring she wore went on and on, and the more people carried on about it, the more Nina was described as not only the mercenary gold digger of yore, but something of a femme fatale besides. She was called a dangerous beauty, having hidden in plain sight for years before she'd taken her shot. Most agreed this was evidence that she was nothing but an evil whore. Still, others countered, her mix of innocence and beauty and a handy sob story made her the only one in all the world who could turn Prince Zeus's head.

Nina found it was less upsetting to read these stories about herself than she'd anticipated. Because it was still nothing more than a character she was playing to match the character Zeus was playing, wasn't it? It was no different than wearing her odd clothes and haphazard hair in a royal court.

Though every night she went to her bed alone and wondered just how much each one of them was playing.

By the middle of the second week, the stories were already changing. Who was this woman who had claimed the unclaimable Prince? Was she truly the disgrace of Haught Montagne, as advertised, or had the wicked Prince simply fallen in love with the lonely orphan girl? For how else was she able to succeed with Zeus?

She had to admit that the paparazzi were thorough in their research. There was a round of pictures she hadn't known anyone had taken, from a hostel she'd stayed at in Spain. But rather than creating a scandal out of the photographs of her at a party, the pictures made her into a different kind of heroine on the ravenous internet.

"Apparently I'm the introvert's mascot," Nina said from her favorite sofa, where she was enjoying another phenomenal tea. "It makes a change, as mascoting goes."

Zeus came over from whatever he was doing on his tablet and plucked the paper from her grasp, peering at the grainy pictures. "You look like a librarian shushing the obstreperous children."

"That's more or less what I was doing, if memory serves." Nina shrugged. "Apparently I'm relatable."

"So my team tells me daily." He handed back the paper, his gaze as warm on hers as if they were out in public where photographers were always lurking. But they were in private. "You're making quite a splash. And not a hen in sight."

But the real test, Nina knew, was the upcoming ball.

At the end of their third week in Paris, they left France and headed to the tiny kingdom of Graciela, tucked away between France and Spain, where the country's newly crowned Queen was having a birthday ball. The expectation was that the guest list would be a who's who of European royalty.

"You look nervous," Zeus said with that lazy drawl that made it clear he was not.

Outside, Graciela was shrouded in clouds as Zeus's pilot circled the small airport, waiting for their turn to land.

"Not at all." Nina tried out a laugh that came out tinny. "Who doesn't love a bit of a swim, surrounded by so many sharks?"

"The trick is to pretend the sharks are minnows," Zeus told her, that green gaze of his a simmering fire even as he gave her that half smile. "And treat them like minnows. Most find it so confusing they spend the rest of the evening trailing about after you, begging for more."

"Sometimes," she said softly, "your cynicism about the human race is heartbreaking."

It was Zeus, so all he did was shrug. No matter how many times she thought she saw something else in those green eyes of his. She told herself it was the hormones They were making her see things that weren't there. And would never be there.

She had to stop looking at pictures of them in the tabloids and imagining what she saw was real, because she knew better.

Nina had to keep reminding herself that she knew better.

There was no what-if here.

"Whatever you do," Zeus told her, something darker in his gaze, "never show the sharks your heart, Nina."

She hoped she wasn't that hormonal.

Nina braced herself once they'd landed and were whisked to the royal castle, but she was surprised to find that the stuffy manners that she'd always found so tedious—mostly because it had been her job to use them in the wake of Isabeau, who did as she liked—were an excellent stand-in for the sorts of masks she used to wear. At first she wondered why it was that royal personages she'd met many times before were suddenly capable of being kind to her as they all lined up to be introduced into the ball.

"What a pleasure to meet you," said a queen here, a sheikh there, and excellencies everywhere. "Many congratulations on your most happy news."

Then she realized, it had nothing to do with her. It was all about Zeus.

Because he might be one of the biggest walking scandals in Europe, but he was still the Crown Prince of Theosia. And everybody knew that King Cronos was not doing well.

"They're already lining up to kiss your ring," Nina murmured as she and Zeus waited for their turn to be announced. Graciela's castle was, like all castles, all about its ramparts and keeps. The ball, thankfully, was being held in the new annex—which meant a grand covered gallery festooned with heat lamps and circulating attendants.

She wanted to laugh, maybe a little hysterically, at the fact that even the rulers and figureheads of Europe had to line up like so many partygoers outside a club.

"A kingdom is a kingdom, after all," Zeus told her, leaning down the way he did now. His mouth so close to her ear that goose bumps prickled down her neck. Or maybe that was because he had curled his hand over her nape. "Theosia might be small and unthreatening, and unlikely to wage war in the traditional sense, but there are always economic pressures that can be brought to bear."

"It's like you're a king already," Nina said with a sigh. She lifted a hand to rub at her neck, as if that could make the shivery sensation dissipate. It didn't. "Already plotting out your wars."

"You have not been paying attention." Zeus gazed down at her, unusually grave. "I've been at war my whole life."

She caught her breath, and her heart pounded—

But then they were being announced.

And she understood why he'd waited for this moment as they stood there at the top of a long stair. Because he had to do nothing but stand there, looking resplendent as ever in his formal attire. He looked even more impossibly beautiful than usual. And he had Nina on his arm, dressed in a gown so outrageous it had taken staff to help her into it.

This was the point all along, she understood as their names were called out and they started down toward the waiting crowd.

This was Zeus's engagement announcement. He'd planned it this way.

But when they reached the floor of the ballroom, he looked down at her and smiled as he took her by the hand.

And Nina…forgot. That all of this was planned. Plotted out ruthlessly by Zeus and his public relations people to create a story. This story. Just as he'd said.

She knew better than to believe any of it.

She knew better, but he tugged her straight out onto the dance floor, then pulled her into his arms. She knew better, but he gazed down at her…and suddenly it didn't matter what kingdom they were in, what ballroom. Who might be watching, or what the papers might say tomorrow.

There was only the way he held her, smiling down at her as he made the belly between them part of the dance instead of an impediment to it.

And Nina wanted fairy tales, the kind she'd dreamed of when she was a little girl.

She wanted all of them, she realized then, as she danced with her very own prince. She *wanted*, when she thought she'd gotten rid of that sort of thing long ago.

Because a girl who wanted in an orphanage was only destined for despair. And a girl who wanted anything at all in service to Isabeau would find nothing but pettiness and backstabbing.

Just like the girl who was foolish enough to have feelings for Prince Zeus was proving herself no kind of shark at all, but a minnow, through and through.

Nina knew all of that, and oh, did she know better. And still, as the music swelled and they danced around and around, she let herself pretend that this was real. That none of this was for show. That the way he looked at her meant what it should.

Tomorrow could do its worst. She had no doubt it would.

What if? she asked herself.

And tonight, she let herself believe.

CHAPTER EIGHT

NINA WAS SITTING at one of the tables set up in semiprivate alcoves dotted around the main ballroom. This part of Graciela Castle was clearly a more recent addition—meaning the last century or two—because each alcove was carefully situated with views out over the tiny kingdom's sweeping valley, covered in snow and dotted with light.

And to make the fairy-tale evening even better, she was waiting for Zeus to return with food. Because, apparently, in the role of Prince Charming that he was playing tonight, he not only danced with her… he fetched things for her.

It was all part of the fantasy she was letting herself believe tonight.

Nina took a deep, steadying breath and wondered if this was what it felt like to truly be happy. No expectations, no regrets. Just that look on Zeus's face and the fire that seemed to burn brighter between them by the hour.

She had no experience with happiness. The closest she'd come was out there on her brief travels—

though even then, she'd still been so aware of what she'd run from.

Tonight she was only aware of Zeus.

And the way she felt when she was with him, the focus of all that bright green intensity.

Nina shivered a little, then laughed at herself. She patted her belly. *I think your father might be a good man*, she confided silently to her child. *When pressed. You'll see.*

The music was glorious, a full orchestra playing music to beat back the winter dark. And Nina almost felt as if she was a queen already, sitting here in sweet solitude as she waited for Zeus's return.

When she looked up and saw Isabeau descending upon her, her usual entourage fanned out behind her, her first thought was that she'd fallen asleep at her table and this was a dream. A dream she'd had more times than she could count. All of those haughty and imperious faces, some already alight with malice. If Nina had been with them, she would have been shuffling along at the rear of the pack, far enough back that she could avoid the poisonous looks they liked to throw her way.

Because they had gained their position with Isabeau through the usual channels—that being by the lucky accident of having noble blood that stretched back through the ages in Haught Montagne, as was proper. Nina had wondered many times if her presence was an insult to these other ladies-in-waiting even more than to the Princess.

The way they were all glaring daggers at her now, she had to assume the insult was universal.

Princess Isabeau came to a stop before Nina in a dramatic manner that she knew very well made her skirt swirl about her while showing her legs to best advantage. She practiced it. And it occurred to Nina that it felt a lot like power to know the things she knew about this woman and no longer have to hold her tongue.

Not that she had to descend to Isabeau's level. But she *could.*

"I can't believe you dare to show your face," the Princess said in her usual cutting tone. "Especially in your revolting state."

Nina understood that she was to take from that the clear message that her face was unpleasant, shown or unshown. Because Isabeau was a classically beautiful, tiny little brunette with a heart-shaped face and perfect bone structure, and she loved to make sure others knew how ugly they were in comparison. She particularly liked to let Nina know this.

It only occurred to her now that Isabeau would not have spent so much effort slapping Nina down about her looks—or her offensive lack thereof—if she hadn't felt threatened in some way. And why would she feel threatened? Only if Nina actually looked the way Zeus made her feel.

The revelation made her smile, far too brightly.

But "Pregnancy is quite natural" was all she said in return. "Some find it very beautiful."

And what a joy it was to say whatever she liked without having to second-guess her words or her tone or the expression on her face. She was no longer Isabeau's little pet. Her pocket orphan that she could pull out whenever someone accused her of being exactly who she was as evidence that once upon a time, she'd had a benevolent impulse.

Nina couldn't seem to tamp down her smile, and Isabeau…actually looked uncertain for once. She brushed back a tendril of her lovely hair, her blue eyes narrowing.

Always a warning sign.

"Who do you think is buying this act? If Prince Zeus was capable of impregnating anyone, he would have had a parade of bastards by now." Isabeau sniffed, then looked crafty. Another red flag. But tonight Nina couldn't seem to work up the necessary concern. "The people of Theosia will rise up in revolt against a grubby commoner trying to pass off her baby as heir to their kingdom."

Nina had not seen that one coming. Maybe she should have. She laughed and took her time standing up from the table, propping one hand on the belly before her, big enough that Isabeau looked askance at it. "I assure you, Isabeau. There is absolutely no doubt about the paternity of this child."

And she wasn't sure she meant to, but she said that in such a steady, distinct way that there could be no doubt that she was announcing—in no uncertain terms—not only her relationship with Zeus but exactly how their baby had been made.

All right. Maybe she did mean to.

It felt…liberating.

Isabeau looked as shocked as if Nina had hauled off and slapped her. "You're nothing," she hissed. "You'll never be anything but a charity case. Don't you know that by now, Dumpy?"

Nina sighed. Not because the nickname hurt. It didn't. It never had. But it was only now that she'd stopped hiding herself that she realized how silly it was that she ever had. And how pathetic Isabeau was to issue taunts like they were on a playground.

That wasn't entirely true. She'd known it all along.

"We could have been friends," she said quietly. "Companionable, at the very least. Instead, you took every opportunity to prove how petty you are. I feel sorry for you."

Isabeau reared back. "*You* feel sorry for *me*? I am a *princess*. My father is a *king*."

"And so will my husband be," Nina replied coolly. "Making me a queen, yes? You will have to forgive me. I don't eat and sleep your hierarchies, but I believe I'll shortly outrank you."

Amazingly, the little coterie behind Isabeau actually…tittered.

Nina could feel everything change in that moment. Not because the courtiers had turned, the way courtiers always did. But because, at last, she truly felt free.

All this time, all the effort she'd spent, whether hiding from Isabeau or, periodically, attempting to placate her—all that was over now. And whatever happened next, she finally understood something she should have realized all along.

Her child would never find itself the plaything of a creature like this. Her child would never be lost. Her child would always know who and what it was.

A prince or princess of Theosia. One day its King or Queen.

Nina had gotten lost after her parents died. But that would never happen again. Not to her and certainly not to her baby.

And once she understood that, how could anything else matter?

"I'm done with you," she said to Isabeau, then swept past her, thinking that she would head across the ballroom to search for food herself.

But she was brought up short to find Zeus standing there just outside the alcove with an expression she couldn't read on his face. Clearly having witnessed the entire interaction.

"Look at you," he said admiringly. He didn't say *little hen*, but it felt as if he had. "It appears you've found your claws."

Then he was looking past her and shifting where he stood, obliquely blocking her from Isabeau. Making his sentiments known.

Again.

"You're supposed to be with me!" Isabeau hissed at him. She stamped her foot. "Our fathers decided it. You can't possibly think you belong with that—that—"

"Princess," Zeus said, in the kind of quiet voice that made a wise person's hair stand on end, "I would advise you not to finish that sentence." He drew Nina closer, and if possible, looked even more like a bronze statue than ever before. When he spoke, his voice carried. "Nina is to be my wife. And, in due course, the Queen of Theosia. She belongs with me. Always."

And as declarations went, it was something. It was even more than *something* coming from him. Nina knew full well that some part of that statement would be on every tabloid around come morning. Maybe that was part of his plan. But she didn't care.

She belongs with me. Always.

Her whole life, Nina had wanted to *belong.* Of all the precious gifts this man had given her, this was the one that made her heart ache.

She didn't care if it was true. She cared that he'd said it.

Nina forgot all about Isabeau. She had the vague impression that her entourage herded her away, but she didn't bother to confirm it. She looked up at Zeus, and suddenly it was as if her belief in fairy tales had spilled over into…everything.

As if maybe it was all real. Complete with a vanquished villainess.

Because she felt powerful and beautiful. Their baby was safe and protected and always would be. And she had Zeus, looking at her as if she was magic.

She belongs with me.

"Remember when I told you not to kiss me?" she asked.

He looked devilish and amused at once. "I remember you spouting such nonsense, yes. I did us both a favor and ignored it."

"You haven't kissed me since."

"But if I'd wanted to, I would have," he said, all lazy drawl and a simmering heat in his beautiful eyes. "That's the key point."

"Zeus," she said. He looked down at her, lifting one marvelous brow. "Stop talking."

And then Cinderella lifted herself up on her tiptoes, leaned forward, and kissed Prince Charming herself.

Because it was *her* fairy tale.

He kissed her back with all the same heat. And then he pulled her with him, laughing, back to the dance floor.

"We cannot leave yet, my wild little hen," he told her. Sternly. "So we must dance."

But the moment they could leave without offending their hosts, he hurried her out of the ballroom and followed his waiting aide to the rooms set aside for them in Graciela's ancient castle.

"What is it?" he asked as they walked in, when Nina laughed. He shut the heavy door behind them and leaned against it.

Nina looked around. Stone walls, tapestries, and an old standing suit of armor in one corner. A fire crackling in an old fireplace. A weathered yet polished wardrobe. And thick, soft carpets thrown all over to mask the chill of all the stone.

"It's just…castles," she said, because it was somehow perfect that they were here, tonight. Making fairy tales real. "They are always the same."

She walked farther into the room, making her way over to the canopied bed that stood against one stout stone wall and running her fingers over the embroidered coverlet.

"Second thoughts?" Zeus asked, his voice a dark temptation, and she remembered that. He had asked that same question on their first night together, but then he had been poised above her.

The hardest part of him notched between her legs, the pleasure already unbearable—she remembered every moment.

She looked over her shoulder at him and smiled. "Not a one," she whispered.

And then she watched him come toward her, dark blond like one of the gods his people sometimes claimed his family had descended from. Green eyes that were darkly intent now and laced with that fire that was only and ever theirs.

He came toward her, then turned her in his arms, and Nina thought that surely now she would feel unwieldy again. Swollen and awkward.

But Zeus held her in his arms, he bent her back, and he kissed her.

Ravenously.

And Nina felt as light as air, as graceful as a dancer.

She met his kiss, all the fire within her bursting into spirals of flame that licked through her body, making her fight to get closer. To feel *more*. To glut herself on this man all over again.

He kissed her, and she kissed him, and it was different now. Better.

Laced through with a kind of reverence, as if neither one of them could believe that they were here again. In a castle, near a bed, just like last time. Nearly seven months gone by now, and it felt like yesterday.

"I looked for you," Zeus said against her lips. "You hid well, little hen."

"I wasn't hiding."

But then she was laughing as he lifted her up as if she weighed no more than a feather and sat her down on the edge of the high bed. His hands were busy beneath her long skirts, and she sighed as he ran his palms up her legs, over her thighs. And sighed again when he only brushed, gently, the place where she needed him most. Then moved on.

She remembered this, too. That Zeus liked to tease.

"Were you not?" he murmured, trailing his fingers up the sides of her dress. "You were hard to find, then, for a person who was not hiding."

But he seemed distracted. He spent extra time on her belly, then found her breasts. Once again, only a glancing caress before he eased her back so he could attend to the complicated fastening of her gown down one side.

"I suppose I was running," she said, because this room felt like a confessional. This night felt like a brand-new start. "But I didn't know where I was going."

His hands stilled. "You only knew you wished to get away."

Nina smiled again. She couldn't stop smiling, really. She lifted a hand and slid it over his hard jaw, strong and solid. And, tonight, with that faint rasp against her palm that made all the fires he set within her kick a little higher. Burn a little hotter.

"Not from you," she said softly. "It never occurred to me that you would come looking. It was my one night with the wickedest, most notorious prince alive." She felt his lips curve as he turned his head so his mouth was against her palm. “That is the Prince Zeus promise, as far as I’m aware. One night. Never more.”

“That is a very strict rule indeed.” He pulled her dress away from her body and then left it open on either side of her, so she felt as if she was being presented to him on a platter of fine Parisian fabric. He moved so he was standing, positioned between her outspread legs. His gaze was a dark blaze as he looked at her, lying before him so wantonly with little more than a scrap of silk between her legs. “But it is for dastardly courtiers. Horrid princesses. Vapid celebrities of all stripes. Little hens are exempt.”

Nina didn’t feel like a hen, she felt like his, and perhaps that was the same thing.

She pushed herself up on her elbows, watching him greedily as he slowly, deliberately, set about ridding himself of his own clothes. Slowly, with that half smile on his face, he stripped himself down and tossed his discarded garments toward the cases his servants had set up. Then he was standing before her, naked.

Far more beautiful out of his clothes than in them.

Zeus came down beside her on the bed. She could feel his sculpted chest against her as she turned toward him, and once again, his mouth found hers.

And for a while there was only that slick heat, that mad spin. As potent as the first kiss. As irresistible as the last.

But he pulled away and directed his attention lower. He concentrated on her breasts first, gazing at them in wonder.

“You astound me,” he whispered in a rough voice, his green eyes nearly black with desire.

Then he used his mouth and his tongue, even the scrape of his teeth. His big, hard hands. Every trick at his disposal to coax her into wave after wave of impossible sensation. It raced from his mouth straight down between her legs and had her moaning.

Nina hadn't known how much more sensitive she was now.

But Zeus did.

And he took his time, showing her all the ways her body had changed.

She began to move her hips, pressing herself against his hard thigh, there between her legs.

And he laughed, the way she remembered him laughing before. That sound of dark, endless delight.

It made her burn all the more.

Outside, the snow came down, but in this room the fire that crackled in the grate was no match for the heat between them. Nina couldn't think what could be.

Zeus worked his way down her body, so slowly she wanted to cry. Maybe she did. And finally he found her belly and laid kisses behind him, everywhere he touched.

Something in her seemed to glow almost bright enough to hurt. That there could be all this heat, all this mad, greedy desire, and yet in the middle of it, a tenderness. Affection. She was making love to a father, not just a man.

This was no fairy tale she'd ever heard of. This was hers, and it was theirs.

And it was real.

But then he wiped all those thoughts away when

he moved even lower, crawling off the side of the bed so he could pull her hips to his face.

His mouth closed over the mound of her softness, and she jolted, even though he had yet to remove her panties.

This was only a test. A temptation. And it still punched through her, a lightning bolt of pure sensation.

Nina made a sound that was neither a sob nor a scream, but somehow both. She lifted up her hips, begging him mutely.

Zeus laughed again.

Then he tugged her panties from her hips, peeling them off her with exquisite slowness. Down one leg, then the next, taking his time.

Only then did he move back into position. He gripped her hips with his strong hands, tilting her toward him. And then licked his way into the very center of her heat.

And this was not the waves of sensation from before. This was a thunderstorm. A whole hard crash.

Nina shattered at the first lick and then never quite came down again.

Zeus, naturally, settled in. He took his time.

And wanting him was nothing new, but Nina knew she had not been this sensitive before. That every time he breathed, her body reacted like this. With a greedy, encompassing joy that she couldn't have contained if she'd tried.

It felt like a gift.

She was limp and sobbing when he finally rose up. He looked down at her like that bronze mask, passion making his features almost stern. If it weren't for that glittering heat in his green eyes, she might have found him frightening.

But she could see how much he wanted her. Looking at the hard jut of his sex made her flush hot all over again.

Zeus pulled her legs around his waist, then angled himself down onto the bed. He propped himself up on one arm and gazed down at her. His chest was moving like hers, like breathing was hard. His gaze was possessive. Commanding.

And all she wanted to do was melt against him, then ask for more.

He gripped his sex with his free hand and guided himself to her entrance. Then he stroked her there, with that hardest part of him that felt to her like bronze.

For a moment their eyes met, and the blaze of intensity there almost sent her over the edge again.

Almost—but then he thrust inside, filling her completely at last.

At last.

Nina could no longer tell if she was at the edge or over it, so intense were the sensations, so wild was this fire.

She gripped his arms as he moved over her, setting a slow, deliriously intense pace.

A rhythm she could feel everywhere, inside and out.

And the dance had been a fairy tale, but this was something better. She didn't think it was hormones any longer, not when her chest ached the way it did and every stroke seemed to open her up more inside. Her heart. Her poor heart.

But it was worth breaking if she could have this.

He dropped his head to pull one nipple into his mouth, hard enough that the electric jolt of it seemed to travel straight down her body into the place where they were joined. And once again, she was sent hurtling.

Hurtling and hurtling, and she heard him shout out her name as he followed.

He flooded her, and she cried out as she shook and shook.

It wasn't until she'd recovered herself some little bit that she realized what she'd said. The secret she'd been carrying all along.

"I love you," she had told him, again and again. "I love you, Zeus."

And she was terribly afraid she'd ruined everything.

CHAPTER NINE

HER WORDS ECHOED inside of him like doom.

Or grace, whispered a voice within.

Zeus had almost forgotten himself, and that never happened. But the taste of her had exploded through him. She had rocked him. He had found no defenses when usually he was the king of them.

The kiss in the ballroom had nearly undone him. He, who had spent his life chasing every sensation available, had nearly been brought to his knees by this woman. In the middle of a ballroom, with the eyes of the world upon them.

And he wasn't sure he would have cared.

Zeus had never cared about making a scene. On the contrary, he went out of his way to cause as many as possible. But he could not bear the idea of further exposing Nina to the same censure.

He'd already done that.

And he, who regretted nothing, had regretted the scene he'd set up in Haught Montagne ever since.

But he shoved those things aside. The rest of the evening had passed in a blur, of faces and names he knew he ought to know, because she'd kissed him.

Nina had dismissed the Princess who had caused her so much trouble with a wave of her hand. Then she'd looked around, every inch the perfect queen, and smiled when she'd seen him.

Then Nina had kissed him.

Entirely of her own volition.

With all that melting, glorious heat.

There could be no concerns that he had seduced her this time. There were no worries that he was exerting pressure on her in any way. Zeus would have sworn to anyone who asked that such things did not concern him—so confident was he of his appeal—but Nina was different.

She had been different that night, and he hadn't been prepared for it.

And now she was the mother of his unborn child. She wore his ring. And she had kissed him like she was the one who'd chosen him from the first.

It was as if that kiss had woken up a part of him he had come to believe no longer existed. Or had never existed. She had chosen him, and she made him believe that he might have a soul after all.

And, more unimaginable still, a heart.

He had felt it pound in him, like it was pounding out her name.

Then they had come to this room of stone and fire, high up in yet another castle filled with so many of the same people doing the same tedious things, and once again, she had humbled him.

She had done it that first night. She did it with ease. She made him new, scrubbed him raw, and he didn't like it. He told himself he *couldn't* like it.

He didn't know what to do with it.

So Zeus had done the only thing he could. He had closed the distance between them, the hunger in him a wild and uncontrollable roar, and he had taken her in his arms at last.

Here, where there were no witnesses. No paparazzi and none on call. There was no press release, no story. No narrative to tinker with.

There was just this beautiful woman who was only his, who had danced with him tonight as if he was a dream come true.

He wanted to be that for her in every possible way.

And then, finally, he'd placed her on the bed and taken her the way he'd begun to imagine he never would again.

It had felt sacred.

Like a vow.

Like a simple, honest truth, stark and irrevocable.

And when she cried out those words she should have known were forbidden, Zeus couldn't bring himself to react the way he knew he should. Instead, he moved them both up in the bed, then pulled the coverlet over them so they could lie there, together.

Because he needed to gaze at her as if he expected, at any moment, that she would be taken from him again. And that, once again, it would be his fault.

"We never talk about that night," he managed to say. His eyes were so greedy on hers, he felt so torn, that he was surprised she could stand to hold his gaze at all. But she did.

"What is there to talk about?" He thought that was a slap, a dismissal. Instead, Nina rolled closer to him and piled her hands beneath her face so she could smile at him. It felt like a miracle. *Maybe she is the miracle*, something in him whispered. "We both know what it was between us. How intense it was. What it meant. Yet it was always going to end the way it did. Because you'd already called them."

The last time she'd mentioned this, he'd deflected. *Were you truly under the impression that I was or am a good man?* And maybe he would never be a good man. Not by any reasonable measure.

But for Nina, he would try.

"I did," he said. Simply enough.

And of all the things he'd done in his life. All the sins, all the scandals. They seemed like nothing to him. It was this admission that cost him the most.

But her smile didn't waver. *I love you*, she'd said. And unlike the many who had mouthed those words before, she knew him. She'd seen him do more than flatter and cajole a night away.

She'd chosen him, not his reputation.

"Zeus," Nina said quietly, her brown eyes soft. "I understand."

Then she leaned toward him, kissing him again. And it was as if she'd flung open the windows and let the noonday sun inside. He felt that light all over him. He felt bathed in sunshine.

He knew that if he bothered to look, it would still be dark outside. A cold winter's night, with snow coming down as if it might never stop, up here in the mountains.

And Zeus had spent his entire life, it seemed, finding new ways to be worse. To be even more terrible than reported. To live down to every low expectation his father had ever set him.

He'd come to think that the reason it came so easily to him was because that was who he was. That all along, he hadn't been acting at all.

But the way Nina looked at him, as if he was the miracle here, made him feel something he had long been certain he would never feel again.

Hope.

"You shouldn't understand," he told her fiercely, his hand going to her so he could grip her, to make sure she was real. "You should hate me. Why don't you hate me?"

"I've tried," she admitted, with that smile of hers. "Believe me, I did try. But it turns out, I don't know how."

What could Zeus do but kiss her again then, with all those things he thought he'd lost. His soul. His heart. Himself.

And he knew that morning would come. As morning always did. He knew that his endgame marched closer every day, regardless of what work he put into selling the world love stories. It would all come full circle soon. He was ready.

But here, now, far away in this castle room where no one could see who they truly were with each other, he let himself be the one thing he'd never been. In all his years of pretending to be this or that. Or everything.

Here with Nina, his Nina, he let himself be nothing more or less than a man.

Not just any man, but the one she loved.

Again and again.

There was a faint hint of light in the sky outside when Zeus woke again to find Nina curled up next to him. The sight caught at him, hard enough to leave marks. This woman who gave all of herself to him, when she, more than any other, should never have let him near her again. That big, round belly where his child grew, safe and warm. He kissed them both. Nina on her cheek, so she smiled a little while she slept. And his baby, too.

His baby. Zeus hadn't let himself truly take in what that meant. That in only a couple of months, he would be able to hold a child of his own in his arms.

He would be able to do it differently. To do it better.

Take what had been done to him, but turn it inside out.

The heart he'd just rediscovered seemed to crack open inside of his chest. He tried to imagine Nina in the role of his mother. Or himself a king like Cronos. He tried to imagine letting all of that weight land on the tiny life inside Nina's belly, and he couldn't. It was too much. He wanted to rage. He wanted to punch the stone walls surrounding him.

He wanted to go back and change everything. Save his mother. Save himself.

And somehow find a way to keep his father from walking the path that had led them here.

Maybe what he couldn't accept—what he'd never been able to accept—was that, given the chance, he'd save his father, too.

He didn't want to feel these things. He didn't want to *feel*. He had always chosen to see himself as a finely honed weapon of a particular vengeance. Nothing less, nothing more. As he had vowed over his mother's grave he would become, so he had done.

Yes, yes, such a weapon, his friend Vin, more commonly known these days as His Royal Majesty, the King of Arista, had said with an eye roll when they'd all gotten together for a drink in Paris.

Perhaps the weapon has grown a bit blunt now that you're impregnating women and parading them about Paris with statement jewelry, Prince Jahangir Hassan Umar Al Hayat had murmured, lounging in the chair opposite in the private club. Jag had grinned. *I recall a time when all you could do was extol the virtues of prophylactics.*

Rafael Navarro, bastard child of the former King of Santa Castelia and long its regent, had laughed. Vin had joined him. Zeus, who knew exactly why they were laughing, forced himself to smile when he would really rather…not.

There are a great many virtues in impregnating the wrong woman and making her a wife, Rafael had said. As he would, having recently scandalized the whole world by kidnapping his own woman from her wedding to another man. Another man who had happened to be Rafael's half brother. *I recommend it.*

I second this recommendation, Vin had said, sounding revoltingly happy.

I have no intention of settling like the two of you, Jag had said, shaking his head at them. *I prefer the time-honored practice of not making my lovers accidentally pregnant.*

His friends and he often cleared their schedules and

made drinks happen in various cities, all these years after Oxford. Zeus had been surprised at how little he had wished to leave Nina in their hotel for even so short a time. He, who had never turned down the opportunity for a social event in all his days. Particularly not when it was with these men. His closest friends.

His only friends.

But he had only shrugged languidly, as if he was still the same *him* he had ever been. *I believe you are all mistaking the matter. I salute your fecundity, truly. Yet I assure you—my situation is not emotional, however accidental. It fits in nicely with my plan or I would not have moved forward with a wedding. Have you met me? Do I seem the marrying kind?*

And he had pretended not to notice how Vin and Rafael had looked at each other then.

He couldn't seem to get that look out of his head now.

Because the way his friends had gazed at each other had seemed ripe with a kind of emotion Zeus would have sworn neither of them could feel.

Yet maybe what he'd been worried about after all was what *he* felt.

What he had always felt.

Zeus kept circling back to the fact that whatever the shape of the weapon he'd made himself into, that hadn't been what he'd wanted. It had never been what he'd wanted.

He'd gone to great lengths to deny it, but at heart, he'd wanted what any child did. His mother. His father. His family.

And it only occurred to him now—here in this

room with a woman who had knocked him off balance from the start—that maybe it wasn't the vow that he'd made at his mother's grave that had motivated him all this time. Not entirely.

Maybe it was the longing of a child, after all.

Zeus told himself he was horrified at his own mawkish sentimentality.

He made sure Nina was covered as he left the bed. He moved over to the fire, pulling the quilt that they'd long since kicked off around his waist. And then he sat, stared into the flames as they danced before him, and, for the life of him, could not understand how things had come to this point without him realizing what he was doing.

Not his own feelings, which he assured himself he could dismiss as he should have long ago. But to *her*. To his Nina. For a man was no man at all who hurt the woman he should protect. Hadn't he learned that when he was young? In the worst possible way? He knew he had. It had changed the course of his life. It had made him who he was.

How could he possibly justify using the woman who loved him, despite what he'd done to her, as a pawn in this bitter game?

The fire gave no answers.

Zeus kept imagining holding his baby for the first time. Staring down into the eyes of his own child. And it was so powerful that it threatened the favorite image he'd been carrying around for more than half his life now. Of staring down at his father on his deathbed, diminished and humbled, and making sure the old man knew that despite everything, Zeus had won.

It was like the two things were at war, ceding no territory.

Tearing him apart.

"You look cold," came her voice, so soft it cut right through him. "Are you all right?"

And Zeus had no idea how to answer that.

Nina was beside him in the next moment, kneeling down with him on the thick, priceless rug before the fire. She drew the coverlet with her, wrapping it around the both of them while she slid her legs beneath the quilt.

He thought she would ask questions, but she didn't. She only sat with him, her thigh against his, until he shifted her so he could hold her before him. She sat between his legs and leaned back, resting her head against his shoulder.

Even then, she only gazed into the fire. As if she knew that simply sitting with him soothed him, somehow. It was as if the heat of her body was hope itself, curling its way into him whether he wanted it there or not.

Whether he wanted to believe in it or not.

He rested his chin on the top of her head. He wrapped his arms around her.

It was only then, in a room dark save for the fire, that he found himself able to talk.

"They say my mother died of heart failure," he told her, amazed at how easily the words came after so long spent holding them in. And letting them poison him. "And in the end, she did. But it was more complicated than that."

"I'm so sorry," Nina murmured.

Somehow that made him want to go on rather than stop, when he would have said he was allergic to pity.

"I told you what a joy she was, but there were many others who did not think so. My father chief among them." He heard Nina murmur something and held her tighter. "I cannot say when I began to understand that the way my father spoke to her made something in her die a little. He was so much older, you see. She had been given to him after his first Queen died, taking his hopes of extending his bloodline with her. That was what he cared about. Bloodlines. The throne. The kingdom. What he did not care about was his young, silly second wife, who he took on purely to breed an heir."

"Maybe he didn't know how to care about anything but those things," Nina said softly. "Do you know what his relationship was like with his first wife?"

That walloped Zeus. Hard. Because in all this time, across all these years and all the bitter hours he had spent cataloging his father's many sins, it had never occurred to him to think of such a thing. He knew about the Queen who had come before his mother. He knew her name and some part of her story. But he'd been so focused on the wrong that had been done to his mother that he had never asked too many questions about the woman who had preceded her.

"I always assumed she suffered the same fate," he said.

"But you don't know?" Nina sighed a little. "Maybe he loved her. And hated that he couldn't have her but felt he needed to have a child."

"Nina." Oddly enough, he wanted to laugh. "Do not defend him."

"I'm not defending him," she replied. "It's not his heart I'm worried about."

His own heart kicked at him unpleasantly. But he kept going. "My mother was soft. It was part of what made her sweet, but she was no match for life at court. The courtiers and sycophants took their cues from my father, and she wasn't like you. She didn't know how to hide herself away. She didn't know how to protect who she was inside. And each harsh word, each bit of malice, each laugh at her expense took more and more from her."

Zeus couldn't remember now why he'd started to tell her this story. But as she nestled in closer against him, something in him eased. Or made room, maybe, so that he could keep going.

"First she would harm herself," he said. "Bruises. Cuts. Not where anyone could see when she was in public. But I saw." He shook his head. "Over time, it became clear that she wasn't eating. That every time someone criticized her, she punished herself for her flaws by taking away food. And then, I suppose, it was not so much a punishment any longer, but how she made her point. How she got the last word."

"Zeus…" Nina whispered.

"They tried to intervene. But in the end, I suppose it was the one place she could assert her will, so she did. And eventually, her heart gave out."

He heard her whisper his name again. He felt the touch of her lips at the side of his neck.

And he had never told anyone this story before.

It was the only story that mattered, and he peddled his stories to anyone who would run with them, but he never gave them this one. Maybe it was that Nina knew tragedy, too. Or maybe it was that she was Nina. And the simple fact of her, sitting here and bearing witness to this tale, made it better.

Not what had happened. But how it sat in him, even now.

"I was eleven years old." Zeus pulled in a breath. "And I was the one who sat with her at the last. And in my rage and grief, that day and into her funeral, I made a vow. I promised her as she was laid to rest that I would keep it."

Nina slid her hand over his chest. It took him a moment to realize she'd put her hand over his heart. He covered it with his.

"It was my father who could have helped her. Who, if not the King? Her husband? He could have stopped what was happening. He could have thrown out anyone who dared speak ill of her. He could have stopped criticizing her himself. There were any number of things he could have done, but he didn't." Zeus heard that roughness in his voice. He knew it told too many truths about him—more than he liked to share. Perhaps even with himself. "I vowed that I would ruin the one thing that mattered to him."

He heard her quick, indrawn breath, though Nina said nothing. But she didn't have to.

"Yes," he said. "I made it my mission in life to tarnish the throne. So that the Throne of Ages would find itself polluted by the most disreputable, irresponsible, unworthy occupant of all time."

That wasn't all of it. But it was enough. Zeus's heart was still jarring against his ribs. He felt outside himself, and that was before Nina turned to kneel before him so she could meet his gaze.

"I know that's the role you play," she said quietly. "But is that really you?"

Something swelled at him, so sharp he assumed it must have been bitterness—though he worried it was something much worse. *Hope*, something whispered in him. "Do you not know? And this the man you claim to love?"

But if he imagined she might look away, or be shamed in some fashion, he was disappointed. She only gazed at him as steadily as before.

"I know what I believe," Nina said with that quiet conviction that made him ache. "The question is, what do you believe?"

There was a roaring in him then. On and on it went. And her gaze was on him, in him.

And he *felt*. He felt…everything.

This woman had haunted him for seven months now, and she haunted him still. And Zeus understood then that it was entirely likely she always would.

Still, that storm raged on inside him. Still, the roar of it was loud enough to blow this stone castle to ash.

Zeus did the only thing he could think of to do.

He bent his head to hers, taking her mouth in a kiss that said all the things he could not. All the things he would not.

Everything he wished he could say to her. Only and ever to her.

Over and over again, he kissed her.

And he moved within her there, before the fire, until the shuddering took them both. Sweet this time, and more dangerous for it. Then he lifted her up, carried her to the bed, and took her once again.

Hot and hard.

As if in the taking, the sweet glory of this maddening fire, he would find the answer. What he believed. What he wanted. Who he was.

And in the meantime, he would hold her like sunshine between his hands and warm himself until hope felt as real as she did.

They had fallen asleep again when a great pounding came at the door.

Zeus rose, pulling on his discarded trousers as he stalked to the door. He flung it open to find the better part of his guard standing outside.

"Your Royal Highness," said the head of his security detail, bowing his head. "I'm afraid there is news of the King. His condition is grave."

For a split second, Zeus thought he had missed it—but no. There were rituals for that. His guard would have knelt. They would have called him *sire.*

He could see from their expressions that they would do these things. Soon.

"How long?" he asked curtly.

"A matter of hours," the man replied.

Zeus nodded, then closed the door. He turned to find Nina watching him, and he braced himself for her reaction. She would fly to him. Offer condolences that he would reject. Try to comfort him, and it might send him into a rage.

But she only gazed at him with what he was terribly afraid was compassion.

"I will find my things and dress," she said.

All Zeus could do was nod. All he wanted to do was reach for her. Turn back time, live in this night forever.

But his father was dying. It was time to go home.

And, whether he liked it or not, honor the vow he'd made so long ago.

CHAPTER TEN

THE FLIGHT BACK to the island was terrifying at first, as the pilot fought the winter weather to get them aloft. But once out of the mountains, everything was smooth. And, to Nina's mind, almost frighteningly quiet the rest of the way until they landed in the bright sun and soft breezes of Theosia.

The moment they returned to the palace, Zeus stalked away, surrounded by his aides. And looking more alone than she had ever seen him.

Nina found herself left to her own devices. Standing in the middle of a palace that was now hushed in dreadful anticipation.

And she'd spent her life mourning her parents' deaths. She had no idea how a person *prepared* for such a thing.

She walked, not sure where she was headed, in and out of the glossy, exquisite rooms that seemed to glisten with their own history. And it was perhaps unsurprising that she eventually found her way into the gallery of family portraits. The Kings and Queens of Theosia, stretching back into antiquity.

Nina looked at all of them, starting as far back in

time as the pictures reached. Slowly, slowly she advanced through the ages until she found her way to the small collection of portraits on the farthest, emptiest wall.

She recognized Zeus immediately. Only a small child in the painting, but undeniably him. The same green eyes. A smile made more of mischief than of studied wickedness, but his all the same. His hair more blond than dark, and the hint of all that austere bronze yet to come.

Then she studied the painting of King Cronos, who she had never met. He had been too ill the whole time she was here. Yet she could see Zeus in the face of the proud man she gazed at now, dressed in all his finery. The same forbidding features. The same hard, sensual mouth.

Beside them hung two very different portraits. One was of a dark-haired woman with eyes of violet and a reserved curve to her lips. Next to her hung a young blonde with emerald eyes and the biggest smile yet in this room full of portraits.

And Nina's heart hurt.

For all of them. But mostly for Zeus. For the little boy with such a big name in the portrait in front of her and the man she'd sat with so early this morning, feeling the clatter of his heart against her back. Hearing each and every betraying scratch in his voice.

She didn't know how long she stood there before she gradually became aware that she wasn't alone. When she turned to look, she saw Thaddeus, Zeus's sniffy butler who had so disdained her on sight.

"Madam," he intoned by way of greeting.

Nina sighed. Maybe it was time for more sad antechambers. "Have you come to encourage me to leave the portrait gallery to my betters?"

But even as she asked the question, she saw that his gaze was on the portrait of Cronos's first Queen, not on her.

"Did you know her?" she asked.

Thaddeus looked surprised for a moment, then something like resigned. He put his hands behind his back and stood taller. "Which 'her' do you mean?"

Nina looked back at the portraits. The reserve in one, the irrepressible life in the other. And the portrait of the King, looking young and mighty. "Either one of them."

"It was my very great honor to have served them both in some small capacity," Thaddeus replied in reliably frosty tones.

Nina smiled at him. Winningly, she hoped. "What were they like?"

"Madam. Of all days, this day cannot be the appropriate—" He stopped himself, but not until Nina had seen what looked like genuine emotion in his gaze. He looked down at once. "I beg your pardon."

"One day my portrait will hang on this wall," Nina said quietly, looking at all the space on this white wall. And trying to imagine her contribution to this long line of people who didn't seem like people any longer, not once they were captured in oil and framed. "And I would hope that if anyone asked, you or someone like you would tell them who I was."

Thaddeus drew himself up. "I would never dream of attempting such an impertinence."

"I'm sure I'll look suitably grand, like everyone else," Nina said, looking over at the rest of the gallery. "But a portrait can't show the truth of things. That I showed up at the palace gates six months pregnant with snacks in my purse. My hair in a mess, and no apparent decency at all. Wouldn't it be a shame if there was no one here to tell *that* story, Thaddeus?"

If she wasn't mistaken, she saw the faintest hint of a thaw in the old man's bearing. Only a hint.

But eventually, the butler cleared his throat and indicated the first Queen.

"Queen Zaria was a childhood friend of His Royal Majesty," Thaddeus said. "They grew up together here on the island and were promised to each other when they were very young. No more than five, as I understand it, and from that time they were always together. By the time they married, it was very clear that they were not only great friends, but very much in love."

Love stories, Nina thought, her heart clutching in her chest. They always ended badly. It was only fairy tales that ended well. *How do people survive these love stories?*

How was she planning to survive the one she was currently living, for that matter? She looked down at her ring, adjusting the way it sat on her finger, and admitted to herself that she just didn't know. Maybe she wouldn't. Not in one piece.

Last night had made it clear that she was all in here, in the very last place she should ever have risked herself. But there was no taking it back.

Nina acknowledged that she wouldn't take it back if she could.

Thaddeus was still speaking, his gaze on Queen Zaria. "They tried for many years to have an heir, with no success. It is my understanding that they were finally successful, but something went wrong. Both the Queen and the unborn heir were lost."

Nina found she had her hands on her own unborn child. "That's a terrible story."

"Look around," Thaddeus invited her. "Look at all the people who hang here. More often than not, they are all terrible stories. Crowns and palaces do not protect anyone. Not from life."

And she couldn't tell if that was pointed or simply true.

"What of the second Queen?" Nina asked.

Beside her, Thaddeus seemed to grow more grave. "The King mourned for some time. Years passed, but he felt he had a duty to his people. Queen Stevi was from a noble, aristocratic family. She had been raised to marry a man of stature. She was innocent but not unprepared." He blew out a breath. "The papers love to pretend otherwise."

"The papers love to pretend," Nina agreed.

The butler bowed his head slightly. Then continued. "The palace had become…dark. It was a place of grieving, with no place for the brightness of youth. The Queen produced an heir quickly and was soundly praised. But it is my understanding that once the task was accomplished, it was felt that she had very little to offer."

And Nina could hear all the court gossip behind those words. All the pain and misery. It was not hard to imagine a bright, happy girl gradually reduced to one more tragedy in a place like this. All the white walls and sunlight in the world couldn't make a toxic environment better. It only made it shine.

Is this really what you want? she asked herself. *For you or your baby?*

But there was a different king then, she reminded herself. A different king than the one who would ascend soon. A different king. Not hers.

"And the King?" she said now, her voice small. She almost didn't dare ask. "Does he yet live?"

"His Royal Majesty clings to life, madam," Thaddeus said. "But barely."

"And Prince Zeus?"

"Has only now left his side."

They both stood there a while longer, staring at the same four portraits, until something dawned on Nina. She turned to look at the crusty old man, standing beside her looking deeply aggrieved he was here.

"Did you come to find me?" she asked. "On the Prince's behalf?"

"Not on his behalf, madam. No."

But Nina understood. She smiled, so wide she made herself laugh. "That does make a change, doesn't it? You tracking me down and then wanting to take me to the Prince. Who could have guessed, all those weeks ago in that musty little antechamber?"

Thaddeus only inclined his head. He looked as if he smelled something rotten.

But Nina felt warm inside. Because she knew, somehow, that this was the beginning of a beautiful friendship. She almost said so, just to see him sneer again without actually sneering.

He didn't lead her to Zeus so much as he walked out of the palace, headed into the extensive grounds, and wound his way down to a secluded cove. Where he left her at the top of a set of stairs with a significant look.

Nina padded down the stone steps cut into the hillside and found Zeus at the bottom.

He was still dressed in the clothes he'd thrown on back in Graciela. He stood and stared out at the sea. Perhaps wishing it would turn stormy and turbulent instead of its offensive deep blue and calm turquoise.

She walked across the sand, then stood by his side, and waited.

"He sleeps," Zeus gritted out.

"Did you speak to him at all?"

Zeus did not move, and yet Nina felt as if he was turning deeper into stone as he stood there. "It is not certain he will wake again."

She remembered asking him about loneliness that night so many months ago. Because she knew her way around it, having had little company but her own her whole life, no matter how many people were around. Much like him, she supposed, if for very different reasons.

But she had never seen anyone more lonely than Prince Zeus now.

It was not lost on her that her declaration of love had not exactly gone down well. Nina had been surprised by it herself. She'd never said those words to another person, not as long as she could remember. She already whispered them to her baby. But they had simply poured out of her mouth last night.

Because somewhere between the ballroom and the bedroom, she had come to understand that it wasn't make-believe with Zeus. It wasn't stories told, or publicity stunts. Not for her. Once they looked at each other, really looked at each other, in Haught Montagne that night, everything that came after had been inevitable.

It felt good to finally admit it.

She had loved him then. She loved him still. And the baby growing ever larger within her was simply one more manifestation of that love. Nina couldn't wait to see who their child would become.

And these seven months of pregnancy had taught her something else, too. It wasn't necessary to know every last detail about a person to love them. It was not even required that love make rational sense. Sometimes it was a look. A quickening. An instant understanding of life forever altered.

Her life was altered. There was no denying it.

She wouldn't take that back, either.

Nina moved closer and took his hand, there before the water that the Theosians beckoned daily, even in these less godlike times. And when he looked down at her, somewhere between shock and astonishment, she squeezed his fingers harder in hers.

"I love you," she said.

And Zeus seemed to shatter, even as she watched. He gritted his teeth so hard she saw the hard cords of his neck stand out. She felt his hands clench, though he did not grip her hard enough to hurt.

"Do you know what I plan to say to my father

should he regain consciousness again?" he growled, his voice gone raw.

But Nina did not let go of his hand.

"I've been planning it since you came here. It is the crowning achievement of my lifetime of disappointing the man." His hand flexed in hers. "And it is all because of you."

He turned to face her, so Nina took his other hand. He stared down at where they were linked and made a low noise, like an animal in a trap.

But he didn't pull away.

"I have all the pictures to show him," Zeus gritted out. "Every scandalous paparazzi shot from the summer, to refresh his recollection. He was apoplectic when it happened. And I've been biding my time, waiting for his final moments to tell him that it is all much worse than he could imagine. Much worse than some pictures in the papers."

She could see that he wanted her to say something, but she couldn't find the words.

"I have been looking forward to this," Zeus continued. "To telling him I'm marrying a commoner, a nobody. An orphan girl who was cast aside by her own country but bears the heir to the throne he loves so much. It will be a masterstroke."

Nina wasn't sure, then, if she felt relief or a hollow sort of despair. Relief, because she'd known that all of this had to be a game. She'd known all along. And little as she minded Isabeau's taunts and gibes, name-calling and spitefulness, she found she minded much more that this was how Zeus truly saw her.

Even if he looked like it tormented him.

But beneath that, that sense of despair. Because she believed he was a better man. The man she'd seen in snippets, here and there. The glimpses she'd seen of him in what looked like the sort of meetings no one would believe the notorious Prince Zeus could sit through, much less command. The man who had slid shoes on her feet so gently and had stood just outside that alcove so that she might handle her former life on her own. The man who could have found her a few gowns for his pictures but had ordered her a queen's wardrobe instead, and who took an obvious delight in dressing her. The man who not only told her she was beautiful but made her feel it.

The man who made love to her like it was a sacred ritual, burning them both clean and new.

She believed all of these things fully. And it felt like a kind of agony that he did not.

"If you wish to say all these things to your father, why are you here?" she asked quietly. "Down on the beach, where if he stirs, it might very well take you too long to race to his side so you can hurt him one more time."

Nina could see the storms in his eyes. The glaze of grief. "You don't understand."

"I do," she replied calmly, though she felt anything but inside. "You saw me choose not to take my revenge on Isabeau. It would have been easy enough to do. It doesn't occur to her yet that I know all her secrets, but it will. I get to take pleasure in not sinking to her level."

He pulled his hands from hers, but he didn't stalk away as she half thought he might. He only stood there, letting the wind move over him while his green eyes were like thunder.

"It is hardly the same thing."

"It doesn't have to be the same thing. I still understand. That's called empathy—but I know they don't teach much of it in prince school."

"Nina."

The broken way he said her name pulled at her, but she pushed on anyway. "I learned some things about your father today. That he loved his first wife. Probably all of his life. And that she died, taking his unborn heir with him."

"Everybody knows this story," Zeus gritted out. "I learned it as a child."

"But you are only paying attention to the *story*, Zeus. I want to talk to you about a man." Nina shook her head when he began to speak again. "To you, he's larger than life. Your father. Your King. The man you blame—and possibly rightly—for making your mother's life so very difficult. All I am asking you to remember is that at the end of the day, he's just a person. And people are complicated. Good and bad. Kind and vicious. They can be all things. And your mother died so young herself, when you were just a child. It's only natural that you hated the person you felt was responsible."

"Because he is responsible. He could have stopped it." He looked ravaged then, but he sounded worse. "He could have *helped* her."

Nina went and took his hand again. She held it between hers, close to her heart.

"Do you have any idea what I would give for a single hour with my father?" she asked, holding his gaze no matter that the look in his eyes was painful. "With either one of my parents? I spent a lifetime wishing I could have another moment. Just one more moment, just enough, so I could tell them the only thing that really matters."

He said something, and she thought it was her name, but the wind stole it away.

"That I love them," Nina whispered. "That I will always love them. That no matter what happened to me, no matter what the years without them were like, I could never let that be what little I have of them. I would regret it forever."

He shook his head, as if warding her off.

"Zeus," she said, low and urgent. "Don't do something you'll regret forever."

"And what if I'm not the man you think I am at all?" he demanded, bringing his face in close, torn apart with emotion. No bronze mask. Just…him. All of him. "What if I am, instead, the creature I have always played? No regrets. No compassion. No love. What then, Nina?"

She reached up so she could hold his beloved face between her hands. And she gazed up at him, only dimly aware of the tears that wet her cheeks.

"Then I will regret it all for you," she promised him. "Your commoner queen, who will love you anyway, no matter how little you love yourself."

And for a moment, he only stood there, as if caught in his own storm. Nina thought she heard the ominous roll of thunder.

Then, as if it caused him physical pain, he pulled

away from her. He staggered back, his green gaze locked on hers.

It felt like a lifetime.

But then Zeus turned away and left her behind on that beach.

Nina wrapped her arms around their baby, promised it all the love neither she nor Zeus had known, and stayed there.

Until her tears were gone.

CHAPTER ELEVEN

KING CRONOS WOKE in the evening, and Zeus was there. The nurses made him comfortable, fluffing his pillows until he frowned and waved them away. Then they left father and son alone in the King's traditional bedchamber.

Zeus had always hated this room. Everything was too martial, too imposing. All about history and tradition. He preferred sunlight and space to all this heaviness.

But he had never thought to ask *which* history his father was mired in. He had always assumed it was all Theosian history and had never cared for the yoke of it himself. But now he wondered if these stout furnishings reminded the old man of something else. Something personal.

Someone.

He didn't ask now. He stood against the nearest wall and gazed down at what age had done to the man he recalled as far mightier than the sun. The true god in this palace dedicated to them.

Back when he had been so small and useless.

Nina's voice sounded in his head. *He's just a person.*

Zeus could admit that he had never thought so.

"I did not think I would see you again," Cronos rasped. And did not look as if he was best pleased to see Zeus now.

Because even at a moment like this, he knew how to provoke his son. Zeus reminded himself that he had not become who he was out of nothing.

"I've been waiting for this moment," he drawled, lounging against the wall in the indolent way that he knew had enraged his father since he was little more than a sulky youth. "Surely you know that. A most indecorous deathwatch, I think all your acolytes would agree."

Cronos only laughed, though it sent him into that rattling cough that had slowly taken him over this last year. "Such is the weight of the crown, my boy. You must wait for the moment of my death to rise. And you cannot mourn for even a moment. You must rule."

Zeus wanted to launch into one of his diatribes. He'd been practicing them for years. He had looked forward to this moment with all that he was. Before Nina, he had planned to vow, here on the old man's deathbed, that he would never have a child. That he would make sure the throne passed out of this family forever, so that all the old man's machinations had been for nothing.

With Nina, he'd thought he'd have an even better knife to stick in, deep.

Because he could still remember sitting with his mother as she slowly faded away, that little smile on her face. So pleased that she had, in her death, done

one thing to please herself completely. He could remember every moment of her last days.

He had been holding them close ever since. Hoarding them so he could build his fury about what had happened, year by year.

But now he was in another room in this palace, at another bedside, and yet his head was still back on that beach. *I will love you anyway, no matter how little you love yourself*, she had said.

And Zeus found he could not bring himself to say the things he should.

"Do you believe I will mourn you, old man?" he asked, almost idly.

And for a moment, he saw again the canny, shrewd King who had ruled his country long and well, through wars and plagues and famines alike.

"It is all mourning, in the end." That gaze of his still packed the same punch. "Remember that, Zeus. If you have any stake in this life at all, sooner or later, you mourn."

And maybe that was the word for what tore Zeus apart. Maybe it was all mourning, after all. For what he'd lost. For what he'd found but had intended to betray in this way. Maybe that made sense of the heaviness in him and the heart he'd only just discovered, broken into pieces.

And all of that wrapped up in an eleven-year-old's rage and grief for the mother who might not have left him if anyone beside him had loved her.

He cleared his throat. "I planned to send you off into the afterlife with the knowledge that I have not only impregnated Princess Isabeau's scandalous orphan, but I will also be marrying her in short order. Forever tarnishing your throne, your reputation, and therefore all you hold dear."

Cronos stared for a moment, and Zeus expected him to start in with the usual outrage. But he didn't feel even remotely as entertained as he'd always thought he would. He felt no rush of glee. No cleansing rush of spiteful triumph.

And it had never crossed his mind that he might find his revenge…underwhelming.

His father began to laugh again, though it made him hack and sputter. It took him a long time to catch his breath again. For a moment, he looked as if he might slip back into sleep. Instead, he roused himself, and when he looked at Zeus again, it was with an expression Zeus had never seen before.

As if his father was almost…bittersweet.

It had his throat tightening up.

"There is no throne in this world that is not tarnished," Cronos said. "It is only that, once the tarnishing has occurred, we all rally about and claim it as gold."

Zeus's pulse picked up then, though he was still. Very still. "And here I thought the only thing that mattered to you in this world was that throne."

"Because it was all I had," Cronos blurted out, as if the words had been tamped down inside him a long while. And the saying of them seemed to exhaust him. He collapsed against his bed, his breath coming harder. But he kept on, looking determined. "I lost everything. The throne was all that remained. And it took me too long to understand that a throne is nothing but a bloody chair. What matters is who sits upon it—and what he does when he is there."

They held each other's gaze for what seemed like forever. Zeus knew that these were words his father never would have said if these were not, perhaps, his final moments. But then, he knew that he would not have listened otherwise. And as they gazed at each other without rancor for the first time in more years than he cared to count, Zeus felt as if a thousand more unsaid things passed between them.

"Father," Zeus began.

The old man lifted a trembling hand. "You have nothing to apologize for, my son," he said, still holding Zeus's gaze. "It is the regret of my life that I did not see what I was doing to your mother, so lost in my own misery was I. And that I remained lost for far too long. I want you to know that if I could, I would go back and change what happened. I would change…" He broke off and smiled, faintly, though his eyes were sad. And his voice was fading. "I would change everything."

And then Zeus found himself doing something he would have sworn he would never, ever do.

He went and sat by his father's bedside. He took the old man's hands and looked deep into his eyes. Because he had stood on a beach and told Nina what kind of man he was, and she had loved him anyway. He knew the power of it.

And how could he deny it to his father now? When he knew how it had felt to hear Nina say those words to him?

I am sorry, Mother, he said inside. *I have been choosing you for a lifetime. But this is the end of his.*

A moment he had been waiting for, thinking he would taint it with revenge. But now he was here, and it was happening, and he couldn't find the will to do it.

He had chosen bitterness his whole life. What would happen if he chose peace?

If he let himself love his father a little, too?

"Father," he managed to say, though his voice was raw. "Rest now. I love you."

And when Cronos's eyes closed again, there were tears on his creased face.

Zeus did not know how long he sat there, but he thought it no more than a handful of minutes. And then his father breathed his last.

And Zeus did not move.

His heart was racing, his ribs too tight. And he knew that he only had a moment left. He only had a single, solitary moment left. One final moment when he was a son sitting beside his father. One last moment when he was who he had always been. Prince Zeus of Theosia.

Not a good man, perhaps. But he had great plans for his future.

First, however, he would step out of these doors and everything would change.

But then, everything had already changed. He was to be a father. There was a woman who looked at him as if he was worthy of her. She did not need him to save her. She wanted only for him to love her.

"I wish we had done it better," he said to his father,

in this last moment that was only theirs. "I wish we'd changed everything together."

He set the old man's hand down. And then he sat back and thought of his mother. His laughing, lovely mother. He was older now than she'd been then. And he had his own child on the way.

So he whispered the words he'd never thought he'd ever utter, not to her. "I forgive you, Mama."

For leaving him. For, in her way, taking him on as harrowing a journey as his father had.

Because in the end, both of them had been too locked in their own misery to care for their child as they should have. He understood that now.

But he did not intend that history should repeat itself. His child would know exactly how much it was loved. Always.

Zeus gave himself one last moment in his chair. Then he rose and blew out a breath. He looked at his father one last time as a son. Then he turned and opened the door.

He had stepped through it a prince. He would exit a king.

And he swore he would do a better job with the new title than he had with the old.

But as his father's attendants rushed inside, he didn't stand there and wait for them all to drop to their knees and "Long live the King" him the way tradition dictated they should. He was moving, rushing through the palace, because he was already King. It didn't matter who acknowledged it.

What mattered was her. Nina.

She was not in her rooms.

She wasn't in the library or any of the galleries.

Zeus was heading back to the beach when he finally found her standing in one of the palace's main halls, contemplating a large bronze mask.

And a thousand things he needed to say stormed within him. He wanted to tell her everything that had happened. Everything he'd understood, almost too late. Everything said and unsaid.

She turned as she sensed him coming, or perhaps he made some noise, and he knew she could see what had happened. Right there on his face. He expected her to call him *Your Majesty*. He expected her to curtsy. He expected that, like every other person in this palace, she would look to his rank first.

He should have known better.

"Oh, no," said his Nina. His perfect little hen. "*Zeus.* Your father. I'm so sorry."

She opened her arms wide, and he moved into them. And then, somewhere in that mess of grief old and new, there was still Nina, and he was kissing her—the heat undeniable.

But all of these other things as well.

And so it was that the brand-new King of Theosia knelt before his scandalous orphan in a hallway where anyone could see them. He wrapped his arms around her.

"Nina," he said, very solemnly. "I love you."

She was crying, and he would have to do something about that, but she was smiling, too.

"I suspect I am very bad at it," he continued. "But I think, if I try, I will figure out how to love you as well as I pretended to disdain everything else."

"Just love me," Nina whispered. "Love us. Everything else is negotiable."

He stayed where he was, his face against her belly, hugging his child and his woman at once.

And when he rose, he wiped away her tears. Then he reached down and retrieved the ring he'd put on her finger. This time, he held her hand while he held the ring up between them.

She was still smiling, though her eyes were still wet. "You already did this, Zeus."

"I did not. Not properly."

"But—"

He lifted her hand to his lips, and she subsided.

"Nina, I love you," he said again, because it could never be said enough. "As I have told you before, I could command you to marry me. But I would rather you do it because you wish to."

And this was harder. So much harder than he'd imagined. Nina was gazing at him, her eyes damp and filled with all the things she'd taught him. Love. Hope.

Forgiveness not because it was deserved or earned, but because it was necessary.

"The King of Theosia will need a queen," he managed to get out past that tightness in his throat, "but I need you. My people will expect me to fail, for that is what I've taught them I do. But you expect me to fly, Nina. And I think that the better I love you, the easier it will be to spread our wings. And I already know that a man is only as good as a woman who imagines him better."

"It has always been yes, Zeus," she whispered. "It will always be yes."

"And in return for these services to man and crown," he continued, though there was light in him now, beating back the shadows. Sunlight, at last. "I will take all the time and energy that I have dedicated to my foolish plans and leverage them on you instead. We will raise our child together, and we will be happy, Nina. If I have anything to say about it, and I do. *We will be happy.*"

"We will be us," Nina said, moving closer so she could reach up to pull his face to hers. She kissed him then. His forehead. His jaw. "Not our histories. Not what happened to us. Not the things we did before we found each other. We will be you and me and the family we make together. We will be *us*, Zeus."

"Forever," he vowed.

And the hall was getting crowded. There were matters of state to attend to—and there could be no more putting off this moment.

Zeus slid that ring back onto Nina's finger, where it belonged. And when she took his hand and held it tightly, all he saw was sunlight. He felt it, deep inside.

I will do it right this time, he told his parents. *I promise.*

"We'll do it together," Nina whispered, as if she'd heard.

And then, hand in hand, they turned to face the future.

The way they always would.

CHAPTER TWELVE

THE FUNERAL PROCESSION took over most of the island. The citizens of Theosia came out in force to mark the passing of their King, whose reign had been long and stable.

They were less sure about their new King.

But a week after his father was laid to rest, Zeus married Nina at last. They stood together in the island's cathedral and spoke all the old words to each other. And new ones that were only theirs. That was the day he made her his Queen, though the coronation would come later.

Not without telling a few stories along the way. The papers were filled with all kinds of theories about the fall of wicked Prince Zeus—and how, perhaps, the most unlikely bride was the only one who could civilize the savage beast.

"This is utter nonsense," Nina complained, sitting with him at the table in his morning room, the light he loved so much making her blond hair gleam like gold. Her brown eyes danced. "You were never a *savage* beast."

Zeus took that as a challenge. And by the time he

was done, she was limp and smiling in the vast bed in the rooms they now shared—his rooms. Neither one of them wanted to move into the King's traditional chambers.

They both wanted that light.

As much of it as possible.

"Your friends have all made a point of telling me that they're disappointed you didn't officiate your own wedding," Nina said at the grand reception after their wedding.

Zeus looked over the press of well-wishers who'd crowded into the palace and saw Jag, Rafael, and Vincenzo standing together. They all lifted their glasses in a mocking toast. He inclined his head in return and reminded himself that he was a king now. He could summon his best friends and call it a treaty summit. He made a mental note to do just that.

"Pay them no mind," he told his wife. "They are shocking reprobates, every one of them."

She made a face at him. "No wonder you all get along."

He and Nina danced and danced. And every day, she was lovelier to him. But perhaps never lovelier than she was then, wearing her stunning white dress, round with his child, and beaming with happiness.

Later that night, they stood on their balcony, looking out over the island that had always been his and was now hers, too. There were fireworks going off in all the villages, celebrating the kingdom's new start.

And what it represented.

Hope.

"You're mine first," he told her, standing behind her

as he had so many times—so he could put his arms around her and hold both her and their future close. "But from this day, you're also Theosia's. You belong to us all now, Nina."

He wasn't surprised to find tears on her cheeks again, even as she smiled with all her might.

"I will do you all proud," she promised.

But Zeus was already proud.

Their son was born late, prompting idle speculation in all the usual places that the new Prince intended to take after his father. And maybe he would one day. But first, there in the palace with the medical staff standing by, he was a miracle.

Maybe an everyday miracle, but a miracle all the same.

Zeus held the tiny bundle with wonder and awe and looked down at the perfect little boy who he knew would take after his mother. If he had anything to say about it.

And they loved each other as best they could, year after year. Wholly. Fiercely. They didn't always see eye to eye, but they fought hard to get back there. Every time.

The commoner Queen of Theosia gave the kingdom not only an heir but three spares. And they loved her for it. She made her royal children work with their hands as much as possible and treated any hint of laziness as a violent illness that required immediate attention. She insisted on kindness. She applauded thoughtfulness. She also loved them all to distraction, made them all feel adored, and was, without contest, the heart and soul of the family. And so, too, in time, the kingdom. Her passion was orphanages and lost children of any kind, and she became a patron of too many struggling organizations to count—at home and abroad.

Princess Isabeau of Haught Montagne, when reached for comment about her once-fiancé and the orphan girl she'd taken into her court so benevolently, never had a thing to say except that she wished them every happiness.

Not in public, anyway.

For his part, Zeus tried to learn from the first part of his life. He tried to love more. He worked hard at being good at all three of his important roles. Husband. Father. King. He hid himself less and less and found it more amusing than anything else how surprised people were to discover that in private, he'd been an excellent prince all along.

He took his stewardship of Theosia seriously but ruled with compassion.

He loved his children. He delighted in them.

But most of all, he loved his wife.

"Are you lonely?" she asked on their wedding anniversary, some twenty years into their beautiful future.

"Never," he replied at once, holding her in his arms in that very same Parisian hideaway where he'd first put his ring on her finger.

"That's a good thing," she replied, turning in his arms and wrapping herself around him with the same bright, hot passion that only grew between them. "But even if you were, I know the cure."

Because she healed him, the way she always did. And over time, he found ways to return the favor.

Mostly by loving her so much and so hard that she never again doubted he always would.

"This is our fairy tale," he told her. "We make the rules, little hen."

"Fairy tales end happily," she liked to tell him as he swept her into his arms. "That's the most important part."

Zeus had to say he agreed.

And that was how a common, possibly scandalous orphan—from nowhere with nothing—married the wickedest, most notorious prince in all the land.

Then tamed him. Just like that.

* * * * *

MILLS & BOON

Coming next month

BOUND BY HER RIVAL'S BABY

Maya Blake

A breeze washed over Amelie and she shivered.

Within one moment and the next, Atu was shrugging off his shirt.

"W-what are you doing?" she blurted as he came towards her.

Another mirthless twist of his lips. "You may deem me an enemy but I don't want you catching cold and falling ill. Or worse."

She aimed a glare his way. "Not until I've signed on whatever dotted line you're determined to foist on me, you mean?"

That look of fury returned. This time accompanied by a flash of disappointment. As if he had the right to such a lofty emotion where she was concerned. She wanted, no *needed* to refuse this small offer of comfort.

Return to her room and come up with a definite plan that removed him from her life for good.

So why was she drawing the flaps of his shirt closer? Her fingers clinging to the warm cotton as if she'd never let it go?

She must have a made a sound at the back of her throat because his head swung to hers, his eyes holding hers for an age before he exhaled harshly.

His lips firmed and for a long stretch he didn't speak. "You need to accept that I'm the best bet you have right now. There's no use fighting. I'm going to win eventually. How soon depends entirely on you."

The implacable conclusion sent icy shivers coursing

through her. In that moment she regretted every moment of weakness. Regretted feeling bad for invoking that hint of disappointment in his eyes.

She had nothing to be ashamed of. Not when vanquishing her and her family was his sole, true purpose.

She snatched his shirt from her shoulders, crushing her body's instant insistence on its warmth as she tossed it back to him. "You should know by now that threats don't faze me. We're still here, still standing after all you and your family have done. So go ahead, do your worst."

Held head high, she whirled away. She only made it three steps before he captured her wrist. She spun around, intent on pushing him away.

But that ruthlessness was coupled with something else. Something hot and blazing and all-consuming in his eyes.

She belatedly read it as lust before he was tugging her closer, wrapping one hand around her waist and the other in her hair. "This stubborn determination is admirable. Hell, I'd go so far as to say it's a turn on because God knows I admire strong, wilful women," he muttered, his lips a hairsbreadth from hers, "but fiery passion will only get you so far."

"And what are you going to do about it?" she taunted a little too breathlessly. Every cell in her body traitorously strained towards him, yearning for things she knew she shouldn't want, but desperately needed anyway.

He froze, then a strangling sound leaving his throat, he slammed his lips on hers.

He kissed her like he was starved for it. *For her.*

Continue reading
BOUND BY HER RIVAL'S BABY
Maya Blake

Available next month
www.millsandboon.co.uk

JOIN US ON SOCIAL MEDIA!

Stay up to date with our latest releases, author news and gossip, special offers and discounts, and all the behind-the-scenes action from Mills & Boon...

millsandboon

millsandboonuk

millsandboon

t might just be true love...